THE SECOND BOOK IN THE FIRST DUO OF PARANORMAL
ROMANCES BY NEW YORK TIMES BESTSELLING
AUTHOR KATY REGNERY WRITING AS K.P. KELLEY!

HAPPILY EVER AFTER...
To some, they're just words signifying a fairytale ending.
For me, Jack Beauloup, they represent an unyielding desire:
Forever with Darcy Turner, the unexpected love of my life.
A love that has placed her human life in danger.

According to Pack Law,
my binding is an abomination that must be severed.
It's ignited a fiery hatred that I must confront and control.
But what is bound cannot be broken.
I will keep Darcy safe.
Even if it means giving up on my dreams.
Even if it means giving up my life.

Boroughs
Publishing Group

www.BOROUGHSPUBLISHINGGROUP.com

IT'S YOU, Book Two
Copyright © 2017 Katharine Gilliam Regnery

ISBN:
978-1-541362-83-3
Interior Format
© KILLION
GROUP INC.

BOOK
TWO

It's
You

KATY REGNERY
WRITING AS
K. P. KELLEY

For Nana Audrey with love.
Thank you for
being the first eyes on this book and
for believing in it all along.
We are so lucky to have you
in our lives.
xoxoxo

Part 3:
Darcy & Jack I

Chapter 1

THREE DAYS. IT'S ONLY BEEN three days since you've seen him.
Darcy sighed loudly from her usual spot on the window seat, taking another sip of her tea. Omnipresent tears burned her tired eyes like acid. At this rate, her face would be puffy for the rest of her life.

Overwhelmed by sadness and confusion, it was almost a relief to feel anger building inside of her since last night, because she'd rather be angry than sad. And she was. She was so angry that she'd turned her back on him, leaving him to drown when he pulled her inside. If she were honest, she'd admit she felt a little bad about that in spite of her anger and fear. Because the thing was…she didn't *want* to still care for him, but she did. Regardless of her anger—her hurt and confusion and hopelessness and fear and revulsion—she still loved him. Which was inconvenient, since she could never be with him again.

Three days without him felt like an eternity. How in the world would she learn to *live* without him?

It was as though time had stopped since she returned from Jack's house on Thursday morning. Just stopped, eking out in painful increments of dragging seconds spent away from him, trying to convince herself she was better off without him.

Nothing was beautiful or interesting or worth her time and attention. Her book had been completely forgotten. She had skipped dinner at her mother's house for the first time in ten years. She hadn't even checked her e-mail to see if she was scheduled to teach next week. She hadn't left the house to do more than wander in the backyard garden for a few minutes yesterday. Wearing whatever she found on her bedroom floor this morning, which happened to be worn-out denim cut-off shorts and an old sweatshirt frayed around the cuffs, she stared out the window at the dim light of the dying day, a book of Métis legends beside her flipped over facedown to hide the charcoal sketch of a gruesome creature.

You're used to not seeing him. You're used to being apart from him. This isn't any different from before, her brain reasoned.

Right, her heart fought back bitterly. *But that was before. This is now. This is after touching him and knowing him and loving him. This is very, very different.*

In her mind, her life was now strictly separated into two distinct time periods: BHW, or Before Honoria's Wedding, when Jack lived in her mind merely as a lovely, poignant memory, and AHW, After Honoria's Wedding, when Jack became the most complex, frustrating, captivating, mind-blowing slice of heaven Darcy's life had ever known.

And then…

This isn't any different? Think again.

…she found out that she was in love with a Roux-ga-roux. A werewolf hybrid. A skinwalker. A dark, depraved creature of the night that hunted humans when the moon was full—or would, if he indulged his nature and allowed himself.

She shivered against the revulsion that made her stomach flip over and pressed her fingers to her lips, bending forward to put pressure on her stomach. The wave of nausea passed. She took a deep breath and a soothing sip of tea.

Flipping the book over, she looked at the picture again, feeling her pulse race as she read the short essay beside the picture for the hundredth time:

THE ROUGAROU (alternately spelled as *Roux-ga-Roux*, *Rugaroo*, or *Rugaru*), is a legendary creature found in the folklore of Laurentian French communities, and linked to European notions of the mythical werewolf. The stories of the creature known as a Rougarou are as diverse as the spelling of its name, though they are all connected to francophone cultures through a common belief that finds its beginnings in the words *Loup-garou* (French pronunciation: [lu ga'ʁu], /'luː gə'ruː/). Loup is French for wolf, and garou (from Frankish

garulf, cognate with English werewolf)
defined as a man who transforms into an
animal.

The creature has been associated with Native American/First Nations legends for hundreds of years, though there is some dispute as to its exact form and function. Such folklore versions of the Rugaru vary from being mild bigfoot (Sasquatch) creatures to cannibalistic Native American wendigos. Some dispute the connection between Native American folktales and the francophone Rugaru.

As is the norm with legends transmitted by oral tradition, stories often contradict one another. The stories of the wendigo vary by tribe and region, but the most common thread in all legends is the appearance of violent cannibalism.

Cannibalism. She stared at the picture for a moment then shuddered again and slammed the book shut. It didn't help. She could still see it in her mind…worse, she could see *Jack* in her mind, coming out of his garage on Thursday morning, his long, yellow claws retracting in the morning sunshine.

Don't be frightened. I'm still me, his eyes had beseeched her.

Yeah, right. You, covered in dried blood with twelve-inch claws!

She swallowed another gulp of tea, glancing at the spine of the book. It taunted her, laughed at her.

Some scientist you turned out to be. Can't even look at a picture without getting squeamish.

Darcy pursed her lips, furrowed her brows, and opened the book again, trying to look at the drawing objectively. She also tried to keep her stomach from revolting as she compared the drawing to what she remembered of her glimpse of Jack.

Overly large, golden, glowing eyes.

Well, she thought, *slight exaggeration.* Jack's glowed, but they were of normal size.

Long, jagged claws hung by the side of the creature in the drawing.

Claws, check. But, they weren't jagged. More like swords or knives. Smooth, but sharp-looking and slightly hooked at the end.

Fangs? Darcy hadn't actually seen fangs, but she assumed they'd probably drop if Jack was fully shifted. So, fangs, maybe.

The drawing showed the creature covered in fur with pointy wolf ears. She trusted that he would grow some sort of body cover when he shifted, and she didn't know about pointy ears, but they were certainly a possibility.

In the arms of the creature in the drawing was a woman, blood dripping out of a gash in her neck, making the fur of his chest slick and shiny.

Darcy took a deep breath, forcing herself to stare at the drawing.

There's a reason it's a drawing and not a photo, Darcy, and that's because no one's ever seen one.

Which meant that some of the facts could be wrong. Jack had indicated he didn't hunt humans, even though his urges might lead him to, if he wasn't locked up. So, perhaps cannibalism was untrue of Jack, even if it was common in others of his kind.

She ran a finger lightly over the eyes, covering them then uncovering them, looking for traces of humanity in the drawing. *He* was still in there, even when he was shifted, wasn't he? He couldn't lose all of his humanity, could he?

Her eyes welled with tears again and she pushed them away, closing the book as she heard Willow's car pull into the driveway. She'd left early this morning to attend to a local patient giving birth at the hospital ninety minutes south in Berlin. Once Willow got to the hospital, it wasn't unusual for her to meet up with doctor friends for lunch, sit in on procedures or purchase supplies for her own medical office.

Darcy had found a note in the kitchen when she finally got out of bed this morning. Four words: *We need to talk.*

While Darcy had spent a good deal of Thursday night crying on Willow's shoulder, they hadn't spoken much on Friday. Willow checked on her before leaving for work and again at lunchtime, but Darcy sensed Willow didn't want to validate Darcy's claims by discussing them. She was treating Darcy like she thought she was crazy. Frankly, she had every right to think so. Darcy couldn't stop talking about skinwalking werewolves, retractable claws, and flesh-eating monsters. It sounded crazy to her too.

The kitchen door opened and closed and she heard Willow taking off her coat. Darcy took a deep breath and braced herself, ready to listen to her friend tell her that she was going utterly and completely nuts.

"Darce?"

"In here."

Willow walked into the dimly lit living room, tilting her head to the side as she regarded her friend with a sad smile.

"How you doing, kid?"

"Oh…" Darcy bit her lip to keep from crying then shrugged, looking down.

She heard Willow take a deep breath and sigh.

"Have you left this spot all day?"

"I walked around the garden for a little bit…"

"How'd you sleep last night?"

"Not bad, actually."

Truth be told, she'd started off the night tossing and turning, remembering the black wolf gasping and drowning in the freezing water, but she had ended up sleeping well. She'd had a dream of the black wolf, of Jack in soul flight form, sleeping at her feet, and it had made her feel safe and loved. She'd slept like a rock with him beside her.

Willow gestured to the book beside Darcy. "Interesting reading?"

"Just trying to figure things out."

"On that note, I need to talk to you."

Willow licked her lips then pursed them together. She took a seat across from Darcy on the window seat and sighed.

"Willow, I know you think I'm crazy. I know you think—"

"You have no idea what I think, kid. Can I speak?"

Darcy shrugged and nodded.

"I talked to Jack yesterday."

"What? What do you mean?"

"I don't think you're crazy, but yes, I was worried for your mental state. I wanted him to stay away from you. You were talking about some wild stuff. Legends coming to life. Cannibalism. Monsters…"

Darcy nodded. When someone else said it, it definitely sounded like she was totally losing her marbles.

Willow took a deep breath then held Darcy's eyes. "Phillip Proctor."

Darcy sat back. Of all the things she thought Willow might say next, mentioning Phillip's name didn't come close to making the list.

"Ph-Phillip?"

Willow bit her lip, her eyebrows deeply furrowed as though second-guessing her decision to say whatever was on her mind.

"Just say what you have to say, Will."

"Okay. You're going to have to stick with me here because there's a lot to get through. So, Phillip came to your apartment that night in college, when you were in grad school, right? You remembered Phillip coming over. You remembered him getting aggressive with you. But the next thing you remembered, you were waking up in a hospital, and you could never quite figure out what had happened. Do I have that right?"

"Yes. That's about the sum of it. But what does that have to do w—"

"Just stick with me. When you left the hospital and went back to your apartment the next day…"

"My kitchen window had been smashed and my living room rug was gone."

"Right. And your necklace," said Willow. "The Métis one I gave to you. That was gone too."

Darcy thought back quickly. "Um…well, I don't know for sure that happened on the same night. I lost it sometime around then. But, actually, Will, I don't think I lost it. I found it recen—"

"Listen to me. Someone took it that night."

"Who?"

Willow tilted her head to the side, looking at Darcy with worried eyes. She reached out and took Darcy's hand.

"Jack."

Jack. Jack? No, that couldn't be. She hadn't seen Jack since that night in high school…until Honoria's wedding. She would certainly remember if she'd seen him in Boston and given him her favorite necklace.

"Willow, what are you talking about?"

"Jack tracked you down when you were at Harvard for your master's. Apparently, he wanted to see you and he found you in Boston. He said he slept on your fire escape for several nights watching you. He knew details about your place. He knew Frank's name."

Darcy felt heat flushing her cheeks even as her fingers got cold. She was starting to feel light-headed, but she needed for Willow to go on, so she swallowed and nodded.

"He was there that night. He watched as Phillip came into your apartment and when he started to assault you, Jack shifted into what he called 'Roug form,' broke through your kitchen window, and—um, took care of Phillip."

"What does *that* mean?" Darcy asked in a breathy voice. "Took care of?"

Willow cringed and looked down.

"What does TOOK CARE OF mean?" Darcy asked again, terrified that Willow would tell her that Jack ate Phillip.

Willow spoke in a rush. "He called it a castration, but technically it was a penectomy."

"What the—what the *fuck* is that?" Darcy could hear the hysterical edge in her tone.

"He cut off Phillip's penis."

Darcy's mouth dropped open and she released Willow's hand, jumping off the window seat and running to the bathroom to vomit. She only made it as far as the kitchen sink. Her stomach heaved and all of her afternoon tea ended up in the sink with a splatter. She coughed, her fingers rigid on the edge of the basin, as she took a deep breath through her mouth. Fumbling with the faucet, she finally got the cold water flowing. She leaned forward, sticking her tongue into the steady stream of clean water then spitting.

She didn't feel Willow come up behind her, but she felt her friend's hand rubbing her shoulder. "Maybe you weren't ready to hear this…"

Darcy rested her elbows on the rim of the sink and bent forward, eyes closed. Willow reached for the tap to shut off the water.

"It's…it's okay. My stomach's just really…unsettled."

"I guess hearing that your boyfriend cut off your ex-boyfriend's…"

Darcy stood up straight, finally taking a breath from her nose. When she opened her eyes, the room wasn't spinning, but her voice was sharp. "Yeah. I got it."

"Sorry," said Willow, coloring.

Darcy shook her head, taking another deep breath and exhaling. She turned to face Willow, resting her back against the sink, still gripping the cool porcelain of the basin. She could feel the tears in her eyes, but she wasn't even sure why they were there anymore exactly. Because Jack was a Roux-ga-roux? Because she loved him in spite of his form, in spite of his nature? Because he had deceived her into loving him as a human? Because she just found out that he cut off Phillip Proctor's penis? Because she just tossed her cookies?

Pick a card, any card.

She felt the wild, frantic urge to cackle with crazy laughter but bit her tongue instead. She brushed by Willow and walked back into the living room, resuming her seat by the window. Willow followed after her, her face grim and worried.

"Finish the rest," said Darcy, quiet but firm.

"Are you sure you—"

"Finish it, Will. Finish the story."

Willow nodded, sitting gingerly on the edge of the window seat but facing the living room instead of her friend.

"He said that Phillip was about to rape you. He said that after he cut Phillip, he picked you up and put you in your bed. He said it was impulsive to take the necklace but he wanted something of yours."

Darcy humphed softly and Willow shifted to face her.

"Apparently he returned it last week, kid. When he brought you the tulips."

"Just walked into our house, huh?" she blurted out, swiping at her eyes and snuffling once loudly. "Well, that's not presumptuous...or creepy."

Willow cracked a weak smile. "That's what I said. But he said that he had waited a long time to return it and he didn't want to just give it to you because it would raise too many questions too soon. So, he left the flowers, put the necklace in your jewelry box and went home."

"What else...with Phillip? Did Phillip die? Did Jack—" She could feel her stomach rolling over again.

Willow looked surprised then recovered. "Oh! No! No, no! I should have clarified that. No, Jack didn't eat—I mean, he didn't *hurt* Phillip any more. He rolled him up in your carpet and took him to the Lakes Region Medical Center in Wolfeboro. Dropped him off there. I read the surgical report. Jack actually made sure Phillip didn't lose so much blood that he'd die. There was nothing to, um, attach back, but they were able to save Phillip's life." Willow took a deep breath and sighed. "Not that he deserved it. If he had ended up on *my* operating table—"

Darcy gave Willow a warning look.

"Let's not go there, huh?"

"Sorry," Willow murmured. "I just—I'm nervous, I guess. It's hard to get my head around it. It was Jack who called the ambulance and waited until it got there. He wouldn't leave until he knew you were safe. And Darcy, it was a waxing gibbous moon that night. Last night before the full. I checked."

More tears filled Darcy's eyes. He should have been back at the Bloodlands by then. He shouldn't have been there watching over her.

"It was risky for him to stay in Boston that long," she murmured.

Willow nodded. "He was cutting it close."

As Darcy processed the meaning behind the obvious basics of Willow's story, tears tumbled out of her eyes. Had it not been for Jack, she may have been raped that night, or worse. She remembered how frightened she'd felt as Phillip pawed at her and she knew she'd made a terrible mistake in letting him come up.

She'd relived the details of that night a thousand times. He'd been so playful over the intercom that even though she knew he'd been drinking, she'd let him come up. And when she'd suggested tea, he'd been polite, accepting a cup from her. It was a few minutes later that she'd seen the swift change in his eyes, from silly and flirtatious to hungry and demanding. And while they'd obviously slept together before, everything felt different that night, and she'd been frightened. As she'd offered him his tea again, he'd slammed it out of her hand, pushing her robe open. When she'd drawn back her hand to push him away, he had struggled with her and the last thing Darcy remembered was the crippling, sharp pain of her head making contact with the corner of her coffee table.

When she woke up in the hospital the next morning, she'd been too frightened to ask the obvious question right away, fearing she'd been raped. But when she'd finally mustered the courage, the nurses had assured her that they'd done a thorough exam and found no evidence of sexual assault. It was then that she had realized that her body had none of the discomfort or bruising that would have accompanied forced sex. What's more, a peace had settled over her and Darcy somehow knew he hadn't raped her. She knew it, like women know visceral, uncompromising truths.

The police couldn't tell her what had happened to the kitchen window, and although no blood was found in the shards, the most popular theory was that Phillip had somehow broken it making his retreat down the old fire escape, in a panic to leave after realizing he had injured Darcy. They also assumed that Phillip had called the ambulance from her apartment phone out of remorse, unable to come up with a better explanation.

For several days, Darcy had stayed with Willow at her apartment in campus housing near the med school until the glass could be replaced and a better lock placed on the window. She couldn't shake the feeling that Phillip might come back and finish the job he'd started, so she was more than a little relieved when she received his postcard sent from Quebec. When she'd received it, the police's theory about Phillip getting away down the fire escape to evade arrest had made perfect sense: Phillip had run to Canada to avoid criminal assault charges, and it was unlikely he'd ever risk coming back.

But Darcy looked at everything through new eyes now. Phillip hadn't broken the window or called the ambulance or gone to Canada, after all. It was Jack. Jack who saved her, who called the ambulance, who sent that postcard to quell her inevitable worries and give her closure.

As Darcy's mind reprocessed the hard facts of that night, her heart softened appreciably toward Jack for the first time since Thursday as she was overcome with a feeling of gratitude, followed by a wave of love for him. He had saved her. He had protected her. He had shifted in front of her, but still managed to keep her safe, and even more, managed to take Phillip to safety. It was a relief to know that she didn't have to be frightened of Jack anymore. As warmth suffused her body, she realized that maybe—after the shock of seeing him had subsided—somewhere inside of her, in her heart, her soul, she knew he would never hurt her.

She glanced down at the Métis book with the frightening drawing and closed it. There was much more to Jack than the vague details of a legend. There was much more to a Roux-ga-roux than she could find out in books that sensationalized a shadowed monster.

Darcy sighed and rubbed her temples. It was a relief to have answers to all of the old questions about what had happened that night in Boston so long ago. But a whole new set of questions had sprung up in the place of the answered ones. How had Jack found her? Why didn't he make himself known to her at the time? Had he been secretly watching her all of these years? And aside from that night, more questions about who he was: Could he control himself shifted? What were the boundaries of his control? Could she possibly learn to live with—?

No. She shut down that hopeful train of thought and told her longing heart to cease and desist. He had irresponsibly kissed her as a teenager and changed the course of her life. He was a dark creature. Her heart insisted she had feelings for him, and her body still heated up at the mere thought of their time together, but her sensible mind knew better: She didn't have space for him in her life. She'd made that clear when she rowed away from him, the howling whimpers haunting her as she left him to drown in the cold, dark water.

It's nice that you're not scared anymore, and you can certainly be grateful that he saved you. But you cannot welcome a monster into your life.

The doorbell rang and Darcy looked up at Willow, who'd been watching her face as she processed this information. Willow looked over at the door then back at Darcy,

"I'll get it," she said, getting up.

Darcy mustered a small smile for her friend, reaching for her hand as she rose. "Thanks for telling me everything, Will. Thanks for listening to him and verifying all of it, and well, just thanks for being my—"

The doorbell rang again and for no reason at all Darcy felt a gathering, a stirring in her heart like awareness. Her eyes narrowed as her breathing hitched and goose bumps popped up along her arms.

"I'm guessing it's a patient," Willow muttered. "With that sort of impatience."

Willow still held Darcy's hand, and as she tried to tug hers away, Darcy gripped onto it tighter, getting up from the window seat and following her friend to the door. She didn't know how she knew, she just did. She just knew in her gut, in her heart, in her head, who was waiting behind the door.

Willow turned the knob and Darcy's stomach exploded into a million bees, humming, buzzing, stinging with delight as the door opened and she beheld Jack's face. Pleasure and pain mingled, her anger no match for the heat of his body before her, the tenderness she saw in his eyes before he shadowed them quickly with indifference.

She locked her eyes with his and felt the current pass between them, the magnet that drew them to one another squeezing her heart with the force of its fierce gratitude for their reunion. Her head swam with dizzy pressure and her knees buckled. With no food in her stomach and the emotional rollercoaster of the last few days overwhelming her completely, her eyes rolled back in her head and she promptly fainted.

Chapter 2

STRONG SMELL. STRONG, TERRIBLE SMELL.

She jerked her head back and her eyes fluttered open as she waved the offender away from under her nose.

"I had just told her about Phillip…too much for her…worried…" She could hear Willow's voice over her head. "Darce? Darcy?"

"I'm—I'm okay. Stop, Will—"

Willow moved the smelling salts away and pressed a glass of water to Darcy's lips.

"Drink."

Darcy was half reclined in her favorite spot on the window seat with two pillows behind her back, and Willow sat beside her, her face inches from Darcy's, worried and cross.

"I'm okay, Will," she said, but took a small sip.

Jack had carried her to the window seat, of that she was certain. She didn't know how long she'd been out, but she could still feel the heat from his arms on her skin, and it felt so good a shiver went down her back. She took a deep breath and sat up a little straighter, pushing back on her hands and moving the pillows until she felt the wall behind her. Then she saw him. Jack sat across from her on the other side of the seat.

Her shoulders dropped in defeat and her eyes teared; she was so relieved to see him, so comforted by his presence after three days of intense sadness, loneliness, and anger.

Aside from the brief tenderness she'd noted when they'd first clapped eyes on each other, before she fainted, there was no further affection in his eyes. His gaze was impassive. Shuttered.

She looked away from him, feeling angry with herself for wanting to see love in his eyes, for the sheer relief she felt to be back in his company. She didn't want to be relieved; she wanted to stay angry. There was no way they could be together, so being around him would just be painful and difficult. The bottom line was that regardless of the leapings in her heart and surges of lust throughout her body, she didn't want him here.

She looked him in the eyes.

I asked you not to come back.

It wasn't my intention to come back.

Then why?

Because I had to.

Darcy swallowed and looked away. It was clear he didn't want to be here. So why had he come back?

"Are you two—are you *talking?*" Willow asked, standing in front of the seat, looking back and forth between them with knitted brows.

"They're Eyespeaking." Another voice. Male. From the dimly lit front hallway behind Willow.

Darcy leaned forward to look around Willow and saw a man there. Almost as tall and broad as Jack, with black hair and dark eyes; she knew they must be related. She whipped her eyes back to Jack.

My brother. Julien.

Well, that's just great. You brought another one here.

His eyes narrowed for just a moment before he gave her a bored look and turned his face away.

"Willow," Darcy said, without looking back toward the foyer and trying to keep her voice calm for her friend. "That's just Julien, Jack's *very docile* brother."

"I know," she answered. Darcy was relieved to hear wonder, not fear, in her friend's voice. "We met while you were…"

Julien stepped forward to stand beside Willow, and Darcy could see him better. His eyes were wide and she perceived a mixture of surprise and what was it? Curiosity? Fascination? Something like that.

"I wouldn't have believed it if I hadn't seen it," he murmured, staring at Darcy then at Jack. "You can Eyespeak."

"That's wild," breathed Willow, her mouth slightly open. She looked back at Darcy, searching her eyes. "Are you talking to Jack right now?"

Darcy looked at Willow, quirking one eyebrow irritably. "How could I—? I'm looking at *you,* Will. Jack and I can't Eyespeak unless we're looking at each other."

"Huh," Willow murmured, still staring at Darcy with her wide, dark eyes.

"You sure you're all human?" Julien now, still staring at Darcy like an alien life form and wrinkling his nose to sniff in her direction.

"Uh, yes. Last I checked."

Jack cleared his throat. "Julien, stop staring at her."

"And smelling her," added Darcy in a sour voice.

"S-Sorry. I just never…"

Jack stood up, glancing at Darcy once before facing his brother and Willow.

"Could you two…" They stared back at him. "I mean, could Darcy and I have a minute alone?"

Julien turned to Willow. "We could go sit on your porch swing?"

"I-I don't know. I don't think I should leave—" Willow started.

"I don't bite," cajoled Julien.

"Very funny," she replied, crossing her arms over her chest protectively. "Promise?"

"You're Métis," he said, as though that declaration should soothe her worries, a small smile tugging at the corners of his mouth.

"How do you know that?"

"He can smell it on you," said Jack quietly.

"You can *smell* that I'm Métis?" Ever fascinated by anomalies of the human body, Darcy could practically see the wheels of Willow's medical head churning with this news. Eyespeak, keen smell. Yep, Willow was in heaven.

Julien nodded. "A quarter, right?"

"Right. But, what does that have to do with you not biting—"

"We're both mixed blood. It's just not…*done*. It'd be like you eating your pet cat or pet dog. You could, I guess, but you just *wouldn't*." He shivered, his face contorting like he'd just bitten into a lime.

"I don't know whether to be insulted or relieved." She paused. "So, that part of the legend is real. You don't feed on Métis. What else?"

Julien was clearly trying not to smile any wider, but losing the fight. "How about this? We go sit on the swing and I'll tell you anything you want to know about Rougs. You ask questions and I'll answer them."

Willow turned back to Darcy with wide eyes, duty tamping down her fascination with Roug biology. "I don't think I should leave you. Are you okay with this?"

"Doesn't look like I have a choice." Darcy looked at Julien. "Don't get too comfortable, though. He won't be long."

The door shut behind them and Jack sat back down on the window seat at Darcy's feet, facing the living room. She flinched as he settled near her, moving her feet away from him.

"Don't touch me."

"Don't worry," he retorted sharply.

He scooted over next to the wall, away from her, folding his hands in his lap. She almost missed the slight movement of his jaw clenching as she watched his profile.

"Why are you here, Jack?" she asked in a gentler voice.

"I need you to come stay with me," he said. His voice was flat and bland. It was a tone you'd use to describe the weather, not make out-of-the-question demands.

"Huh. That's *so* not going to happen."

Jack looked down, licking his lips. Darcy hated the way warmth pooled in her belly remembering his mouth on hers. Her heart beat faster and her breathing felt deeper and more deliberate. She shifted her legs, trying to distract herself by looking out the window.

"Me too," he muttered.

She turned her head to him and saw the copper flakes stir and burn in his eyes.

You too what?

My body wants yours as badly as yours wants mine.

Darcy narrowed her eyes and looked away, at the darkness outside. His cockiness made her next words a little easier.

"Jack, the only thing I *want* is to never see you again. I'm not going anywhere with you. I need you to leave and not come back. That's all I want."

"*That's* not going to happen, Darce." His voice was low and taut and unyielding.

"WHY NOT?" Angry tears burned her eyes as she pulled her knees up to her chest, staring at him with furious eyes, the loneliness and frustration of the past few days tumbling out in a sob. "You're ruining my life! I want you out of my house. I want you to leave! Why can't you just leave me alone?"

"Why? WHY? Do you think *I* want this? Do you think I *want* to be bound to you? Do you think I like it that I can smell you from where I'm sitting and all I can think about is burying my body inside of yours? You think I *want* you in my head…in my *heart*?" He choked on the word "heart" like it was acid in his mouth and it made her wince. "Damn it,

Darcy! I get it. You left me to *die* in that water. Believe me, I'd leave you alone if I could!"

His voice had picked up volume and momentum as he spoke and he almost spat out his last few words. He had also slid closer to her as he spoke and she could feel the heat being thrown off his body as she continued to stare out the window, forcing herself to remain calm, despite the direct effects of his words.

He was right.

She wanted him every bit as much as he wanted her.

Her body screamed for his and her heart beat for him with the same fierce, unspeakable longing she heard in his voice. Her insides throbbed with the physical memory of him moving inside of her, bringing her to peak after peak of perfection. The swirling and tingling began low in her belly just in response to his words—his angry, passionate, inadvertently loving words. She was wet and ready for him, despite everything. Despite the fact that they had no future together.

Somewhere in her mind, she also processed his words: *Believe me, I'd leave you alone if I could.* She couldn't deny they hurt. Even as she pushed him away with both hands, she wanted him to want her, she wanted him to love her. She longed for it. She hungered for it.

She leaned the slightest bit forward, toward his body, watching his face, his lips, suddenly needing reassurance, suddenly needing to know that he loved her as much as she loved him, not because he was compelled to through the binding, but because he wanted to love her, because he was powerless to stop his heart from belonging to her. She closed her eyes, felt her resistance buckling.

Her mind roared a warning. *NO! No, Darcy. You don't want the life he can offer you. No! Tell him you don't want him.*

She pulled back quickly, jerking her eyes open, confusion making her voice wobbly and her words weaker.

"Please," she begged him, tears making their way over her lashes and down her cheeks when she opened her eyes. He glanced over to see her tongue dart out to lick a tear away from her lips and she heard him groan lightly and lean away from her. "Please let me go, Jack. I don't know how else to say this: I don't want you. I don't want you in my life."

That's a lie, her heart bellowed, warring with her mind, but her mind didn't retract it.

He winced and her heart clenched with the pain she was causing him. If it was anything like the pain she was causing herself, it was bad.

"I don't care. You need to come stay with me," he said again, his voice soft but hard at the same time. "You're not safe."

"Not *safe*?" she snorted. "I think I'm a hell of a lot safer here than in a remote house in the middle of the woods with you and your bro—"

"You're not. You're in danger."

"D-danger?"

"Yes."

He answered softly and she knew he was trying not to frighten her, but it only served to increase her panic.

"What do you mean?"

"My sister. I think she's…" He shook his head, working his jaw as he stared at his lap. "I think she's coming for you."

Jack swallowed and started telling Darcy about Lela. He told her about his father's mistress, Lynette, and her accidental death, falling into a sharp knife during a heated argument. He said that she left behind a child, Lela, who had been raised by his parents. He shared that his father had recently passed away and Lela was hurting and angry. She was looking for a sur-rogate father figure and resented that her brother was bound to a human. Jack said he wasn't positive, but he thought there was a good chance that Lela was coming to take out some her sadness and anger on Darcy.

"Tell her she doesn't need to come here. Just go home. Go be a father to your little sister."

He looked up at Darcy and she saw regret brimming in the beautiful dark eyes that she wished she didn't love.

"It's not that simple."

"Sure it is. Go back home. If she comes here, I'll tell her you're gone."

"No, she won't give up that easily. She wants me to herself."

Darcy shrugged, frustrated, wondering if she was getting the whole story because the song he was singing didn't make any sense to her.

"She's grieving. She might do something crazy." His face flushed and she knew he was withholding something, but she didn't know what, and he didn't want to tell her. "I'm afraid she'll track you down. I'm afraid she'll try…"

"She'll try to what, Jack?"

"To break the binding," he sighed.

"That's not possible. You've said a million times! I belong to you and you belong to me. It can't be broken. You said we're bound until death."

Jack nodded, staring at her, and although she hadn't meant the words to sound tender or as any assurance of her feelings for him—he had rattled them off so matter-of-factly—she could see the momentary glimmer of hope in his eyes as he looked at her.

But the voice she heard in her head wasn't soft or tender. It was hard and blunt.

That's right, Darcy. Until death.

It took a second for Darcy's brain to follow his meaning.

"Oh my God! She wants to *kill* me? You think she's coming here to *kill* me? Just because you're bound to me?" No wonder he was trying to hide the truth.

In her mind, you're in the way, so yes, she might try to hurt you. And you're not a Roug. You can't defend yourself from her. Julien and I are here to protect you.

Darcy covered her face with her hands. His abrupt return suddenly made sense to her. He wasn't here because he loved her and wanted to convince her to be with him. He wasn't here with flowery words of love or cajoling promises to get back into her good graces. He was only here out of duty—to protect Darcy from his sister.

She wished this realization didn't hurt. It should have somehow soothed her—after all, she didn't want him either—but it didn't. It ached that he wasn't back because he wanted her or missed her. He was only back out of obligation, out of a sense of duty or responsibility for her safety. And it bothered her. A lot.

Not to mention some crazy half-sister of Jack's who wanted her dead was actually coming to Carlisle to hurt her or kill her and God-only-knows-what-else to get her way. If Darcy stayed in her house, she was not only a sitting duck, she was a threat to the safety of the people she loved, like Willow and her brother. She had to go with Jack to lead this Lela away from her loved ones. She had no other choice. She was trapped.

And just like that her feelings of hurt and longing departed swiftly, replaced by anger—*anger* such that she'd never felt before. Cold, hard anger that blighted out her other thoughts. It was as though her life wasn't her own anymore, and the fury inside of her rushed forth like a tidal wave of bitterness.

She lowered her hands.

"You've destroyed my life," she said softly, feeling her eyes narrow as she stared at the black hair of his bowed head. "I will *never* forgive you for this."

"Well, I guess I'll have to live with that," he answered acidly, failing at trying to sound casual. His voice was laced with an anger as compelling as her own.

She wanted more of a reaction from him. She wanted him to own her anger and frustration, and the words poured out of her mouth without her thinking.

"Let's be clear about one thing, Jack. Don't think I'm going to suddenly just jump back in your bed."

When Jack looked up at her, his eyes were burning. Gold, churning, seething, undulating lava.

"Fine," he gritted out through clenched teeth.

"I mean it," she sneered, crossing her arms over her chest and staring at him. "Don't touch me."

His nostrils flared with hurt as he stared at her with yellow, narrowed eyes. She heard his voice in her head—a low, furious, dangerous growl.

You'd have to beg me first.

Her chest heaved from the impact of his words and she looked away from him. He stood up and made his way to the front door without looking at her again.

"Pack a bag," he threw over his shoulder, his speaking voice strained and low. "I'll wait for you outside."

HE OPENED THE FRONT DOOR and stepped outside, taking a deep breath of the cold night air. It felt like a balm on his hot, angry skin. He clenched his fists together, wishing he had something to hit, or better, wishing he could shift and hunt. He couldn't remember feeling so frustrated and angry at once. Fuck. Shit. Fuck. *Fuuuuuck!*

While Jack hadn't expected her to jump up and down for joy at the expectation of his protection, he still hadn't quite anticipated the quiet fury of her words. *I'll never forgive you for this.* He cringed, his breath shuddering as he exhaled through clenched teeth. It was clear how utterly repulsed she was by him, and he wasn't just angry and frustrated. He was hurt. A lot.

Whatever hopes he'd had when she opened the door were dashed by the fury in her eyes and the coldness of her voice.

Her voice that he loved so well. His heart had just about beat out of his chest when she'd opened the door with Willow. He'd felt the binding more solidly in that moment than he had since he'd kissed her so many years ago. It was like a tangible, touchable thing between them, this life force of energy that bound them to one another.

He saw her eyes roll back in her head a moment before she fainted and in one quick lurch forward, he had her in his arms once again, exactly where he wanted her when he'd left Portes de l'Enfer hours earlier. He'd felt a surge of tenderness holding her limp body in his arms as he had the night he almost killed Phillip Proctor. As he walked to the window seat, he thought about holding on to her, being the first face she saw as she woke up, touching his lips gently to hers and telling her that he loved her above all living beings on the face of the earth…but the memories of her little row boat cutting through the freezing water had stopped him. He settled her on the window seat and backed away, waiting for Willow to rouse her.

He ran his hands through his hair, leaning against her front door. Damn it, he *was* sorry that he had ever kissed her. He *was* sorry that he'd ruined her life. He *was* sorry that she had to come and stay with him against her will. But he had never intended to hurt her, and if she didn't want him anymore, fine. She could have it her way. As long as she was safe, he'd steer clear of her over the next few days. He certainly wasn't going to beg her to love him when she so clearly didn't.

He took a deep breath and exhaled loudly, gradually aware that Willow and Julien were staring at him from the swing at the end of the porch.

"Are you okay?" asked Willow, eyeing Jack suspiciously. "That was a marathon."

"Was it?" Jack asked.

Willow glanced at her watch. "Almost an hour."

"You get your questions answered?" he asked her.

Willow glanced at Julien, giving him a brief, pained look before turning back to Jack, her wide, dark eyes searching his face with worry.

She didn't answer him.

"How's my friend?" she asked instead.

"She's coming to stay with me for a while." Jack massaged his jaw with his thumb and forefinger, bracing himself for another attack from another angry female.

"Is that right?" She gave him a wary look then stood up gracefully and folded the blanket that had been draped across her lap as she sat next to Julien. She turned to Jack's brother, offering a weak smile. "Thanks for telling me so much."

Julien winked at her. "You sure?"

She shrugged at him then looked at Jack, hands on her hips, her small, wiry body sturdy on firmly planted bare feet. "She *wants* to stay with you?"

"She *needs* to," he answered, holding her eyes.

"She's not going anywhere if she doesn't *want* to."

Jack looked down at the dark-haired wisp of a woman with admiration. He was almost certain she didn't know what she was, the power she could wield once she accessed it. Until then, he could break her in half while still in human form, but she was standing up to him like a warrior Roug. She had backbone, he'd give her that.

"Then I guess you'll have to go talk to her."

"I guess I'll do that." She approached the front door then paused, looking back and forth between the brothers. "I want you both to know…I've never felt as happy to be Métis as I am right now."

"Yeah," said Julien, pursing his lips to avoid a grin. "Métis taste terrible."

"We wouldn't know," Jack retorted in a sour tone, giving his brother a look before pushing open the front door for Willow to go inside.

Once she was gone, he sat down next to his brother in the space vacated by Willow's departure and the old swing creaked under the difference in weight. He sighed, resting his elbows on his knees and bowing his head.

"Didn't go so well, eh?"

"Nah," whispered Jack. "Not great."

"She pretty much hates you?"

"That's about the lay of it."

"I couldn't believe it when you two were Eyespeaking. She's *human. Just* human. Full-blooded. No Roug blood. Not even Métis."

Jack sat back, looking over at his brother. "Told you."

On the drive down from Portes de l'Enfer, the brothers had talked about Darcy in depth, Jack sharing the entire history of his relationship with her. Their kiss, the incident in Boston, and their more recent meeting at Honoria's wedding. Jack left out some of the more intimate details of their weekend together, but spared none as he described her reaction to him in shifted form and her actions as she rowed away from him during *Dansmatête* last night, leaving him to drown.

Julien had gasped at this, knowing that the feelings and actions shared while inside with your mate were just as consequential as the ones you shared while fully conscious. What Darcy had done to Jack was not unheard of in Roug culture, but it was incredibly dangerous and bordered on taboo. If the vision had gone on longer, it could have even been life-threatening to Jack in real life.

"Maybe you *should* let Lela find her," Julian snarled quietly.

Jack's right hand had found Julien's neck in a split second without ever taking his eyes off the road. As he squeezed the tender skin around Julien's windpipe, Jack had articulated his words in a dark, uncompromising tone.

"*Nobody* hurts her. Not while I'm alive."

Julien had reached up, struggling to remove Jack's hand and Jack had finally released him. Julien sputtered and coughed, massaging his aching throat.

"Nod that we're in agreement, Julien."

Julien had nodded, exclaiming in a raspy voice, "*Merde! Vous êtes fou, Jacques!*"

"You think I'm crazy? Watch what happens if you—or Lela—touch a hair on her head. She's mine, Julien. I'll protect her with everything I am."

"Okay. Okay. I get it. Calm down."

As they sat on the swing, Julien nudged him. "Your mate's um, pretty, I guess. For a human. So, you never said if you two…"

"What?"

Julien grinned, enjoying Jack's discomfort. "You sorta glossed over the part about *being* with her. How did that work out? Were you able to…?"

Jack tilted his head to the side, his face curdling, and Julien's eyes sparkled.

"Did you or didn't you? Come on, Ja—"

Julien quieted abruptly, clearing his throat, as the front door opened and Darcy stepped onto the porch with a colorful, floral duffel bag on her shoulder. She was still wearing those cut-off shorts and Jack's eyes lingered on her long legs before raising them to her face. Her hair was pulled back severely in a ponytail and under the glare of the porch light he could see how puffy and blotchy her face was. She'd been crying. He could smell the salt on her skin.

"I need to get a few things from my office," she said quietly, refusing to look at him. "At least I can *work* while I'm in exile…"

She looked at him pointedly and he took her bag as she walked past him toward her office over the garage. He watched her go, realizing that the twenty feet from the porch to the garage even felt too far. As angry with her as he was, he didn't want her more than an arm's length away from him. Not with the threat of Lela.

Willow looked guarded and unhappy as she stood in the doorway. She trained her eyes on Jack.

"So what am I supposed to do if what's-her-name shows up here?"

"Lela. Her name's Lela, and she won't hurt you," said Julien. "She respects the old ways. As soon as she smells your scent, she'll know what you are."

"That's hugely comforting," said Willow, crossing her thin arms over her small chest.

"Send her to me," said Jack. "I'll be waiting for her."

"Maybe Julien could stay here?" she asked, flicking her eyes to him, and then coloring with the boldness of her request.

Jack shook his head. "Julien's hunting Lela while I stay with Darcy. Believe me, Lela won't hurt you. She may try to scare you, though, Willow. She could shift to frighten you."

Willow's eyes widened.

Jack and Julien exchanged looks, and Jack nodded slightly.

Julien cleared his throat and Willow looked over at him. "Do you want to see me shift? A little? To show you what it's—"

Willow reached out and grabbed Julien's arm, pulling him into the living room without another word and closing the door behind her.

Well, that should be interesting.

Jack looked up at the garage. He could see Darcy's silhouette against a drawn shade near her desk window. He watched the graceful movements of her body as she gathered books and notes together in a pile, finally shutting off the light.

Willow and Julien emerged from the house. Willow looked pale.

"Are you okay?" Jack asked.

Willow's wide, black eyes regarded Jack solemnly and she nodded.

"Sure?"

She nodded again and Jack could see that her eyes were filled with tears. He put his hand on her arm.

"We're still just Julien and Jack. Neither of us wants to hurt you."

She pulled her arm back from him, crossing her chest protectively. "It's just a lot to, um, process."

"What is?" asked Darcy, offering a heavy canvas bag filled with files and textbooks to Jack.

"N–nothing," muttered Willow. "Just, um. Everything. All of this."

Jack noticed as Darcy's eyes narrowed at her friend. She looked at Jack and he looked away, gesturing to Julien. They headed to the car, giving the women a chance to say their good-byes.

Julien got in the backseat, and after waiting for Darcy for a second, Jack decided to let her open her own goddamned door. To hell with chivalry.

He sat down in his own seat and cracked his window, trying to hear some of their conversation.

"…remember Boston. He cares for you…"

"…stop, Will. Enough…"

"…keep an open mind…"

"…you're trying to help, but just…"

"…just stay safe…"

"…you too."

Darcy hugged Willow then made her way down the porch steps, opening her door and settling into the passenger seat without a word. She buckled her seatbelt then turned to Jack.

I guess you got what you wanted.

I never, ever wanted this for us.

Then he turned from her, put the car in gear, and headed home.

Chapter 3

T HEY DROVE IN ALMOST TOTAL silence except for Julien's two half-hearted attempts at polite conversation with Darcy, questions which she answered with monotone, monosyllabic answers. She had zero interest in casual conversation with Jack's brother.

She should probably feel more frightened of Lela, but after Willow's revelations about Jack's behavior in Boston, she knew he would protect her. Of course he'd have to do it without touching her, which made her remember his response: *You'd have to beg me first.*

She glanced at Jack's hard profile, feeling cold inside. Since he'd reentered her life two weeks ago, he'd been so anxious to be with her, spend time with her, touch her…so loving and longing and tender. It felt strange for him to be pushing her away. And she grudgingly admitted that it didn't feel good. In fact, she'd never felt so alone. Not even when he was gone.

A chill went through Darcy and she hugged herself more tightly.

"You're cold," murmured Jack.

She pointedly ignored him. The air was heavy between them and she sensed he expected her to say *I didn't think that,* but she was determined not to fall into intimacy of any kind with him. The best way to ensure her defenses stayed high was to refuse to be baited into even a modest sociable rapport. When asked a question, her plan was to answer it in as few words as possible. Otherwise, she wasn't available for small talk and other gateway conversations.

The reality was that she didn't feel like she had much control over her life anymore and she didn't like it. Her binding to Jack was chosen for her, and his nature was an unpleasant surprise about which she could do nothing. She wouldn't be able to go down to Dartmouth this week to teach or visit her samples, and now she couldn't even live in her own home.

Not to mention, her heart—her treacherous, traitorous heart—wouldn't listen to the ample reason offered by her head and insisted on doing its own thing: loving Jack wholly and unreservedly, in spite of what he was. And her body—her weak, eager, panting body—wouldn't stop leaping and catching and tingling and shivering like a wild animal in heat just because he sat beside her.

Well, she thought, *you two can suck it. My mind's in charge. And my mind says NO.*

Her mind said no to loving him and no to wanting him. No to feverish skin and losing time and a life spent with a creature of such depravity. No to sisters who want you dead and customs you can't comprehend. No! No! No!—

She heard Jack's voice ask a question and whipped her head to him.

"NO!" she blurted out.

"Whoa!" He looked confused, brows furrowed. "Fine. Carry your own bags. I was just trying to help."

Darcy looked around. They were parked in front of his lodge and she saw Julien through the windshield walking over to the garage. She'd been so deep in thought she hadn't even noticed the car had stopped.

She looked up at the dark house and realized she'd never seen it so still and dark. *No lights on.* Which meant he'd come to her first, directly, not even stopping at home first.

"I don't want your help," she muttered.

"Fine," he said again, his voice terse and growly. "You know, it's going to be a delightful few days if you're planning to be this unpleasant."

"Huh." She turned to him, tapping her chin with one finger, forgetting her rule not to engage in conversation with him. "Am I not being pleasant enough for you? Pray tell me, master of comportment, how I am meant to behave when the man I have loved *my whole life* turns out to be a werewolf who eats people and has a little sister who wants to kill me? Am I not being *delightful* enough for you?"

He had sucked in a deep breath as she yelled at him and his narrowed eyes widened with tenderness as his face softened, his lips parting in surprise.

What? What did I just—

She sighed, biting her lower lip in frustration, realizing what she'd said. Damn it. She'd just told him that she'd loved him her whole life.

"Say it again," he demanded softly, his voice breathless, deep and rich, laced with wonder, naked in her ears, saturated with the full measure of his desperation. He reached out to touch the hand closest to him, covering it with his as it rested on her bare thigh.

His face. The hope and tenderness on his face was so beautiful—so heartbreakingly beautiful—he looked like the boy she'd loved so desperately in high school, striding toward her in the darkness, a year's worth of brooding suddenly replaced by gentleness, by hope, as he pressed his lips to hers and changed her life forever.

"*Please*, Darcy."

She winced at his words and at the heat—the dazzling, perfect, familiar heat— of his hand covering hers, his flesh melting into hers, her defenses wavering as his eyes besieged hers. Her heart slammed against her ribcage, making it hard to draw a deep breath, and a small strangled sob escaped her throat as she gazed at him. It was just enough to jar her from her thoughts, from her feverish, fathomless longing. She reached inside, clawing for her anger, and, unearthing it, she pulled her hand away. She looked down, clenching her teeth together as her mind resumed control with one searing, deliberate, blistering word:

"No."

Then she turned and opened her door, swinging her duffel bag up on her shoulder and breathing deeply as she beelined to the house.

Her life might be in utter chaos, but what small authority she still had over her words was hers and hers alone, and while she might need to stay with him for her own safety, she didn't have to like it.

GOD DAMN IT! DAMN IT. Damn it. Damn it. Fuck!
He quelled the urge to slam his hands into the steering wheel, curling them into fists instead, feeling his eyes brighten to gold with frustration. She had caught him utterly and completely off guard. He never even dreamed he'd hear the word love fall from her lips when she flashed her eyes at him, using that sarcastic, smartass, condescending tone. And now that he'd been teased with it, he ached to hear it again. Her refusal felt cruel and left him cold.

Damn it. What a fucking mess.

He exhaled loudly, puffing in frustration.

She didn't want him? *Fine.*

She wanted to hate him for destroying her life? *Have at it.*

And if she wanted to think of him as nothing more than a sinister, cannibalistic monster all the live-long day until the cows came home? *Great!*

She could stay in her snit and he'd give her a wide berth. If that's how it had to be? *Aces. Fabulous. FINE!*

She stood by the front door with her back to him. She refused to turn around, even though he was taking his time in the car. His nostrils flared with frustration and he clenched his jaw together until it throbbed.

He didn't want her rigid and angry, repulsed by him, suspicious and spiteful. He wanted her loving and warm, pliant beneath him, whispering her everlasting love. He shuddered as he heard her words in his head again—*the man I have loved my whole life.*

Regardless of what she'd inadvertently said, and how good it felt to hear it, he seemed closer to China than to getting Darcy back in his bed, and now to know—on some level, no matter how much she wished she didn't—that she loved him, just made it worse. *Damn it! Damn, damn, damn!* After a lifetime of waiting for her, and then actually having her, facing her coldness was beyond frustrating. Especially when he could tell that whether she liked it or not, she still wanted him too.

Stubborn woman.

When he had covered her hand, he felt her heart rate speed up, felt her lungs compress from the pounding beat. He could smell the sudden rush of wetness between her thighs, the way her body heated up almost instantly, preparing itself for him. He'd read the lust in her eyes before she'd looked away. It softened Jack's anger to realize how hard she was fighting against her feelings for him and attraction to him.

He suddenly heard Tombeur's words, still fresh in his head from last night. *Never saw a binding as strong as yours.*

He sat back in his seat, watching her thoughtfully through the windshield—the way she had her hair pulled back into that severe ponytail at the nape of her neck. He could tell that her arms were crossed over her chest, her posture guarded, even from behind. She was in a defensive position, which made his eyes widen in realization.

She *did* want him.

She *did* love him.

She wouldn't *surrender* to him.

And she wasn't just fighting him; she was fighting herself. It struck him with clarity and poignancy as he watched her shiver once, shifting her weight from one foot to the other, still refusing to turn around. This wasn't about her heart or her body. This was about her head.

Jack took a deep breath, processing his thoughts. She was a scientist, suddenly surrounded by circumstances that made no sense to her. In a Roug to Roug binding, this wouldn't have been an issue—both mates would have long ago acknowledged their nature and gifts, embraced the strange, iron bond that compelled them, and enjoyed the special connections that accompanied it. He felt a wave of compassion for her as he realized how difficult it must be for her to accept who he was and who they were as a bound couple. He was expecting her to accept the realities of his supernatural world, which had to be painfully, shockingly impossible for such a logical mind.

And then he knew: *You want her body and her heart? You're going to have to win her mind.*

A gentle smile spread across his face as he resolved upon what he needed to do, loading and locking a battle plan into his head that would frustrate his body in the short term, but hopefully reward it later with her trust. *She thinks she doesn't want you? Doesn't need you? Then give her exactly what she wants. Treat her like one of the humans you used to bodyguard in Boston, with respect and deference, but nothing that even hints of intimacy.*

He thought about how easily she used Eyespeak now, how quickly she rattled off the facts of the binding. How would she feel if he treated her like a normal, unbound human he was being paid to protect? *That's what she thinks she wants, what she says she wants, so give it to her. Free her mind to figure out what she wants.*

Put the heat on the back burner. Quit looking at her body. Don't touch her and don't provoke her. Take your body and your heart out of the equation for now so she can too. Don't force your nature and your world on her. No talking about Rougs. Don't refer to the binding. No Dansmatête. No Eyespeak. Don't force her into your world. Give her mind the space to decide whether or not she wants the life you can offer.

Treat her like a human while she finds her footing, not like your mate. Give her space to want you and miss you. Space for her heart and body to work on her head. It was her head that would—or would not—allow her heart and body to surrender. It was her head that would finally have to see that she still belonged to him, in spite of his nature, regardless of his DNA, despite the seeming impossibility of being together.

The bottom line? *Give her what she wants: space, respect, and indifference. And see if maybe—just maybe—you get what you want in the end.*

HE'D CERTAINLY TAKEN HIS TIME getting out of the car, but once he did, he was perfectly affable as he unlocked the door, flicking on the lights and gesturing for her to precede him inside.

She walked into the vestibule, keeping her duffel bag securely on her shoulder, like it could protect her, the only familiar thing in an unfamiliar life. She didn't look back at the door when he closed it. The last time she'd been up against that door—

"Let's get the lights on, huh?"

Jack walked around her, not touching her, and flicked on the lights in the living room as he headed for the kitchen.

"Do you want anything? I'm making tea."

She would kill or die for a cup of tea.

"No," she answered, one foot stepping into the wonderfully high-ceilinged room where they'd first made love.

Her memories assaulted her immediately. The weight of Jack's body over hers. His mouth covering hers. His lips sucking on her nipples. His tongue licking the most intimate part of her, the strong, hard, length of him filling her until they both—

"You sure?"

"Huh?" she moaned in a dazed whisper, looking up. He was filling a teakettle at the sink, his eyebrows raised expectantly. She took a deep breath and composed herself quickly. "Uh. No. I mean, yeah. No tea. I'm sure."

"Okay." He approached her from the kitchen, stopping a good five feet in front of her and offering her a friendly smile. "If you change your mind, please feel free to make your own. I'm sure you can find whatever you need. If you can't, just ask. I hope you'll make yourself at home."

He was being perfectly pleasant, which was throwing her off a little. She wasn't used to him being so…normal. He was usually so brooding and intense with his dark eyes, or *burning* eyes, making her body feel too many things at once. She still stood under the arch that led from the vestibule into the living room, unsure of herself and suddenly very, very tired.

"Hey," he said lightly, glancing at her eyes and then away quickly. "I bet you're tired. How about I show you to your room?"

He turned and started up the stairs without approaching her or offering to take her bag, so she traipsed behind, following him up the stairs.

"I have a comfortable guest room for you. Opposite side of the house from my room, so you'll have your privacy."

His voice was light, yet warm, and void of any suggestive undertones about his room.

She thought of his bed—his huge, downy bed where she had slept all night with him lodged intimately inside of her. The warmth of his body behind hers. The hair on his chest against the smoothness of her back. His strong, corded legs intertwined with hers as his hands rested lightly under the weight of her breasts.

Her mouth felt dry and she swallowed, forcing those memories away and remembering the *last* time she was in his bed: waking up after fainting on Thursday morning to find him watching her, his face a mask of worry and regret.

She circled the banister, following him to the right, away from the side of the hallway that housed his bedroom.

"Here we are," he said, pushing open the last door at the far end of the hallway, next to the bathroom where she'd showered after getting caught in the rain last Saturday. She remembered he'd left his robe on the sink for her. And socks. Thick socks for her freezing feet.

She looked up at his face, catching his eyes, but all she heard was a buzzing noise, a hum, like white noise, like nothing. She raised her eyebrows and he gave her a modest, polite nod, looking away.

He stepped back from the door so she could enter the room. It was simple but comfortable, exactly the sort of guest room she would choose for herself. A full-sized, walnut sleigh bed with a blue and white toile comforter dominated the cozy room. Two end tables, each with a simple brass candlestick lamp and cream-colored silk lampshade, flanked the bed. The floor was hardwood, with a thick coat of shellac making it shine, and a wool throw rug with a periwinkle hydrangea lay on the floor at the side of the bed. There was an antique dresser on the wall across from the bed with a mirror and doors on either side.

"Left door is a closet. Right is a bathroom." He opened his palms. "Sure you don't want some tea?"

Darcy placed her bag on the bed and looked back at Jack, who still stood in the doorway. He glanced at her, then stepped back into the hallway, his hands clasped in front of him like a hotel porter.

"No. Thank you," she murmured, looking into his eyes again. Buzzing. Nothing more. It annoyed her not to have access to his thoughts. She'd become accustomed to hearing his voice in her head.

Where are you? she wondered distractedly, catching his eyes. *Can't you hear me?*

"Well, then." He pressed his lips together, giving her a light smile. "I guess I'll say good-night."

"Yes, I… Good-night, Jack."

"Sleep tight." He turned away from her and she listened to his departing footsteps until he opened his bedroom door and closed it behind him.

H E FLOPPED DOWN ON HIS back, exhaling.
       Merde! This is not going to be easy.

When she asked, *Can't you hear me?* it had taken all of his self-control not to flinch, not to think, and not to respond. His hands had twitched to reach out and touch her hair, cup her jaw and crush her lips with his. So he'd pressed them together, giving her that polite, milquetoast smile.

He sighed. *Stay the course, Jack. She needs space from Roug ways.* He knew that everything needed to feel more normal for her peace of mind and for her to decide what she really wanted.

He ran his hands through his hair, staring at the ceiling, his bedroom painful and soothing at once. Darcy's scent was everywhere. It was in the sheets that he refused to change, in the wood fiber of his headboard. All over his rocking chair where she'd sat naked. In the curtains that flanked the windows where she'd gotten up to watch the moon. And the thing was? He wanted her scent to surround him. He just wished she was here too.

But it wasn't lost on him that her tone had softened in the small space of time since they'd entered the house. She'd thanked him when he showed her to her room and she'd told him good night in a much softer, less combative voice than earlier.

Give her room to figure out what she wants. But, for God's sake, distract yourself, Jack.

He hadn't showered since returning with his father last night, and since a cold shower would help ease his desire for her, he started there.

After, with his hair wet and tousled, he threw on some jeans and left his room to find Julien.

He was surprised to hear her door open at the end of the hall as he approached the stairs.

"Jack?"

He hadn't bothered with a shirt, and he watched her eyes widen as they ran slowly over his upper chest, down his abs, finally resting on the muscular V that led to—

Even from fifteen feet away, he heard as she sucked in an audible breath, her mouth open and soft. Finally she raised her eyes to his.

You're so beauti—

"Did you need something?" he asked, cutting off her thought, trying to sound blandly polite as he crossed his arms over his chest.

"I, uh…yes." He knew she probably didn't mean to, but she smiled at him. "I forgot my charger. For my iPhone. Do you…"

"Have an extra? Sure. I'll find it and leave it outside your door."

"Thanks."

Suddenly her forehead wrinkled and she grimaced as though she couldn't believe what she was seeing. Then she was moving toward him, on a mission, closing the distance between them. Her eyes were trained on his shoulder and he stopped breathing as she raised two fingers and pressed them against the pink, jagged scar tissue of his recent gunshot wound. Her eyes flicked to his then back to the scar, which she lightly caressed with her cool fingers. Jack felt his body responding to her touch—the first she'd voluntarily offered him since they said good-bye in his car last Sunday. He clenched his jaw together. *Control. Control. Control.*

"Oh, Jack," she whispered, staring at the angry, twisted skin, her fingers resting like a cool brand against his skin. "What happened?'

He stared at her bowed head, trying to think of words. Any words other than: *A member from another pack took a shot at me while my mentor and I carried my doped-up father into the woods before shifting to take him home to die.*

With all the strength in his body, he stepped back from her, leaving her fingers dangling in midair as he fixed a neutral expression on his face, glancing nonchalantly at his shoulder.

"It's nothing." Then he shrugged, turning to head down the stairs.

"You were hurt," she murmured. "You were hurt on Friday night. I—I felt it."

More than you can possibly know, he thought to himself, still looking away from her, remembering the feeling of his body losing the battle against the icy cold water.

He stood immobile on the stairs for a moment, fighting the instinct to say these words aloud and tell her how deeply she had hurt him. He clenched his jaw, holding his tongue, and realized she wasn't referring to the first time he pulled her inside, but the second, as he fell asleep, after his father died. She must have felt his pain and sorrow when he'd pulled her inside, when he'd fallen asleep at her feet. He looked down quickly, the moment almost unbearably charged with unsaid things.

Get away from her. Now.

He wanted to grab her around the waist and pull her up against his body, plunge his tongue into her mouth until she moaned his name and wove her hands through his hair. Until she told him she loved him and would never hurt him again as terribly as she had last night. His fingers trembled and he felt his hips shift to turn around and face her.

NO! Go now, Jack. Now!

He made his feet move down the stairs without turning back to look at her, tossing, "I'll find you that charger." over his shoulder as he left her.

DARCY WATCHED HIM GO, DAZED and confused, her fingers still warm from where they had briefly rested on his skin. She backed up to her room then turned, shutting the door behind her.

He had backed away from her touch, ended their conversation as quickly as he could, and left, barely looking at her. He was so cool, so politely impersonal.

He wouldn't meet her eyes, not that she'd been able to hear inside his head since they'd returned to the lodge.

It felt like he was pushing her away.

Looking at herself in the mirror, she saw the confusion on her drawn face. Making a choice to push Jack away was one thing…having him do the same to her was quite another, and she had to consider how she felt about getting exactly what she asked for.

"What do you want?" she demanded from her reflection in a hiss. "What the hell do you want from him? If you don't want him, you're getting exactly what you want. Be happy."

But she wasn't. At all.

In fact, she would go so far to say that if it continued—this disinterested politeness, this protection based on duty instead of love—it would be *unbearable* for her. She flinched at the thought of losing his teasing smile, his burning eyes, the touch of his hands on her body, his lips moving hungrily over hers. *You belong to me, and I belong to you...*

She wanted to weep with confusion and frustration.

Of course she wanted him.

Of course she loved him.

She just wished he was a human being. Just a regular human being.

No, a voice inside her heart whispered. *No, you don't, Darcy. You're drawn to him—to all of him—and that includes his darkness. You wanted it from the beginning. From the very beginning. Make no mistake: Part of what you love most about Jack Beauloup is acknowledging his darkness but believing that you can brighten it. Sun to his moon. Day to his night.*

When she'd seen him that very first time in the library, she'd been blinded initially by the sun in her eyes. Then as the clouds had shifted to dull the light, the first thing she'd been able to focus on was the inky blackness of the stranger's hair at the far table. And when their eyes met, her heart had leaped in her chest in recognition, in sympathy, almost in *reunion,* two halves of a whole finding one another after a long, lonely exile apart. She'd watched his cold, brooding eyes warm just for a second as they held hers, and she'd felt the truth deep inside where her mind and heart and body formed a perfect trinity of understanding: *I could be the light in your darkness.*

She took a shaky breath and sighed at her face in the mirror, still moved by the fierce connection she'd felt to him so long ago.

She looked away from her face and grimaced as another reality surfaced: She didn't like the packaging. She wasn't frightened of Jack, personally. She knew that he wouldn't hurt her, felt strongly in every fiber of her body that he would expend his own life protecting hers, if necessary. But she didn't know how a shape-shifting Roux-ga-roux could fit into her life, and vice versa. It wasn't that she didn't want him physically—she did. It wasn't that she didn't love him—she did. The problem was that she simply didn't see a way to be together.

Big tears welled in her eyes and a lump rose in her throat until it hurt to swallow. Her hands dug into the soft wood of the antique dresser until her fingers ached and she left a neat set of eight small indentations.

She turned and sat gingerly on the bed, picking up her cell phone charger and carefully coiling it before hiding it in the zipper pocket of her duffel bag.

Then she lay back on the bed, her head swimming with confusion and despair, and allowed the quiet tears to run free from the saturated wells of her eyes.

JACK STRODE INTO THE NIGHT'S cool air, fighting the urge to shift and run off all of his frustration and want. It would feel so good to run, to feel the branches swipe at his protected body, his feet thumping on the floor of the woods. If he was quiet enough, he might be able to stalk and kill a deer. *Blech.* He didn't love the taste of raw deer—it was bitter and tough compared to human meat—but the mere act of the kill would quench some of the fire in his chest, and tasty or not, the blood would quench a bit of the fire in his belly.

Oh, yes. That'd be perfect, Jack. You'd come back with blood all over your body, your hair and beard wild, covered in leaves and dirt. The way your luck's been lately, Darcy'd be standing at the top of the stairs waiting to see it.

No. No hunting. No shifting. Save it for Lela.

Lela.

Jack crossed the front courtyard, briefly admiring the almost-perfect half-moon, oddly called the Three-Quarter. The math came easily. Twenty-three days 'til full.

Entering the garage, he climbed the stairs to the writing studio where Julien would be staying, and found his brother sitting at the desk, typing on his laptop.

"Looking for fresh kills?"

Julien nodded, scanning the police notices for Quebec City. "Not finding any, though. None reported, anyway. I don't think she's traveling shifted, Jack. Which is good. It'll take her longer to get here if she doesn't run."

Jack plopped down on the loveseat that he'd had upholstered for Darcy in soothing moss green tones. "You want to stay in the house?"

"Nah. Best your, um, *mate* doesn't see me coming and going too much. Didn't get a very friendly feeling from her. She can pretend she's just there with you."

Jack scoffed. "She'd rather be anywhere than with me."

"Yeah," Julien swiveled in the chair, facing Jack. "Sort of picked up on a little *tension.*"

"Tension? She's pushing me away with both hands."

"Sorry, brother. That's gotta hurt."

"Doesn't feel great." Jack sighed. "Nothing I can do about it, though.

I'm giving her space."

"Women hate space. They think they want space, but they hate it and they make you pay for it later."

Jack rolled his eyes, changing the subject. "What'd you talk to Willow about?"

Julien scratched his thick beard. "She had a lot of questions. How does it feel when we shift? She made me detail what happens. She asked about hunting and killing. I left out some details of that. I told her about the bindings. She asked if I felt yours was legit. I said it was, but that I'd never seen anything like it. I mentioned the re-bindi—uh…um, I mean, we talked a little bit about Natalia. She asked about the stuff Nat had been hooked on. Seemed real interested in that. She's a smart little *Enchanteresse.*"

Jack leaned forward. He hadn't been listening carefully, distracted with thoughts of Darcy's fingers on his shoulder, but he perked up at the word *Enchanteresse.* "Do you think she knows?"

"What she is?" Julien shook his head. "Nah. She wouldn't have been nervous around us at all. In fact, when *I* realized what she was, *I* got tense for a minute, but I'm positive she didn't know. I mentioned the word and she didn't flinch."

"She's also a doctor. A Western doctor."

"Some combination," murmured Julien respectfully.

Jack had researched Willow's family but there was nothing concrete about her *Nohkom* or father being blooded *Enchanteresses.* It was possible she was a first-generation enchantress, but he'd only know if he asked her directly and he wasn't interested in opening that conversation.

"Maybe it's weak," said Jack. "She's only a quarter."

"Pfft. Didn't feel weak at all to me. Felt like if she wanted to cast or conjure, it'd be just as sealing as any other full-blooded *Enchanteresse.* But, I could be wrong. Humans aren't my strongest point. I guess you'd know better…" Julien shrugged. "She's cute too. I'd bed her, you know, if I wasn't looking for Lela. Then again, things go south with an *Enchanteresse,* BAM! You're suddenly a field mouse or a—"

"Don't even think about it."

"Huh?" Julien looked up, surprised, then smirked. "Why not? What do you care? She's not your mate. She's Métis. I could scratch her itch and she could scratch mine—"

Jack leaned forward, sitting on the edge of the couch. "I'm asking you to leave her alone."

Julien shook his head, annoyed. "Save your growls. I'm not getting tangled up with an *Enchanteresse*—I don't have a death wish. Besides, I intend to bind myself to Lela as soon as she gets here."

"You sure about that?"

"Yeah, I am. Been sure on it forever. Felt it before I bound to Natalia and just about the second that binding was broken. Lela can't feel it because she's been fixed on you, but yeah. She's the one."

"She's a handful of trouble, Julien."

"Oh, she's two handfuls of trouble, Jack. But I've got two hands. She's *mine.*"

Jack heard the warning in his brother's voice. He understood better than anyone that sometimes you were pulled to someone for reasons you couldn't nail down. Your entire being cried out to them and there was nothing you could do about it but answer the call.

"Speaking of my dear little sister, did you catch a scent yet? At all?"

"Nothing. She hasn't been here."

"Yet," said Jack, sitting back. "What's the plan?"

"I'll patrol around your place and Darcy's house every few hours until I pick up her scent. Once I find it, we wait here. She'll come looking for Darcy."

"And then?"

"You'll have to restrain her so I can spark to her, Jack."

"Restrain her?" Jack scowled at his little brother. "Shifted? You're going to try a Shifted Binding?"

Shifted Bindings were not impossible, but incredibly intense. Because every body part was on high alert, it could turn into a very passionate, very explosive, very *immediate* mating in full Roug form.

"If I have to. She'll still probably try to knock my teeth out, so you better hold her tight. But as soon as we're bound she won't hate Darcy anymore. She'll barely remember why she came here in the first place."

"Julien, I can't overpower her unless I'm shifted."

"That's right."

"But Darcy's here."

Julien nodded then gave Jack a look and shrugged. "Might want to show her first."

Jack took a deep breath. He hadn't considered that in keeping Darcy safe he might need to shift in her presence. He'd decided long ago to never risk losing her by shifting in front of her. Hell, she had freaked out just seeing his claws retract. How would she react to seeing him in full shifted form?

Julien smiled. "The little *Enchanteresse* took it well."

"Stop calling her that. *Willow*."

"*Oui, Jacques! Saule, la belle Enchanteresse.*"

Saule meant "willow tree" in French, and Julien looked very pleased with himself. He grinned and continued. "Gave me ideas, seeing her eyes go all soft and shocked and wide watching me shift. It was pretty hot, Jack."

"You're an idiot."

"Says the one of us bound to the human who's never even seen him in full-blooded form." Julien rolled his eyes, standing up. He pulled his shirt over his head and shucked off his pants. "Enough about *la belle Saule*. Time to go sniff out my mate."

"Not here!" exclaimed Jack. "What if Darcy's looking out the window? Go shift in the woods. Where she can't see!"

Julien shook his head. "I'm not ashamed of who I am, Jack. You should try it."

"IN THE WOODS."

It was too late. Julien's eyes burned gold and Jack watched as his claws started protracting by his side, inch by inch. Watching the prickly fur emerge from Julien's skin made Jack itch. Julien's fangs dropped and his feet splayed larger, thick calluses forming on the pads and sides. His body grew in height and width, the muscles in his chest and thighs expanding to thrice their human size until he stood fully formed: a tall, broad, burning-eyed, fanged, clawed, fur-covered creature. He turned to the window, throwing back his head and howling at the moon before speeding down the stairs, out of sight, lightning fast.

Jack heard one more howl about thirty seconds later, about half a mile away.

He bit his thumbnail, annoyed.

I'm not ashamed of who I am.

Yeah, you are.

I'm not.

But, was he? Was he ashamed of being a Roux-ga-roux? Would he give it up if he had the chance? He had a quick, clean flashback to that night he first kissed Darcy. He'd forgotten after all these years, but yes, he had wished he wasn't Roug. He had admitted how much he hated the killing side of who he was, how much he wished he could just be a full-blooded human so that he could be with Darcy. So that he could have her.

He hung his head between his legs in dismay. Fate had only gotten part of the order right that night—sure, he could have her, but only as a full-blooded Roug. And having her, of course, wasn't exactly working out since she despised him and wished he'd never come near her in the first place. And just when things didn't look bleak enough, Jack's hopeless thoughts were compounded by another:

Julien was right. With Lela coming and a possible confrontation, it was likely that Darcy would see him in shifted form in order for him to protect her. He thought of the way she seemed to soften toward him as he acted more "human" tonight.

All of that hard work for nothing.

Chapter 4

DARCY HEARD A LIGHT KNOCK at her door the next morning and roused herself from sleep to answer. The hallway was empty, but on the floor she found the cell phone charger in a neat coil with a note that read simply: *Coffee's ready.*

She looked down the hallway again, but hearing nothing, she picked up the charger and returned to her room. Unzipping her duffel, she took out a pair of soft, worn jeans, frayed to white around the waist and cuffs from years of wear. She clutched them to her chest as she looked out the window, watching the rivulets of rain snake down the glass of her bedroom window. It would be a chilly day, not that it mattered since she'd undoubtedly be spending it trapped inside under Jack's watchful eyes.

She chose a soft pink, scooped-neck, long-sleeved shirt to wear on top then twisted her hair up into a loose chignon, tendrils falling around her face and no pins to keep them up. *Oh, well.* She touched the necklace she'd been wearing since she found it—the eternity symbol that Willow had given her so long ago, that Jack had stolen for fifteen years.

She considered taking it off, but then recalled his disinterested politeness last night and couldn't resist leaving it on. *Go ahead and act like you don't see it. In fact…*

She pulled the barrette out of her chignon and let her hair tumble in silky waves around her shoulders. She lifted her breasts in her bra and tugged her shirt down to maximize her ample cleavage. Fishing around in her purse, she found her lip gloss. She ran the spongy wand over her lips, pursed them and smiled.

There we go. Now try and treat me like your Great-Aunt Harriett. I dare you.

Her triumphant smile slowly faded as her head played devil's advocate.

You called him a monster. You told him to go away. You told him that he's destroying your life and you'd never forgive him. He's respecting your wishes and you're teasing him. It's not fair.

She took a deep breath and released it through her shiny lips. Regardless of what she'd said to him in anger, she *wasn't* ready to let him go yet, and starting this morning she was going to make it as difficult as possible for him to treat her like his dowager aunt. She wanted a reaction; she needed to know he still wanted her and—even more importantly—that he still loved her and wasn't just protecting her out of a sense of duty. Determined, she pulled the bedroom door shut behind her and headed downstairs.

As she approached the kitchen she could hear Jack's voice, and its deep, animated sound made her stop, lurking at the bottom of the stairs, around the corner from the kitchen where they couldn't see her.

"...couldn't believe it. I'll give you this—that took some balls."

"When she said your name I just about fell over. She's always had a thing for you," said Julien.

Darcy felt like she'd been slapped. Or doused with a bucket of freezing water. *What? Who? Who's always had a thing for Jack and what did "she" do that took balls?*

"Oh, come on. She just looks up to me."

"There's no *just* about it. Made me crazy my whole life. Jacques this. Jacques that."

"*Pére* was always MIA and I was the oldest. That's all it was." He paused and Darcy could barely get her head around the ramifications of this statement before he continued. "Who knows? Maybe you're right. I'll be honest, though, I'm pissed at her, Julien, pulling that stunt, making me kiss her at the Gathering."

Making. Me. Kiss. Her.

Darcy's eyes widened; her nostrils flared and her lip curled. If she'd been Roug, her eyes would have been on fire, because even as a human she felt her blood heat up to boiling. Her face felt blistering hot and the shell of her ear was on fire.

Someone had kissed his lips.

Someone had kissed what belonged to her.

She felt dizzy from the rush of adrenaline that made her want to find this "her" and slam her fist into the unknown bitch's mouth again and again until it split and bled. Until the memory of Jack's lips was replaced by the memory of Darcy's fist.

She turned the corner and walked into the kitchen, stopping in the doorway, crossing her arms under her breasts, which lifted her heaving chest up and outward. She found Jack and Julien at the kitchen table and made eye contact with Jack over Julien's head.

Who did you kiss?

Jack's eyes dropped to her breasts and he sat up straighter, his mouth parting lightly. Finally he shook his head and looked down quickly. When he looked back up at her he was smiling politely, doing the Great-Aunt Harriett's dutiful nephew routine again.

"Morning, Darcy. Did you sleep well?"

Julien turned from his seat at the table, his chipper smile fading as he came face to face with the generous swell of her chest, rising and falling with the force of her breathing. He quickly raised his glance, taking in the redness of her face, neck, and chest. He gestured loosely to her face.

"You look a little…flushed."

Darcy flicked a narrow-eyed, terse glance at him then returned her eyes to Jack.

WHO, GODDAMNIT? WHO DID YOU KISS?

He blinked at the tone and volume of her voice in his head, but it was her only indication that he had heard her.

"Coffee?" he asked, congenially, gesturing to the coffee maker on the counter.

Her eyes burned from holding them open and she blinked twice, feeling tears gather. He had kissed someone during the short time he was away from her and now he was trying to act like it didn't happen.

"No," she murmured.

Julien looked back and forth between his brother and Darcy then stood up, awkwardly waving toward his chair. "You want to sit? I was heading out for a run anyway…"

She sat down without dropping Jack's eyes and Julien quietly made his way out the back door.

More buzzing. More white noise. She gritted her teeth in frustration that he was ignoring her. She switched gears. For now, she needed to know…

"Who did you kiss?" she finally whispered aloud.

He winced. It was so slight and so momentary an expression, if she hadn't been watching closely, she would have missed it. But, she was watching closely. She couldn't possibly look away.

"It doesn't matter," he said softly, his voice bland and even.

"It does to me."

His nostrils flared in his apathetic face and that second brief show of real emotion was a relief to her even as his face quickly resumed a façade of dry boredom.

"And why exactly is that?" he asked.

She folded her hands on the table before her, not surprised to see the backs flushed deep pink. Her whole body was on fire. Jack belonged to *her*. To her alone and no one else, and certainly not to whomever he was kissing.

"Who?" she asked again, her voice gravelly and low in her dry mouth, the cogs of an engine grinding to a full and complete stop.

He shook his head back and forth and spoke softly. "Why do you want to know? No, a better question is…why do you care? You asked me to leave. You said you didn't want to be with me. You let me—"

"Who?" Barely a breath now.

He raised his mug to his lips and sipped before replacing it on the table. "One of the girls in my pac—at home. She forced a sparking with me."

"Forced a sparking?"

He sighed. "She wanted to bind herself to me."

Darcy's eyes flew open in fury and she balled her hands into side-by-side fists on the table in front of her. "You're *already* bound to someone."

"Is that right?"

"Yes, that's right," she said sharply, clenching her jaw.

"Well, that's funny, because you pretty much left me for dead on Friday night."

She stared at him for a moment—saw the depths of pain in his eyes, and couldn't bear it that she had hurt him so terribly—before looking away. She knew the new flush of color in her face had more to do with shame than anger.

His voice was softer when he spoke again. "Nothing happened when I pressed my lips against hers. Nothing."

As Darcy processed his words, she felt her shoulders lower incrementally and her fists relax, her nails easing back from the soft pillows of her palms. She took a deep breath through her nose, looking up to find his eyes, the words forming before she could check them.

You belong to me, Jack.

The familiar copper flecks leapt around his dilated pupils. She knew he couldn't stop them from hissing and sparking as he heard her thoughts loud and clear. But he didn't reward her by completing the declaration.

He cleared his throat and stood up, crossing to the counter to pour himself some more coffee with his back to her.

She knew that leaving the black wolf to drown had been wrong, but she couldn't help the confusion, fear, and desperate anger that she'd felt at the time. After two days of reading grotesque reports and terrifying stories, she wasn't ready to see him or be with him. When she found herself in the little boat all she could think was that if she could row faster and faster she could get away from him, from the nightmare of his nature, from the darkness, the heat, the unsolvable problem of their binding. By the time she'd realized she was making a mistake, she was sitting back on her window seat. When he'd returned to her later in the evening, pulling her back inside with such quiet tenderness, she was so relieved that he wasn't dead or hurt that she shivered, waking up just enough to let him know she wanted him to stay. And she had fallen back to sleep with the heat of his body warming her feet.

Part of her wanted to apologize to him…to tell him that before hearing Willow's story about Boston and Phillip, her mind had been in turmoil. She *was* sorry that she rowed away. If she could go back in time, she'd never, ever make that same decision again.

"Are you sure you won't have some coffee?" he asked from the counter, that dreadful polite tone back in place.

"I'll get my own," she muttered. Something else was bothering her as she quickly reviewed Jack's conversation with Julien about the woman Jack had been compelled to kiss.

"Suit yourself," he said lightly.

She turned to face him. "This girl you had to kiss. It was your sister, wasn't it? The one who's coming for me."

He spun around slowly, searching her eyes warily before looking away. "My half-sister, yes. Lela."

It all made sense. "So, she's not just coming to kill me because she wants her *brother* to herself. She wants you for a—a *husband*?"

Jack shrugged, holding her eyes.

"Your *sister* wants to bind herself to her own—"

"Half. Half-sister."

"Still…that's…that's…," Darcy murmured, staring at the table, unable to finish the thought. *Disgusting. His* sister *wanted to be bound to him? What kind of new depravity was this?* Any time it felt better, it got worse. Any time he felt possible, she was reminded he wasn't. Her head hurt and she felt like crying.

"I brought in your bag of books and your laptop. I can give you the Wi-Fi password if you need it. I put the books next to the coffee table in the living room in case you wanted to do some work today."

She nodded, her head swimming with confusion and longing and revulsion and jealousy and anger.

"Darcy," he started.

She turned, drawn by the low, gentle sound of his voice; it wasn't just polite—it sounded like Jack, *her* Jack. He stood by the counter with his back to her and her breath caught at the sight of him, the way he filled out the jeans he was wearing and the muscles of his back that she could see through the button-down shirt whose tail hung loosely over his butt...the way his black hair grazed the collar, drying ends curled under and over and teasing her to run her fingers through its thick softness.

"I don't approve of half-sibling bindings," he said quietly. "But I didn't have a choice."

Then picked up his coffee cup and walked out of the kitchen. She waited until she heard his footsteps on the stairs before she bent her head to silently cry.

H E'D NEVER FELT SUCH SWEET relief in his entire life.
Regret. He'd seen regret cross her face when he mentioned the drowning. It was as plain as the nose on her face. She felt ashamed. And then she'd repeated the binding vow, telling him that he belonged to her. He closed his eyes against the rush of tenderness he felt for her. It was like a heavy weight was being lifted off his shoulders. Like maybe, just maybe, she would be able to find room for him in her life.

He ran the water in the shower, willing himself *not* to go downstairs to check on her. He knew she was upset, but talking about his Roug roots and obscure loopholes in ancient binding laws wasn't going to bring them closer together until she was good and ready to talk about them. For now, it was best to keep things polite and calm.

Which was difficult when she was throwing jealousy off her body like heat. He had never felt owned by her—personally—before. He'd felt owned by the fact that he was bound to her and when he had made love to her, he felt the binding strengthen. But he'd never felt the white, furious, heat of possession he felt from her just now.

Frankly, he couldn't think of anything more arousing than the sight of his bound mate red-skinned with fury that he had kissed someone else. He exhaled low, stripping off his clothes and stepping into the cold shower with an erection the size of Mt. Washington. Seemed like cold showers were becoming his best friend.

Keeping his head in their conversation had been difficult, to say the least.

When she walked into the kitchen he knew immediately that she had overheard them, but he was shocked—and fascinated—to see her reaction. She looked like a goddess, a warrior, someone wild and hot and demanding, and his blood spat and hissed and boiled to see her so undone, so *possessive* of him, as imprisoned by the strength of their binding as he, regardless of her protestations.

He'd had a sudden notion of grabbing her and pushing down her jeans, ripping her panties away and bending her over the table to enter her pulsing heat from behind in one fast, hard thrust. He would have reached forward to push up her pink shirt and bra, and covered her breasts with his hands, grasping them, kneading them, finally pinching the nipples with his thumb and forefinger in time to every rhythmic pump until she arched her back up against him and screamed his name. Then he'd grasp her hips and plunge into her one final time, his hot, virile come spurting into the sweet, tight heaven of her body.

He moaned, resting his head against the tile wall under the shower, feeling his sex pulse with the fierceness of his thoughts, his terrible desire for her. Every muscle in his body tensed, peaked, and then shuddered... once, twice, thrice...*Darcy, Darcy, Darcy*...ahhhhh. His fists curled and he groaned aloud as he came forcefully onto the wall in front of him, riding the waves of pleasure as the cool water skimmed down his body and his eyes reflected like melted gold off the shiny white tiles.

IT WAS HARD TO CONCENTRATE.
No.
It was impossible to concentrate.

When he came downstairs, his hair was wet, again, and he'd asked if she wanted a fire in the fireplace. She had shrugged noncommittally which apparently he had taken to mean, *Yes, I want a fire. Please make one squatting in front of the fireplace showing off the hard muscles in your thighs and the gap of hot, toned skin between your lower back and your butt so that I can't get a thing done.*

While she pretended to be reading notes about *Parmeliaceae* and *Lycopodium clavatum,* she was really fantasizing about those thighs straddling hers and her hands stroking that gap of skin while he—

"What're you reading?"

He hadn't turned to her. He was still poking at the fire. Poking at the fire instead of poking her, she though petulantly.

"Oh! Um…" She cleared her throat, pressing a cool palm against her hot cheek. "I have this theory about um, lichen and mosses."

"What's your theory?" he asked, twisting a little to glance over at her. The motion made his t-shirt ride up and she could see a bit of his waist now too.

"Uhhh…," she breathed. "Theory. Um, my theory. My theory is that mosses and lichen have unknown healing properties. Medicinal. Did you know that *Parmeliaceae* contains a cousin element to olivetolic acid? You know, from cannabis?"

"Wow! Let's go smoke some Parmel…whatever it is."

Darcy chuckled. "We'd have to find it and synthesize it first."

"Good thing I know a botanist! You lead the way?"

His eyes sparkled and she felt herself grinning at him. He was so handsome crouched down in front of the fire, with his half smile and still-wet tousled hair. His beard was trimmed and short, neat but emphasizing his hard, manly jaw. She looked back up at his eyes. Surely when he shifted she would still see him in those yellow eyes.

You're still you, aren't you? Even when you—

"Tell me more," he said gently, and she saw the slightest tightening of his jaw as he turned back to the fire, breaking eye contact with her.

She knew he could hear her in his head, but he refused to engage in Eyespeak. He refused to engage in intimacy of any kind with her, and yes, she was getting exactly what she asked for, but no, she didn't like it. She didn't like Polite Jack at all. What's more, she didn't want it.

She didn't like him treating her with passionless deference. She didn't want him keeping his distance, and she definitely didn't want him kissing anyone else. It's true she had been relieved by his words indicating his disapproval of Lela's behavior, but it didn't change the fact that the last lips to have touched his were Lela's and not Darcy's, and it was taking all of her strength not to remedy that situation.

"How about I show you?" she murmured and heard the thickness in her own voice, her words surprising her.

He twisted to face her, his bare feet swiveling soundlessly on the stone hearth.

She held her breath at her boldness.

His eyes darted to her breasts, which threatened to pop out of her t-shirt with the force of her breathing, then back to her face. Their eyes locked and she saw the flames catch, copper fire leaping and crackling.

"I was just going to make some tea," he said, his voice raspy and tight. He stood up, replacing the poker, and then walked through the living room, by the couch where she sat, into the kitchen.

Tea! Tea?

Darcy's cheeks flushed with embarrassment as he passed by. She blinked, trying to figure out what had just happened.

He doesn't want you. That's what just happened, dummy.

He didn't want her?

Oh, my God.

He didn't want her.

It squeezed her heart like a vise. She swallowed back the lump in her throat, cheeks still blazing. One truth in her life was becoming increasingly more apparent. As Jack pulled away, Darcy's longing for him doubled, tripled, was starting to consume her. There was no mistaking the change in her feelings. She wanted him. All of him.

As much as she hated the Roug part of who he was, it was still part of the man she loved. And aside from the binding, during which he unintentionally changed the course of her life, he'd done nothing to hurt her. He'd only tried to connect with her, to strengthen their bond, to keep her safe. And what had she done? She'd pushed him away, called him names, told him she didn't want him and left him for dead. And all the while other women were throwing themselves at him.

She hadn't even thanked him for what he did that night in Boston… that terrible night when Phillip could have raped her—or worse. She winced, her fingers moving of their own volition to touch the eternity symbol hanging from her neck. It was hot against her skin, as though it retained some of his heat from all those years spent with him.

Her thoughts were jarred by the sound of the mug he placed on the table before her. He didn't linger near her. He selected a book from the bookcase flanking the right side of the fireplace then settled in a chair several feet away to her right, turning on a reading light behind the chair and taking a sip of his tea before setting it on a table beside him. He opened his book.

"Jack?"

"Hmmm?"

She swallowed, suddenly nervous, rubbing the charm between her fingers like a talisman.

"That night in Boston…"

He looked up. His eyes clouded over for a split second, narrowing at her before he picked up his mug and took a deliberate sip, eyeing her from over the rim.

More buzzing. More white noise.

She didn't care.

She stared at him, pouring her thanks into her eyes, feeling the connection with him even as he wouldn't let her in.

You saved my body. You saved my life. You kept me safe even though you were shifted. You took care of everything—everything—and I never said…I mean, I just want to say…

"Thank you," she whispered.

She saw the Adam's apple in his neck bob slowly as he swallowed hard. His eyes flicked from her face to her breasts then to her lips and back to her eyes. Slowly. Like he was undressing her, touching her with his eyes. Did she imagine she could feel the searing heat of his body from across the room or was it true that she actually felt it? And was he remembering that night or thinking about right now? She desperately hoped for the latter.

Before her eyes the copper cooled to brown, stopped dancing, withdrawing from her, and she felt and saw his mask slip back in place. He gave her a friendly nod before placing his cup back on the table, and then he raised his book and continued reading.

THE WORDS ON THE PAGE swam before Jack.

Cold shower.

Cold shower.

Another

Cold shower.

IT CERTAINLY WASN'T THE REACTION she'd hoped for, but as he buried his nose in his book it was clear that it was all she was going to get.

She picked up her notes and re-read them, trying to concentrate.

> Referred to by many names, including Wolf's Foot Clubmoss, it has a pale yellow pollen from which Lycopodium, a substance used to treat various health conditions, is derived.

He doesn't want to sit with me. He refuses to Eyespeak with me. He hasn't pulled me inside since Friday night. Is this dreadful politeness just a result of anger and hurt, or have his feelings for me changed?

> In medicine, *Lycopodium clavatum* uses range from treating upset stomachs, food poisoning, kidney problems, and muscle cramps...

How could they change already? Could he want someone else? The image of a young Roug woman sprang to mind. Tall and muscular with fully developed breasts and a small waist. Black hair like Jack, with wild eyes that would glow hot as he made love to her and skin that wouldn't burn red when he touched her, and—

Stop! Stop thinking about it.

> ...to serious conditions such as hepatitis and pneumonia. It can also be used to treat irritability and other emotional problems that manifest physically, like *alcoholism* and eating disorders.

What if he wants her? What if the kiss with her did mean something and I'm only here with him because he feels an obligation to me? His father cheated on his mother and his mistress bore a child. Jack could do the same. He couldn't find orgasmic pleasure with someone else, but he could find companionship and affection. He could leave me and return to Quebec and find someone like him, who would understand and embrace his strange ways. Make a life with her and never return to me…

Her heart clutched with the thought, and her chest physically hurt when she imagined Jack loving another woman, watching *her*, touching *her*, his tongue in *her* mouth, his lips moving over *her* skin, his strong body thrusting into *her*, giving *her* pleasure.

She whimpered lightly and felt a sudden tightening in her throat, following by a rush of bile in her mouth. Trembling, she reached for her tea, taking a sip, trying to calm down. She had thought she felt repulsion when she learned about Jack's nature last Thursday, looking at drawings of Roux-ga-roux, and even hearing him say his sister wanted to be bound to him. But even all combined, it was nothing against the revulsion she felt at contemplating Jack being intimate with someone else. The idea of Jack with anyone else felt like death. No. Death would be a relief from the pain of him being with someone else. He *belonged* to her.

She glanced up at him from over her notes. His legs were long in front of him, crossed at the ankles. She considered them for a minute, the bold lines of the bones in his ankle running down to his toes, a sprinkle of hair on the top of each foot and on each toe. The arch was high and the toes were long—

She blew out an exasperated sigh, looking away.

Jack leaving her was the very last thing she wanted. She wanted him. All she had *ever* wanted was him. She had to figure out if he still wanted her. If he did, she would apologize for her behavior. She would reassure him that she had spoken harsh words out of confusion and anger. She would make it clear that her heart still belonged to him and always would.

H E FELT HER LOOKING AT him. Just as he had in high school. He could hear her too, the soft whimper, the way her breathing was more deliberate when she was looking at him. He could smell, a moment ago, when her body swelled with slickness, right before she looked away, huffing.

It was taking all of the control he had learned throughout his lifetime not to throw his book on the floor and jump on her. It was a sort of an unreal, acute torture to know that she wanted him physically but still withheld herself emotionally. Pushing her now wouldn't ensure anything. He needed to wait it out a little longer; he needed her not just to want him, but to trust him, to choose him. He needed her to be responsible for welcoming him into her life, into her body. There was no room for coercion or pressure; the ball was firmly in her court, and must remain there until she made a decisive, direct move on him. Not because of the binding, but he sensed that her head was close to surrendering, along with her heart and her body. And only then would he trust that she really, really belonged to him.

He risked a quick peek at her from over his book.

Damn.

Her strawberry-blonde hair draped like silk over her shoulders as her head bent forward over her notes. The ends just brushed along the way-too-plunging edge of her t-shirt, a deep, shadowed valley between her breasts teasing him as he salivated. He swallowed painfully, staring at her breasts, remembering the softness of them, their taste in his mouth as he suckled on them, the way the nipples beaded at the touch of his tongue, how she had arched her back, pushing up against him, welcoming him into—

He cleared his throat, tearing his eyes away, his mood darkening with desire for her, with the torture of having her near and not having her. He lifted his book and sighed.

"Jack?" she asked.

"Hmm?" He tried to sound disinterested, even as every nerve ending responded to his name on her lips.

"Why'd you come back yesterday? Just to, um, just to protect me?"

He glanced up at her, scratching his chin in what he hoped looked like an absentminded gesture.

"I feel responsible for your safety," he said quietly, evenly, his voice well controlled, despite the emotional turmoil he felt inside. "It's my duty."

She seemed disappointed in his answer—he saw the muscle in her jaw twitch as she clenched it. As much as he wanted to stare at her, he forced his gaze back down.

"Is your—I mean, um, is Lela beautiful?"

"Yeah." He didn't look up. "She's pretty."

"How pretty?"

"Very."

"Prettier than me?"

He kept his eyes down. *No one's prettier than you. Not to me.*

He shrugged.

"I bet she's dark haired and dark eyed…"

He kept his eyes on his book and tried to keep his voice neutral. "Darker than you, lighter than me."

"Do you, do you wish the binding—I mean, when you kissed her…do you wish it had worked?"

She was killing him with these questions. He sensed she wanted reassurance and he longed to offer it to her, but he didn't trust her motivations. Did she want reassurance because she was jealous of another woman? Or because she loved him and wanted to be assured of his love for her? Jealousy wasn't enough. He wanted her love.

He shrugged again, looking at his book.

"Jack!"

He looked up, trying to appear casually interested in her questions.

"Hmm? What?"

"Do you wish you were bound to Lela?"

If Darcy were Roug, her eyes would be on fire, greenish and silvery, maybe, because she'd retain her birth color when she wasn't shifted and turned Rougs burned silver, not gold. He'd met several turned Rougs in his lifetime and they always gave themselves away with their silvery eyes.

"It doesn't matter what I want," he finally answered. "I have a duty to you."

Her eyes widened in anger and her mouth dropped open. She winced, snapping her book closed around her notes and hugging the messy pile to her chest.

"Duty! Well! I'm so sorry you're *trapped* by your *duty* to me," she hissed at him, making "duty" sound like a truly dirty word. "I'm sure you're very sorry that you ever kissed me."

She stood up, putting one small, pink hand on her hip as she faced him. He wished he could kiss every freckle on it. Thousands of kisses that would take all afternoon, leaving her panting, leaving him breathless. He ordered his tongue to stay in his mouth and not lick his lips. But, damn, he wanted her bad.

"I *am* sorry."

And he *was*; he was sorry that he had "destroyed her life," as she put it yesterday.

"Oh!" she gasped. Her mouth dropped open again, as if he had slapped her, and her eyes suddenly glistened with tears.

He forced himself to stare at her impassively, maintaining the growling, humming noise in his head.

"Well, it might just shock you to know that I'm…I'm *not*, Jack. I'm *not* sorry you kissed me," she continued in a huff, tears burgeoning in her eyes. "Do you hear me? It was—it was the most—oh, you know what, Jack Beauloup? Just, just screw you!"

Then she turned and hurried out of the room.

A moment later he heard her bedroom door slam. Hard.

He felt like a dog for hurting her and it took every bit of strength inside of him not to run after her, comfort her, pull her into his arms and tell her how much he loved her, how he never, ever would or could want any woman but her. But he also had to admit that hearing her say that she didn't regret the binding made her pain worth it.

She regretted letting him drown and she didn't regret the binding.

Clearly Julien had no idea what he was talking about, because if the end goal was having Darcy in his life, one thing was certain: Giving her space was definitely working.

Chapter 5

HAD THAT JUST *HAPPENED?* HAD that *really* happened?
She stood with her back against the door she'd just slammed feeling bewildered, feeling numb.

Jack was sorry that he'd ever kissed her.

The pain in her heart was so excruciating, so all-consuming, she pressed her hands to her chest to try to assuage the pressure. Her eyes burned like he'd thrown acid in them. She couldn't take a deep breath. His words—I *am* sorry—had reduced her to a shell. A shell of the person who used to be Darcy Turner.

She sat down on the bed in his guest room, her whole body aching as she concluded the truth of the facts as she saw them: *Binding or not, he doesn't want you anymore. And once the threat of Lela has passed, his obligation to you will be met and he'll be gone.*

A new wave of searing pain accompanied this realization and knocked the wind out of her lungs. She felt the same strangling sensation she'd felt as a teenager in the girls' bathroom with Willow when she'd learned he had moved away and was never coming back. When she had thought to herself, *I* don't *belong to you, after all, and you* don't *belong to me.* Only this time it wasn't about whether or not she belonged to Jack, it was about him not wanting her in spite of the fact that she did.

She lay back on the bed, resting her head on her pillow, and drew her knees to her chest, words entering her consciousness and refusing to leave.

Belonging to someone like you belong to Jack is an "all in" sort of true love, Darcy, and you've just realized you're "all in" too late.

Her face crumpled and she held herself, sobbing quietly, until she finally fell asleep.

She woke up a few hours later feeling…awful. Her eyes burned from so many tears and her face was puffy and hot. She swung her legs over the side of the bed and looked out the window at the setting sun. The days were getting longer now, but the rain continued, making it darker early today. She was grateful for the greyness of the early evening—sunshine would have just compounded her sorrow at wanting something that was no longer hers.

No longer hers. The words shredded her composure and she hugged herself, wishing that her body didn't want him…

Wishing she didn't love him…

Wishing that she didn't want him in her life…

But her body longed for his, her heart belonged to him, and life simply wasn't worth living without him. Whether it was the binding or her own feelings, it didn't matter anymore. Whether he shifted into a Roux-garoux for three nights a month didn't matter; she knew he wouldn't hurt her and he had, in fact, structured his life in such a way that he wouldn't hurt anyone else. In truth, nothing mattered. Nothing mattered but Jack. The loss of his warmth and intimacy after a lifetime of feeling his presence? The mere thought of him with another woman? She couldn't bear it. Belonging to Jack wasn't about some kiss when she was a kid. It was about her heart recognizing his in the great, grey chaos of the world and claiming it. Her mind had accepted the truth a few days too late: It wasn't about loving him when it made sense—it was about loving him even when it didn't.

She slid her body to the edge of the bed until her feet touched the floor and, wrapping a blanket around her shoulders, made her way to the window. The rain on the glass blurred the scene before her—she could make out the stream that had burgeoned from the rainfall, rushing in white foam over the almost-covered rocks. Her eyes moved to the right toward the rustic bridge, taking in the small patch of bright green courtyard almost directly below her room. She looked all the way over to the garage and thought—for a moment—that she saw Jack looking up at her from in front of the garage, eyes blazing gold.

Say it again.

His voice was so clear in her head, it was as though he had whispered in her ear. She whipped her neck around, but the door to her room was closed and she was still completely alone. She turned back around and rubbed at the glass to clear the fog of her breath, but if he *had* been standing by the garage, he wasn't now. She didn't see anyone.

Say it again. Hm. That's what he'd said yesterday when she'd blurted out that she had loved him her whole life.

Say it again, he'd begged her with his eyes, but she had refused.

But why would he have said that if he'd only returned out of duty to her? Why would her declaration of love matter to him if he didn't love her back, if he wished he'd never been bound to her? Why would he demand with such fierce intensity that she say the words again if they were meaningless to him?

She stepped back until her thighs hit the mattress and she lowered herself slowly to the bed. Was it possible that it wasn't too late? After all of the terrible things she'd said to him, that maybe he hadn't given up on her? That he had returned not just out of duty, but out of love? Was it possible that after she'd yelled at him, insulted him and rejected him, he could still love her?

"Say it again," she whispered aloud. She took a deep breath and sighed. *Please let him still love me. Please.*

She took a shaky breath, pulling the blanket around her.

One thing was certain: She couldn't bear to let him know she loved him only to be rebuffed, to discover that when his duty was fulfilled he'd be leaving her. As much as she wanted him—*needed* him—in her life, she also needed some sign that he still belonged to her.

She swallowed, feeling stronger. If he still loved her, still wanted her, all she needed was a word, a look—anything, anything to give her courage—and she'd willingly fall into his arms and never leave them again.

SHE'D STAYED IN HER ROOM for the rest of the day, not even opening the door when he asked if she'd join him and Julien for dinner.

"No, thanks," she'd responded softly. He'd heard the hurt in her voice and that, along with her absence, was really starting to bother him.

As he lay in bed that night, acutely aware of her just a few feet down the hallway, he started to have second thoughts about the waning merits of Operation Give-Darcy-Space. Showing her what life would look like without their intimate connection was forcing her to think about him, yes. But maybe he'd overplayed his hand by allowing her to believe that he regretted the binding. Maybe Julien was right and women *did* hate too much space.

Jack took a deep breath, determined to try a slightly softer approach tomorrow.

The next morning she walked into the kitchen wearing a pair of flimsy, silky pajamas like she used to wear when she lived in Boston: short-cut boxers and a tank top that skimmed her breasts and left nothing to the imagination. She poured herself a cup of coffee, grabbed a banana, turned and walked right back upstairs to her room without looking at him or saying a word.

He scowled at his omnipresent erection, watching her hips sway gently as she headed back toward the stairs. This was getting ridiculous now.

He sat at the kitchen table for an hour, hoping she'd come back down, but she didn't, and by midmorning he couldn't take it anymore. He rapped lightly on her door armed with the best enticement he could think of and ready to set misinformation to right.

"Darcy?"

"What?" Her voice was soft and vulnerable and felt too far away.

He crossed his arms over his chest, feeling like an idiot talking to her door. "The uh, the rain's finally stopped. Want to come for a walk in the garden? I haven't shown it to you yet."

Silence. He knew she would want to. He had a sense that it bothered her to be cooped up as much as it did him, and by now she must be going a little crazy. But she didn't answer. He couldn't hear a sound through the door.

Time to employ that softer approach, Jack...

"I, uh, I miss you and I was hoping we could talk, Darcy. Will you please—?"

He heard her feet hit the floor and take two steps toward the door. She opened it and stood in the doorway, her arms crossed over her silky little top.

The sight of her so close after hours of having her so far away gave him relief and started a burning inside of him at the same time. Damn it, he wanted her more than ever and felt his body hardening as he looked slowly up and down her form, missing nothing, missing everything. Would he ever be able to control his longing for her? Ever?

His hungry eyes finally made their way back to her face. She'd been crying and she also looked nervous, like she was a little wary of him, but there was something else almost buried beneath the baggage—hope.

"I didn't know you had a garden," she said softly in a small voice.

He was surprised that while her tone wasn't exactly warm, it wasn't especially cool either. He couldn't very well keep letting his gaze drop up and down her body, so he glanced over her shoulder into her room and noticed the bed covered with papers, books, and her laptop. She'd been working. He was glad of that.

"I'll give you a tour if you come down."

She seemed to consider this for a moment, and he suddenly worried she'd refuse him and shut the door. He couldn't let that happen. He looked at her directly, holding her green, worried eyes tenderly.

Please, Darcy.

Her eyes widened a fraction as she sucked in a surprised breath and a sudden, relieved smile tilted the corners of her mouth upwards as though she recognized him, as though she'd been waiting for him. Seeing her so vulnerable, her face so naked and open, made his breath catch.

It's you, Jack. You're back.

He grinned at her, ridiculously pleased to hear her voice in his head. He didn't want to hope for too much, but he couldn't help it. He had missed her too.

"See you downstairs," he said lightly, turning away from her door.

Ten minutes later she joined him, dressed in the soft, broken-in jeans from yesterday, a scooped-neck black t-shirt that, thank God, didn't make her breasts flow over the top like the pink shirt yesterday that had tortured him, and muddy hiking boots. Her hair was pulled up in a bun and her eyes seemed marginally brighter, if still guarded.

"You brought your boots," he observed, tearing his eyes away from her face to look at the caked, well-worn boots.

She took a deep breath and he looked up to find her considering him. What was she looking for?

"Always."

"So, what have you been up to?" he asked politely, anxious to keep their rapport friendly. He gestured toward the front hall and she started toward it.

"Research mostly."

"Getting a lot done?"

"Some."

He could sense she was still upset and he hated it. He hated how they'd left things yesterday. He hated that he'd barely seen her since.

"Darcy," he said softly, his hand on the front door where he'd made love to her for the final time last Sunday morning.

She looked up at him and he could see the worry in her eyes.

"I never answered your question yesterday. You asked if I wished I'd been bound to someone else."

Her face flushed red and she swallowed, looking down as if she knew the answer would break her heart.

"No, baby," he said gently. "The answer's no. I don't want anyone else. There's never been anyone for me but you."

She raised her face to him and he saw the surprise in her eyes first, quickly followed by relief, chased by tenderness, which settled there. Relief and tenderness. And then Jack knew. That's what she'd been searching for—reassurance. It made his heart catch that he'd made her wait for it, but he couldn't help hoping that her uncertainty had solidified her feelings for him.

"I'm sorry that kissing you destroyed your life. But I'm not sorry I kissed you. I'm not sorry I'm bound to you. I'll never be sorry. No matter what."

She held his eyes, taking a deep, shaking breath and he opened his arms to her. Without even a moment's hesitation, she stepped into him and he pulled her against his chest, his eyes closing slowly as he rested his cheek against her head, inhaling her scent, grateful to be allowed to touch her again.

"It hurt me when you said that," she mumbled close to his neck.

"I could feel it. I'm sorry."

"Oh, Jack," she sobbed. "I'm sorry I said such awful things to you. I'm sorry I didn't turn the boat around. I was just so confused and I just—"

"You don't have to explain," he murmured, pressing his lips against her hair.

She leaned back and he moved his thumb to her face to swipe away the tears.

"You didn't destroy my life," she said softly, placing her palm on his cheek. "I'm so sorry I said that."

He wanted to kiss her but stopped himself. He finally felt as though they were making headway and didn't want to risk it by making a move on her. But if he didn't release her soon, he wasn't going to have a choice in the matter.

"Want to see the garden?"

She nodded and smiled, and he released her reluctantly, taking her hand instead and opened the door.

"It's behind the house. Follow me."

For the year his mother had lived here, she had spent a good deal of her time clearing the land behind the lodge and creating a pretty sizeable vegetable and flower garden. Tallis had believed strongly that vegetables and flowers were bound to each other, the flowers attracting the bees that pollinated the crops. Jack had hired a local gardener to clean up the badly neglected garden last fall and he was hopeful that after the last frost in May, he'd see some vegetation. He had cleared an additional area to add an herb garden, sure that Darcy and Willow would take a personal interest in it. He was pleased to see that his instinct had been correct.

"Jack!" Darcy exclaimed, dropping his hand as she preceded him through the white picket fence into the well-manicured space. "How did I not know this was here?"

"The living room's at the front of the house. My bedroom too. And yours. And it was so rainy last weekend, I guess we missed it…"

Just saying the words made him think of the things they didn't miss, staying inside his house, dry from the rain, wet from the raw passion she drew from him. A shiver went down his spine and he squeezed his eyes shut, grappling for control, only opening his eyes when he heard her gasp.

"It's a wonderful garden!"

He watched her pick her way through the flagstone paths, squatting down here and there to look at the neat rows in the middle that would bring forth vegetables, and the mulched borders that would spring forth with shrubbery and flowers in a few weeks' time.

"Over there is an herb garden," he said, gesturing to the smaller, fenced garden within a garden.

Darcy smiled at him then made her way over, opening the little white picket fence and stepping gingerly over the bricked walkways that separated five neat rows. She squatted down and chuckled with delight as she realized that carved bricks labeled the rows.

"Oregano…sage…thyme…parsley. You've got all the ones I would have suggested. Most kitchen herbs can't hang on in this climate. Willow's tried everything, but she has to bring most inside by Halloween. Long winter. Short growing season. These'll do well."

"My Mom planted these twenty years ago," he said softly.

"Did she? Your mother's a gardener?" She looked up at him.

"She is," he answered. "She has a nice garden at her place."

He stopped, smiling at her gently, gesturing to the fifth row. "That one's empty. I don't know what she had there. I thought you might…"

His voice trailed off as he realized what he was about to say. He thought she might like to have her own space to cultivate one day and he'd left it empty for her.

"Recommend something?"

Close enough. He nodded. "Any ideas?"

"It's an unusual suggestion and you'd need to line the bed with plastic so it doesn't run riot, but horseradish would be a nice addition. It thrives in this climate and it's practically pest-resistant."

"Horseradish."

"Hot," she said, grinning up at him, eyebrows slightly raised.

He licked his lips then looked away from her, clearing his throat. *Don't kiss her. Not yet.*

"I'll look into it."

It was feeling more and more impossible not to reach for her, so he turned away, opening the gate and leaving her in the herb garden. He made his way across the vegetable rows, finally sitting down on a small stone bench under a crab apple tree. It was just starting to show real signs of life. In another week or so, it would explode with white flowers.

What would his life look like in a week or two? Lela would surely be handled by then, but would he be with Darcy or apart from her? And in less than eight weeks he was supposed to attend the re-binding. *His* re-binding. He'd barely had a moment to consider how to handle that. He needed to iron out the situation with Lela first. Then he could turn his mind to it.

"Penny for your thoughts?"

Darcy sat down beside him, her body pressed lightly against his on the snug garden bench.

He shrugged, blisteringly aware of her body so close to his. "They're not worth a penny."

"I'm the one buying and I say they are," she said, turning her face to his. She caught his eyes and he looked away.

"Jack, *please* don't push me away anymore."

Her voice was a whisper, so soft and low he could have almost mistaken it for a breath if he hadn't been listening carefully. He heard the pain in it too, the confusion and regret.

"I'm not pushing you away. I thought it's what you wanted—"

"I can't bear it," she said softly, her voice quavering on the cusp of a sob.

"I thought you needed some space to think," he answered simply, looking straight ahead at the garden, feeling her eyes on his face. "I went about it all wrong...how I told you about us. I frightened you."

It surprised him when she leaned her head on his shoulder. "It's a lot to try to understand, Jack."

He swallowed, nodding. He couldn't tell for sure where she was going. He hoped like crazy that she'd been able to make room for him in her life.

They sat in silence for several tense minutes until she continued. "Here's what I kept going back to: Why would you save me from Phillip one day just to hurt me another? All you've ever done is try to protect me. You said it was your sacred vow and I believe you. I'm not frightened any-more."

He clenched his jaw, feeling overwhelmed by her words, a rush of hope stinging his eyes. The light weight of her head on his shoulder felt per-fect, felt like home, and suddenly, wildly, he wanted countless years sitting with her like this—*exactly* like this—in their garden, until they were old and grey and their children's children frolicked amongst the neat rows of flowers and herbs.

What she said next surprised him.

"Your father cheated on your mother."

"He did." Jack confirmed, omitting the news that his mother had cheated on his father too.

"So the binding isn't...foolproof."

"Maybe they were fools," Jack said softly. Which he suspected they were for not working harder at their bond.

"I didn't think—I mean, I thought once you were bound to someone you couldn't..."

"You can still *sleep* with someone else," he clarified. "You just won't achieve, um, the same *satisfaction*, the same *completeness*."

"So, a man could still father children outside of his binding."

"Yes, it happens," confirmed Jack, thinking briefly of Lela and Julien.

The sun was still high for late afternoon. The days were getting longer now. They'd keep getting longer until the Solstice. The Solstice.

Darcy moved slightly closer to him, her side flush against his, her head still resting on his shoulder.

"What happens to *us*, Jack?" she asked quietly.

He was surprised by her question, taken aback by the directness of it. Her use of the word "us" almost took his breath away, but he reminded himself to tread softly, to choose his words carefully.

"I don't know. It's not only up to me. What do you want, Darcy?"

She answered with another question. "After Lela's caught...will you stay?"

He shrugged lightly. He didn't have an answer for her until he knew what she wanted. If she wanted him to go, he'd go. If she wanted him to stay, he'd stay. He wanted to stay. He wanted to stay with her and ask her to marry him. Although Rougs didn't have any binding ceremonies, other than Gathering Bindings, he wanted to respect her human traditions. But, he hadn't really dared to dream that far except in his best, wildest, most unlikely dreams.

"If you went home," she started, her voice thready with emotion and, he suspected, more tears. "You could find a Roug girl. Not your…not your sister. But, someone who understood everything about who you are. Someone who you could, you know, live with and h-hunt with, and have ch-children…"

She stumbled on the last words and finally her voice trailed off. He felt her swallow against his shoulder.

"I could do that," he replied in a whisper, sensing the fragility of the moment, the fleeting nature of this precious common ground. "And you could find a nice human, buy a house in town with an herb garden, and have barbecues with your neighbors, and your kids would be…"

His voice broke, so he stopped speaking, taking a deep breath through his nose, trying to ignore the throbbing pain that such a vision accompanied. He swallowed, feeling miserable. He looked at the pale orange hair pulled back in a bun, resting on his shoulder, and he realized that more than anything else in the world, he wanted what was best for her; he wanted her to be happy. It gave him the strength to say what needed to be said.

"If that's what you wanted, I'd leave you alone. I'd never pull you inside again, Darcy. I'd let you go and I'd never come back. I promise."

She lifted her head slowly from his shoulder and he reached up gently with his thumb to brush away the tears that fell in streams down her face.

"Why do you *have* to shift?" she sobbed.

"Because it's what I am. Because I can't change it and there's no remedy for it." He raised his other hand to her face, cradling it tenderly, his fingers flush against her damp cheeks, thumbs resting by the corners of her mouth.

"Are you s-sure?" she managed through tears.

"It doesn't exist. I wish it did. I wish to hell I could control it completely, but for those three nights, I can't. I can't, Darcy. I can't." He shook his head back and forth, his eyes burning with Roug gold and human tears as he looked down, ashamed of his emotions, ashamed of who he was, desperate for her light in his life and knowing there was no way she would ever agree to stay.

He felt her small, cool hands reach up to cover his, her fingers lacing through his to rest on the skin of her own cheeks. She leaned her head forward until her forehead rested softly against his.

After a moment, he pulled back, his watery eyes capturing hers. He couldn't read her face. It was almost expressionless, but that didn't make it less intense. She held his eyes with a fierceness he couldn't recall ever seeing in her gaze before.

You belong to me and I belong to you.

He inhaled sharply, wincing at the power of her words, and his eyes shuddered closed. *Please, please, please,* he pleaded with every god of the universe, every power that ever was or had been or would be, even though he knew he had no right.

He opened his eyes and looked into hers.

I love you, Jack.

His eyes leapt with fire and he jolted forward, finding her lips with his.

DARCY PLUNGED HER HANDS INTO his hair, pulling his head to hers, moaning as he thrust his tongue into her mouth. Drinking him in like a thirsty wanderer in the desert, she couldn't get enough. She sucked greedily on his tongue before releasing it to stroke hers, sending shivers of pleasure down her back all the way to her toes, which curled inside her muddy boots.

Jack lowered his hands to her shoulders, pushing her t-shirt down until her shoulder was exposed, then he abandoned her mouth, kissing a trail along her jaw to her neck to her shoulder, murmuring her name—"Darcy, Darcy, Darcy"—like a litany as his lips moved insistently across her skin.

She pulled the hair on the back of his head hard, jerking his head up and smashing her lips into his. She felt their teeth clash and tasted blood on her lip. Jack growled into her mouth, his hands dropping to her waist and moving urgently under her shirt. He pushed her bra aggressively upward and she felt his hot, huge hands covering her liberated breasts, his thumb massaging her nipple until it stood at attention, almost painfully erect.

She slid her hands down his neck, running her hands over the rippling ridges of muscles under his shirt, then over his stomach, one hand straying lower until she felt his belt buckle, and then lower, resting on the enormous bulge in his jeans.

He groaned into her mouth, squeezing her breasts sharply, eliciting a sob of pain-pleasure from her throat. She felt for his zipper under the buckle and pulled it down, wiggling her hand inside. She gasped as she made contact with the unconfined, hard, satin length of him, her fingers curling around the top half of him, stoking the head of his rigid shaft with her thumb as he had caressed her nipples.

Suddenly he broke off their kiss, lowering his hands from her breasts and pulling hers away from his erection. He panted against her face, resting his forehead on hers, eyes closed.

Darcy grimaced in frustration, trying to pull her hands away from his to touch him again. She didn't want to stop. She never wanted to stop. But he held her wrists firmly.

"Why?" she finally sighed with frustration, her voice breathy, heavy, stonewalled. "Don't push me away—I want you, Jack. I choose you. Why can't we—"

He leaned back from her.

Because…

His chest heaved up and down with the force of his breathing and his eyes burned from wanting her.

…my brother's standing behind you.

"Looks like you two made up."

Julien's amused voice was like a bucket of cold water. Her wrists relaxed and Jack released them. She discreetly reached up and tugged her bra down, readjusting it over her breasts as Jack zipped up with a low groan.

He stared at Darcy with hunger and longing, his hands resting lightly on her thighs, but spoke softly aloud to his brother. "Your timing is incredibly shitty, Julien."

"Yeah. Sorry about that."

"Is this about Lela?"

"No. Nothing yet. I just came to say that after spending two days with you two, I felt I deserved some real company that didn't scowl or growl at me this evening." Darcy turned at the waist to look at him, torn between feeling bad for him and wanting to smack his face off for interrupting them. He grinned at her. "So, when I was checking out your house early this morning, I invited Willow over for dinner."

"Really?" Jack's tone was surprised if not amused. "And what are you making for her?"

"*Oh non, mon frère.* I promised your *coq au vin.*"

"Is that right?" Jack asked.

"And I even did the stealin—er, shopping."

"I don't even want to know," muttered Jack under his breath.

Darcy turned back to him and grinned. "I wouldn't mind knowing how you make it."

I wouldn't mind seeing your naked body in my bed.

Her cheeks flushed hot and ached from the sudden width of her grin.

Later.

Promise?

She stood up without answering and took his hand, unable to keep a joyful laugh from rising up out of her chest as she pulled him back into the house.

DARCY SAT ON THE COUNTER beside him as he chopped vegetables for the *coq au vin*, chattering about her lack of expertise in the kitchen. She plucked a carrot off the cutting board and observed to him, in a teasing voice, that he could always give cooking lessons if he needed a little spare cash.

He winked at her, feeling happy.

It was true. He was completely comfortable in the kitchen; he'd learned how to cook from the most exclusive chef in Boston. After a decade with the Council he had taken a job in Boston doing private security for humans, and working with such wealthy and privileged people had exposed naïve, backwoods Jack to the best food, the best wine, the best of everything, including their personal staff, which always included a chef willing to teach tricks of the trade to an eager student after hours.

Regardless of the soft, stupid work, exposure to the super wealthy had only served to feed his ambition—he wanted those things in his life. He wanted to be able to offer them to Darcy someday. So Jack had worked hard, learned quickly, and acquired a sterling—if expensive—reputation. Being the best in his field meant a lot of money, and living simply meant amassing a small fortune.

It was unusual for Rougs to seek employment in the human world. In fact, it was so unusual, there was a name for it: êtreseul. Literally it meant "to be alone," and while it wasn't exactly frowned upon—many of the Rougs close to Quebec had jobs working for or with humans—it wasn't commonplace for members of the pack from Portes de l'Enfer. Money was far better when they sought employment in the human world, but it was always risky. You had to be able to hide or explain your three-day absences from work, control your temper and impulses, but more than anything, it meant that you didn't have the support of the pack around you.

While Jack had missed his family, working in the human world was important to him for two reasons: One, he knew he needed to make a lot of money to be able to renovate the old Southern Bloodlands lodge for him to share with Darcy, and two, he needed to learn how to blend in with the humans.

Working for the CE had toned his body and taught him important self-defense techniques, and he and Tombeur had long mastered control at all times except *Pleine Lune*. The reality was, however, his superior sense of smell and hearing, even while in human form, gave him a distinct edge over other employees. After a short stint guarding a warehouse in Waltham, Massachusetts, his excellent record and good looks got him assigned to protecting a wealthy family who lived in Weston, Massachusetts, in a ten-million-dollar compound. His salary jumped from $25,000 to $160,000 per year, and with only modest living expenses and one extravagance in his life, the rest of the money was banked.

The extravagance? The mostly empty brownstone apartment he'd rented that had a mattress on the bedroom floor, his clothes in the closet, and a little bit of food in the fridge. After scaring the owner to death (well, almost) by shifting on the fire escape and scraping at the kitchen window, she'd moved out in a haste, claiming the apartment was haunted, and Jack had stepped up to sign a lease within a day of her departure.

It was Darcy's old apartment, of course, from her Harvard days. She had lived there for four years, which meant that remnants of her scent were everywhere in the small dwelling. Finally surrounded by her smell on a consistent basis for the first time in his life made Jack feel more at home than he'd ever felt in Portes de l'Enfer. It reminded him every night what he was working for, where he was going. He would hold Darcy's Métis necklace up to the light of the moon through the bedroom window, the light reflecting through the holes of the figure eight like eyes, as he made his plan to include her in his life, to reclaim his mate. He'd close his fist around the necklace as he slept, the cool metal imprinting on the heat of his skin, never allowing him to lose sight of his life's destination: the arms of Darcy Turner.

And now here she was, sitting beside him on the countertop of his kitchen, wearing the very necklace he'd held onto for so many lonesome nights. Suddenly overcome with relief and gratitude for the miracle of her presence in his life, he stopped chopping the onions and carrots, and put the knife on the counter.

"...but it's okay. My mom's a great cook and I don't really have anyone to cook for anyway except myself and—"

He put his hands on her knees, capturing her eyes.

...and I can cook for us, he told her, finishing her sentence. His eyes flicked to her lips, lingering for a moment before looking back into her eyes.

She put down her carrot and raised her hands to his face.

Us.

She smiled at him, but it faded as her eyes darkened to evergreen, her legs parted to welcome him closer, and he pressed against her until the erect tips of her breasts brushed against his chest.

He eased his hands up her thighs, finally resting them on her hips. He could smell her arousal and it made him harden wanting her. He would never stop wanting her like this. And all he wanted right now was to pick her up off the counter and carry her up the stairs to his bed. He was distracted by her tongue running over her lips. He watched her teeth gently bite into the pillow of her lower lip and his eyes slammed up to seize hers.

Kiss me, Jack.

He heard the low growl leave his throat at the same time his lips came crushing down on hers. He pulled her roughly up against his body and she raised her legs, wrapping them around his back, locking them. He plunged his tongue into her mouth and she moaned, arching her body up against him, running her hands through his hair.

She wiggled her hips to fit more closely to him and he groaned, pushing into her softness, only holding onto the edge of his control with a thread. If they didn't stop, he was going to rip off her pants and take her on the kitchen counter beside the chopped carrots until she screamed his name and ran her nails down his back.

As if sensing this inevitability, she pulled back from him. Her lips were rosy and puffy and her eyes were heavy with arousal.

"Can you please finish cooking *quickly*?" she panted, lowering her hands from his hair.

He dropped his head to her shoulder, feeling laughter bubble up from a joyful place in the middle of his body. Yes, Lela was coming. Yes, Solstice was coming. Yes, they were having guests for dinner. But this impossibly sweet, bright angel was his, and nothing could dampen his hope for them. Not in that moment.

He finally drew back and looked at her.

"Going to be hot," he said, licking his lips, kneading her hips under his hands, making no move to pull away from her.

"Dinner?" she murmured.

He shook his head back and forth slowly. Damn, his body didn't want to calm down, and he needed another few minutes to prepare the food before he could carry her upstairs and have his way with her.

"Nope."

She raised her eyebrows in question.

"My bed. In about"—he glanced at the chicken about to burn in the sauté pan then back at her—"ten minutes."

"Promise?" she asked saucily.

The look on her face was killing him.

He nodded, taking a deep breath, backing away from her and picking up the knife again.

She picked up the carrot she'd been nibbling on and popped it onto her mouth. He watched as her lips settled over it, and suddenly wasn't sure he'd actually make it ten minutes.

She watched him with those heavy, aroused eyes.

Quit it, he told her.

She withdrew the carrot from her mouth slowly, letting it make a popping sound at the end, and Jack groaned, licking his lips, feeling his eyes brighten dangerously.

I mean it, Darce. Stop.

She smiled at him, glancing at the enormous bulge in his jeans, and he could see how much she was enjoying his pain.

"Just wait," he growled, cutting the vegetables with more speed and less precision than before.

"For what?" she breathed in a low, husky voice.

"You'll see," he groaned, imagining her spread-eagle on his bed, his face buried between her thighs as she writhed under him, bucking up against his face. Yep. He'd get her back for her carrot antics.

He worked in silence for a few minutes, transferring the carrots and onions to the crockpot and turning the chicken once more before she spoke again.

"You're good with knives," she said and Jack made a mental sigh of relief that she wasn't using that low sexy voice that had him dying to mate with her.

"I should be. I worked for the Council Enforcement for ten years," he said, deftly moving the salted and peppered chicken, thigh by thigh, to the waiting Crockpot.

"Doing what?" she asked. "Or do I want to know?"

"Keeping order, mostly," he said quietly, adding red wine to the mix of chicken and vegetables, averting his eyes. *Hunting rogue Rougs, enforcing hunting boundaries and kill limits, arbitrating bitter feuds between neighboring packs.* It wasn't easy work.

"In…your pack?" she asked, and he could tell she was testing out the words for the first time.

"Mm-hm. Well, mine and the seven others. There are eight packs in the Northern Bloodlands. The Council is the governing body. It's made up of representatives from the eight packs."

"I've heard you talk a lot about the Northern Bloodlands. Is there a Southern?"

He turned to her and nodded. "Yep."

"Where are they?"

"Umm…here, actually. Carlisle was the Southern Bloodlands, Darcy. From Carlisle to Colebrook. Used to be three southern packs on this land and five up north."

"How long ago?" she asked with wide eyes.

"A long, long time ago."

"When Proctor Woods was *Bois Loup Garou*," she said.

"You remembered." He looked up at her and marveled that they were able to have this conversation. She was discussing his life, the history of his pack.

"How many of you are there?" she asked, taking another bite of carrot.

Jack sighed. It meant everything to him to hear her say that she loved him, but he still didn't want to scare her away with too much information.

"About a thousand," he said, whisking a mixture of flour and chicken stock to pour over the mixture and finally be done with it for a few hours. *Or two,* he thought averting his eyes.

"That's at least a thousand kills per month," she gasped.

"No," he said, shaking his head. "It's not. Not at all. The young don't hunt. Only adults. And bound couples share a kill with their families.

There are strict rules."

"It still must be several hundred," she murmured. Jack hated the fear in her voice.

"Many think like me, do what I do, hunting wild game instead. Especially the ones who keep company with Métis partners. Others have contacts at the morgue, at ceme—"

He saw her hand whipped up to cover her mouth and he stopped talking, wincing as she heaved twice, her shoulders rolling forward. Finally she uncovered her mouth and took a deep breath, looking down.

"We don't all hate humans," he said softly, pouring the stock mixture over the chicken and covering the Crockpot. He dusted his hands on his jeans then put them on her knees. "I think things might be changing. But, change is slow."

"It has to start somewhere," she breathed. She covered his hands and nodded bravely.

His heart swelled with love for her, and he slid his hands slowly up her leg, pushing his fingers between the V of her thighs, seeking the hot, sensitive skin buried beneath too many layers of clothes. Dinner preparation was done for now. There were other things that needed his attention and that definitely needed hers.

He looked up at her and she held his burning eyes with her clear green ones.

I want you, Darcy. Now.

I want you too.

With his eyes locked with hers, he put his hands around her waist, slowly pulling her off the counter. Her body slid down the front of his until her feet touched the floor, and every nerve ending in his body demanded more.

"I love you," he said simply. "No matter what."

"I love you too," she answered.

He brushed lips against hers then took her hand and pulled her toward the stairs.

Chapter 6

THE DOOR CLOSED WITH A click and she turned to face him.
Say it again.

She smiled at him. "I love you."

He tugged at the hem of her t-shirt, pulling it out of her jeans and over her head.

Again.

"I love you."

He spun her around gently, unclasping her bra and sliding it gently down her shoulders with lightly trembling fingers, down her arms until it dropped soundlessly to the floor, then he turned her back around.

Again.

"I love you."

He unzipped her jeans then dropped to his knees in a single graceful movement, tugging them down over her hips, catching his thumbs in the waistband of her panties so that he slid everything down her body at once. She lifted one foot out of the pool of discarded clothes and he kissed the soft insole of her foot, listening to her breath quaver and catch before setting it down and lifting the other. He nibbled it gently, pulling her jeans away before releasing her small, perfect foot to the floor beside him.

He gazed up at her on bended knees...*Naked. Blissfully, exquisitely naked before me*...worshipful, in awe of her trust, her faith in him, her hope for them, her light and her goodness and now, her love.

Again.

"I love you, Jack. I love you forever."

He reached up and put his hands on the soft, pliant skin of her backside, and he pushed her toward him, burying his face in the soft triangle of melon-colored hair between her legs.

"Jack!" she gasped as his tongue found the sensitive nub nestled in the folds of hidden skin.

Her head fell back as a low moan escaped from her throat. Her knees threatened to buckle, but his strong hands held her up as his tongue licked, sucked and swirled, and a delicious pressure built inside of her.

Her hands, which rested lightly on his head, flexed and stretched, threading through his hair, as her insides melted into lava, coursing through her body with abandon, a wild fluttering bringing her closer and closer to heaven until the heat was unbearable. She exploded, screaming his name as she tremored and shuddered and her knees gave out and her body surrendered.

Her eyes were still closed while her muscles spasmed, contracting and releasing, her insides flooded with heat. She felt him pull away, but instead of falling into a limp heap at his feet she was swept into his arms and he laid her gently on his bed.

She heard the buckle of his belt hit the floor and a moment later the weight and heat of his body settled beside hers, his lips capturing hers in a slow, decadent kiss. His tongue licked her lips, running over the smoothness of her teeth to find hers and stroke it gently. She tasted the salty sweetness of her own body in his mouth and it roused her from the aftermath of her climax. She opened her eyes with renewed vigor wanting one thing alone: for him to know the same awesome wholeness, the same perfection, the same physical embodiment of love that he had just rendered to her.

She pushed against his chest and as he leaned back looking at her quizzically, she put her hands on his arms, pushing gently until he understood and smiled, falling back onto the bed so that she could lean up and kneel beside him.

Darcy looked at his enormous, thickly veined shaft, which pointed straight up toward her and seemed to pulse with the beating of his heart.

She flicked her glance to his eyes, smiling.

Is that for me?

He smiled back at her, his chest rising and falling rapidly, nodding his head on the pillow. Then he unleashed a tense, strangled sound as she bent her head over his chest, taking a nipple in her mouth and sucking it into a quick point.

She looked up at him again.

More?

Pain and excitement crossed his face as he nodded again.

She bent over him, her soft hair brushing against his short, curly, wiry hair, and she captured the other nipple between her lips, flicking it with her tongue before gently using her teeth to make it pebble-hard in the space of a moment.

Looking up at him once more, she ran her tongue over her lips and smiled.

More?

He must have been holding his breath because it came out on a low hiss as he nodded his head one final time, throwing an arm over his eyes as he winced with fevered expectation of what was surely to come next.

She leaned over his chest again and as her fingers encircled the base of his cock, she touched the very tip of her tongue to the glistening head, swirling once before taking him entirely in her mouth, into her throat, in one smooth, soft, slow motion.

The muscles in his stomach flexed and he groaned, his fingers curling into fists in the sheets on either side of his body as her breasts skimmed his stomach and she released him briefly before sucking him back into her mouth again. The heat of her mouth…the hot, wetness of her mouth on him was like nothing he had ever felt before in his entire life, and his nerves screamed for more, more of her tongue, her soft wetness, the mind-blowing suction, the strong, slow pumping motion of her hand. His eyes rolled back in his head and he felt a gathering inside, stronger and stronger until he was sure he would—

How she did it, he'd never know, but one moment he was in her mouth, and the next she had straddled him, lowering her body onto his pulsing, quivering erection, and he thrust instinctively once, twice, reaching for her hips and opening his eyes.

Say it again, baby.

She smiled slowly and he could see it on her face—he could see that she had never loved anyone as she loved him, that she would never again love anyone in her life as she loved him. His eyes burned and teared, and if he had died right there, his life would have been worth living for every moment that led to this one.

I love you, Jack. I belong to you.

She bent down and bit his upper lip as she came with a loud moan, her insides quivering and trembling around his shaft. His muscles clenched tightly in preparation just as he fell over the edge with her. He reached up to clasp the sides of her dreamy, spent face, plunging his tongue into her mouth at the same time he kissed her womb with the tip of his hard length, letting go of any remaining control as his body exploded, shattered by the pleasure of Darcy's body climaxing around him. He growled her name into her throat, spilling his strong, full-blooded seed into her waiting, willing, beloved perfection.

"WHAT TIME IS IT?" SHE asked him, resting her head on the damp hair of his chest. The skin beneath was hot on her cheek, but she couldn't bear to pull away. She sighed, never wanting to leave his bed. Never wanting to be further away from him than she was right this second.

He moved slightly, the hand caressing her hair stilling momentarily before resuming its gentle stroking.

"Four," he murmured. "We have time."

"That's a relative expression for us."

He didn't make a sound, but she heard his chest rumble lightly and he ran the backs of his fingers over her cheek before returning to her hair.

"I love your hair," he said, quietly, reverently. "I've always loved it since that first day you walked into the library. Like an angel with a halo walking out of light and into my life. I dreamed about it for years and years."

"When we were apart," she murmured, propping herself up on his chest to see his face. "What were those years like for you?"

"Awful...hungry...desperate...hopeless..." he shook his head, his face stricken and tender at once. "Those four days I spent in Boston? Watching you when you were in grad school? They were the best of the bunch. Four days in twenty years."

"Did you do that a lot? Find me? Watch me?"

He shook his head. "No. Not a lot. A handful of times." He looked sheepish for a moment. "I know the woods around Willow's house pretty well. And you always made it easy, sitting in the window seat. But I never stayed very long after getting so attached in Boston. Minutes. Hours. Just enough to see you."

"Jack," she murmured, searching his eyes as hers filled with tears. "I'm so grateful you were there."

He kissed her softly. "Me too, baby."

"I wish I'd known you were there. I wish I hadn't had to wait so long to see you again."

"You felt me, though?" he asked, stroking her hair out of her face and lovingly tucking the strands behind her ears.

She nodded, smiling at him sadly. "Going inside kept you fresh in my mind. I've always felt connected to you. Always. Even before that night backstage. I wanted you so much from the very beginning. From the first time I saw you across the library, I wanted you in my life."

He reached for her, cradling her against his chest and kissing the top of her head. The heat of his skin was searing, but it felt too good to pull away.

"You too. You walked into that library bathed in light. I think I would've happily died for a moment with you."

"Instead we get a lifetime," she breathed, feeling happy, feeling like Jack was her home, her choice, her heart, her life.

He didn't speak again right away, but his arms tightened around her and he buried his face in her hair as if overcome by her words. When he spoke again, his voice was soft, emotional.

"I did everything I could to figure out how to be with you. But there were so many dark moments, Darcy. How was I supposed to make you understand? How could I ever have what I wanted most in the entire world? You seemed impossible to me."

"Possible." She smiled, reaching up to trace his lips with her finger. "You figured it out."

"Have I?" he asked, his brows furrowing with uncertainty and hope. He searched her eyes. "Are we...are you..."

She tilted her head to the side, anxious to reassure him, but looking for the right words to express her feelings for him. "Jack. I don't—"

"No!" His face turned to stone and he gripped her arms almost painfully. "No! I can't lose you now. I won't let you go. I won't. You can't leave me—"

"Jack!" she exclaimed softly, wincing as she looked at her arms. He relaxed his crushing hold on her. "Let me finish."

He swallowed and she watched his throat bob with the force of it.

"I don't..." she started again. "...know how to live without you now."

He exhaled in a rush of breath. Putting his hands under her arms, he pulled her on top of his body, clasping her to him fiercely, like he would never, ever let her go. *You're mine, you're mine, you're mine.* She felt the furious rhythmic thumping of his heart against hers and felt her heart respond in kind, *I'm yours, I'm yours, I'm yours.*

"The thought of anyone else…like this…with you." Tears filled her eyes as she placed her hands on his cheeks, gently pressing her lips against his and then drawing back to look at him. "I'd rather die. Do you hear me? I'd rather die than live another day without you."

"So we'll figure it out?" he asked in a rush. "We'll stay…together?"

She nodded and watched his face change from uncertain to relieved before her eyes. His eyes fluttered closed for a moment and she knew he was having trouble controlling the depth of his emotions as his eyes glowed under his eyelids.

"We will," she whispered, smiling at his handsome face, "stay together."

Like lightning, he flipped her gently back and swung his body over hers, his erection hard and pulsing against her thigh. Her body flooded hot and wet, instantly ready for him again. She arched her back to meet his quick, smooth thrust and his eyes seized hers, his burning, seething, beautiful glowing eyes that she would read with clarity for the sum total of her days and hours and minutes from now until the end of time.

I love you.

I love you too.

I belong to you.

And I belong to you.

Forever.

Forever.

And then they were one, seeking, finding, needing, having, unrequited finally, finally, finally requited.

"WHAT TIME IS IT?' SHE asked again, her face resting on a pillow across from his.

He turned to look at the clock on his bedside table.

"Almost five."

She looked troubled. He knew that "losing time" bothered her and wondered if he couldn't try to offer some explanation.

"Do you want me to try to explain why it happens?" he asked.

"You know?"

"Not for sure. Nobody I know has ever been bound to a human, so I sort of had to figure it out for myself, but I have an idea."

"Please?" she asked. "Tell me?"

He leaned forward and kissed her nose then leaned back.

"My theory is that you lose about two hours a day when you're with me."

"Why?"

"My body lives on a lunar calendar, on a lunar cycle. The moon takes 29.54 twenty-four-hour days to make a full return to *Pleine Lune,* to Full Moon. 29.54 times twelve months is 348 days. Your calendar year is 365 days. That's a difference of twenty-seven days. 648 hours. Roughly two hours every day. When you're with me, you lose them."

"Why don't you lose them?"

"Because I never had them. They never existed for me."

"Why do I?"

"Because you're bound to me. And the nature of the binding is Roug, so I think it forces you to comply with Roug time when we're together. This isn't written down anywhere. But I think I'm probably right."

"Will I age faster?"

"I don't know, baby," he answered quietly, running a finger up her arm from her elbow to her shoulder. "It bothers you?"

She nodded, moving her other arm under her head and looking away.

"It makes you sad?"

She shrugged lightly, but a tear escaped from her eye and ran down her nose, dropping with a plop on the sheet between them.

"I'm sorry," he said gently.

She rubbed her eyes and mumbled something.

"What?" he asked.

She lowered her arm, finding his hand and entwining her fingers through his.

"Small price," she repeated, taking a deep breath and closing her eyes. "I'm so tired. I wish I could sleep for a few minutes."

He smoothed the hair back from her forehead and kissed her lightly. "Sleep a little. I'll wake you up right before seven."

She took a deep breath and sighed. "Jack, when Lela comes..."

"Mmm?" he murmured.

"I know you'll keep me safe," she whispered softly, her voice already heavy with impending sleep.

"Don't worry, baby," he breathed, kissing her forehead again.

In a moment she was breathing deeply and he knew she was asleep. He watched her for a few minutes, marveling that just last week he was sure she was lost to him, and now here she was—delivered to him, surrendered to him. For the first time ever he believed not just in the power of the binding, but that Darcy Turner belonged to him because she chose to give herself to him. Not because her destiny had been chosen for her, but because she had decided to claim it: to love him, in her own mind, from her own heart, with her own body.

And suddenly Jack knew why his binding had always felt different—why, as Tombeur had observed, it was so extraordinarily strong.

Because among all Rougs he was an exception. His binding hadn't just been given to him. He'd had to earn it. And now that he had, he'd hold onto it with every breath, every bit of strength and courage that he owned.

He'd need it all, he considered bitterly, watching her sleep.

Solstice is coming.

Chapter 7

"*...*JEMMA'S SCREAMING AND JACQUES*...UH, AIDE-MOI, Saule.
Comment dis-tu, uh, glapier?*" Julien's dark eyes found Willow's across
the table, flicking briefly to the neckline of her black V-neck dress before
catching her eyes again.

If Willow noticed the look, she didn't acknowledge it. She just smiled
at him, giggling, her lips stained from red wine. "Yelped?"

"*Oui!* Jacques *yelped* and our parents came running! But it wasn't poisonous. Just hairy."

Darcy, who sat at the head of the dining room table, chuckled with Jack,
Julien, and Willow, and then turned her eyes to Amory beside her, who
looked down at his bowl of half-finished *coq au vin* with narrowed eyes.
He picked up his wineglass and drained the rest. Clearly Julien's glance at
Willow's small but pert assets hadn't been lost on her brother.

They hadn't expected Amory to join them, and Darcy had rushed to set
the table for five instead of four when he showed up unexpectedly with
Willow. She couldn't hide the worry that must have crossed her features
because Jack had come up behind her, wrapped her in his arms and kissed
her neck, whispering in her ear, "It'll be okay. I promise."

Jack had been right. It had been okay. It'd been better than okay. It
felt so...*normal.* Julien entertained them with perfectly normal stories
from their Beauloup childhood and Darcy could almost forget that she,
her brother, and her childhood friend were dining with two men who
turned into bloodthirsty creatures at the full moon—one of whom, she
had decided firmly this afternoon, was her life's mate, her beloved. She
glanced at him beside her, his omnipresent stubble shadowing his strong
jaw, his black hair just a little wild, his dark eyes crinkling with amuse-

ment. She felt her heart swell with love for him, with hope for them.

In fact, the only immediate fly in her ointment was the attention that Julien was paying Willow and the way she was lapping it up. Darcy didn't like it. She didn't like the way it was affecting her brother. Her brother didn't know the untold dangers lurking in provoking an argument with Julien.

"You're scared of spiders, Jack?" giggled Willow, whose cheeks were cheerfully flushed, from either a little too much good French wine or a little too much bad-boy French attention from across the table.

"I'll be honest, Willow, they're not my favorite."

"Not his favorite, he says, forgetting he screamed like a *fillette* at the sight of one," said Julien, elbowing his brother beside him.

"That one could have eaten you for dinner, *mon frère*," Jack advised him, shaking his head and curling his fingers around Darcy's hand, which rested on the table beside him. Even that small, encouraging touch sent a blast of heat from her fingers up her arm to her neck where it connected with her pulse, making it flutter faster.

She turned away from him to look out the French doors that led to the garden behind the lodge. From where she sat at Jack's huge, rustic, farm-house table, she had a good view—the perfect view, in her opinion—of the small stone bench under the cherry blossom tree where she and Jack had kissed a few hours earlier, deciding that a life spent apart was no longer possible. She twisted her wrist so that their palms were flush and married, watching her fingers settle softly on the back of his hand as his readjusted around hers.

Julien cleared his throat loudly and Darcy looked up. Her cheeks flushed with heat to realize that everyone was staring at her and Jack. Julien winked at her suggestively, a knowing smile playing on his lips.

"Jacques, my compliments!" he said, kissing his fingers. "This was divine. And I am happy to wash the dishes if *la belle Saule* will help me."

Julien cocked his head to the side, looking adorable, and winked at Willow—*Willow!*— who simpered.

"*I'll* help you," said Amory quietly, staring at Julien.

"*Mais, non*," said Julien, his charming smile unwavering even as Darcy noticed the new chill in his tone. "You're our guest, Amory."

Amory stood up, picking up his bowl and Willow's, then heading into the kitchen without another word.

"Ça va," Julien said quietly, nesting Darcy and Jack's bowls over his and following Amory.

As soon as they were out of earshot, Darcy turned to Willow, her eyes serious. "What are you doing?"

Willow had the temerity to look innocent. "What?"

"You're going to get Amory hurt."

"Amory can hold his own, kid."

"If you two are together, stop messing around. I mean it. He's my brother, and no offense, Jack, but I don't trust yours."

"None taken," said Jack. "I think Darcy has a point. Julien can be slippery about humans."

Amory strolled back into the living room on his own and three sets of eyes looked toward the kitchen door, which swung back and forth lightly with no sign of Julien.

"Julien left," said Amory, sitting back down between Darcy and Willow.

"Did something happen?" asked Darcy.

"Uh, yeah. I suggested that he might want to stop checking out my girl's tits, at which point I thought he was going to try to deck me. But all of the sudden he wrinkles his forehead and juts his nose into the air like he's sniffing for breakfast. Then he just turned and left out the back door." Amory shrugged.

Darcy's eyes widened and she looked out at the garden apprehensively before catching Willow's worried eyes. Jack squeezed her hand gently and she turned to him.

"It was weird. No offense, Jack." Amory seemed oblivious to the sudden change in the energy around him.

"None taken," Jack murmured to Amory, but his eyes were wide and worried, trained on Darcy.

She's here.

I know.

Darcy's eyes flicked to Willow and Amory then back to Jack.

Willow will be okay. What about Amory?

There's no time for them to leave. It wouldn't be safe anyway. Between me and Julien, we'll outnumber her. But, Darcy, I meant to…I meant to show you—

What?

I may have to shift. To help Julien.

She stared at him, hoping that her face didn't betray the fear she suddenly felt. She loved him. Completely. But she didn't know that she was ready to see him shift.

"Hey, Willow," said Darcy, turning to her friend, a calm smile fixed on her face for her brother's sake. "Jack has this awesome media room on the third floor. Why don't you guys go get a movie started and we'll join you as soon as we finish the dishes?"

Amory grinned at Willow. "Sounds good to me."

Darcy mouthed *Lock the door* to her friend and Willow nodded quickly, turning to Jack. Her eyes implored him to take care of Darcy and Jack nodded once, his hand still holding Darcy's.

Amory pulled back Willow's chair and Darcy watched as they walked up the stairs together.

"It'll be okay," said Jack, low and gentle once they were out of earshot.

"I know you'll keep me safe," she said and he leaned forward to press his lips to hers.

"As long as I'm alive, no one will *ever* hurt you."

"Then stay alive."

"She's just a girl." He smiled at her. "Don't worry about me."

"All in a day's work, huh? I'm suddenly really glad you used to work for the Council."

She drew her hand away and pushed back from the table, standing up. He stood up beside her, opening his arms and she stepped gratefully into them. She leaned her cheek against his chest, flattening her hands against his back as his strong, hard arms encircled her.

"I want you to go up to the media room with Willow and Amory. Lock yourselves in. Don't open the door. I'll stay down here and hopefully you won't see or hear a thing until I come up to tell you it's all over. Don't come out, Darcy. No matter what you think you see or hear. Don't come out."

Her nostrils flared at his tone. He was worried for her.

"Do you think you'll have to shift?" she asked. She wanted to prepare herself with the little bit of time she had.

"Almost definitely. Julien's going to spark to her and I'm going to need to hold her."

"You two are going to *force* her to—"

"Just a kiss. Nothing more. We'd never hurt her. He needs to kiss her to see if they're meant to be bound. If they're not bound, we'll have to deal with her. Probably lock her in the vault for a while, which is why I can't have you hide there. It's the only place that could possibly hold her…"

"Do you think she and Julien will…?"

"*He* does. He seems sure that she's the one for him." He whispered into her ear, "I know how that feels."

He leaned back and pressed his lips against hers, brushing softly, reverently.

"I *definitely* know how that feels."

"Me too," she whispered, tilting her head to the side and reaching up to thread her fingers through his black hair. She chuckled softly. "If she wasn't here to kill me, I'd sort of love seeing it happen. A binding."

"You probably won't see it. But, if you do, I'll be shifted, and just remember…"

"I know. You're still you." She smiled at him gently. "I choose you. No matter what."

She felt him shudder as he clasped her tightly against him, pressing his lips against her hair. "I have to go. I–I'll walk you upstairs. Remember… don't come out. No matter what."

"You don't have to walk me," she said, pulling back gently. She touched his cheek with her palm and felt it tremble with the fears she was trying to keep at bay. "The faster you go help Julien, the faster it'll be over. The faster we can get back to us."

He turned his head so that his lips could press softly against her palm, and then he looked at her face, holding her eyes.

It'll be okay. Don't be frightened.

She nodded gravely.

I love you, Darcy.

I love you, Jack.

Then she pulled her hand away and turned toward the stairs.

A S SOON AS DARCY WAS out of sight, Jack slipped out the back door, threw his clothes down on the back step and shifted, anxious to find Lela before she found Darcy. He turned to the moon and howled, lifting his black nose to the sky to catch Julien's scent and track it. He was distracted by Lela's scent too, but he ignored it—she had probably watched them from outside before retreating into the woods. Having Willow and Amory over for dinner had been a bad idea, taking the edge off their vigilance.

Jack ran through the woods, leaping over fallen tree trunks, the jagged terrain of the forest floor no hindrance for his leather-tough, fur-protected feet. He finally found Julien about three miles from the lodge.

He howled a greeting and Julien howled back.

Where is she? Jack asked.

Having trouble pinpointing her, responded Julien, and Jack could hear the frustration in his growl.

What's the matter with you? First Roug you've ever tracked? Jack asked impatiently.

You try it. Her scent's everywhere!

Jack breathed in then ran full speed to the west, but her scent eventually petered out and he returned to Julien. He raised his nose to the moon again and ran east at a clip, finally slowing as he realized her scent was fading yet again. He ran back to Julien and as he did, he went by a spot that was particularly strong-smelling. He circled the trunk of a tree then approached it and sniffed, wrinkling his nose. Lela's saliva ran down the bark in a frothy stream.

Merde! She had marked the woods.

Instead of trying to hide her scent, she had zigzagged all over the woods, spitting on tree trunks and boulders. Since Roug saliva held their venom, her smell was strong everywhere. It was impossible to figure out where she was. She could be anywhere.

Jack ran back to Julien.

We're not going to find her, he growled. *She marked the woods.*

Julien threw back his head and howled in anger.

Then we'll just have to keep searching until we do.

One second he was staring at his brother, the next—for the first time since his binding to Darcy twenty years ago—*she* pulled *him* inside.

DARK AND COLD. SO DARK and cold and misty.

His pads flexed over a pile of wet, soggy leaves and he turned his head to the left then right, orienting himself, letting his eyes adjust to the pitch darkness. The forest near his house. Up high. How jarring to suddenly be pulled inside.

Softly—softly enough to be very, very far away—he heard her cry and took off at a high speed run toward her. *Distress.* He could hear it in her voice. *Fear.* Racing down the slippery hillside, he yowled and yelped, hoping she could hear him, hoping she knew he was coming.

His muscles ached with the speed of his run but despite the hard bends and twists in the course, he didn't slow down. She was in trouble. All he knew was that he had to get to her. He had to find her.

Her cries were closer and closer and still he raced until he found himself in front of his house, in front of the lodge. He raised his yellow wolf eyes to the top window where he saw her looking out the jagged glass of the media room window, a single claw resting against the white of her throat.

Their eyes locked and he whined, his tail curving between his legs, feeling the terrifying strength of her fear.

HELP ME!

Jack's eyes flew back open, blazing and burning. He turned to Julien beside him, threw back his head at the moon and howled. Then he raced back to the lodge, fervently hoping he wouldn't be too late.

D ARCY SENSED THAT SOMETHING WAS wrong as soon she got to the third floor stairs, only to find the door wide open. Had Willow misunderstood her? She'd been clear about locking the door.

"Willow? Am?" she said quietly in a trembling voice, walking up the stairs, her adrenaline starting to pump through her body uncomfortably.

Three more steps and she could see that the lights weren't on, nor was the TV. There was only moonlight filtering into the room as far as she could tell. She took a deep breath, wondering if she should run back downstairs and call for Jack, but he'd been more than clear about her staying upstairs.

As she reached the top step, she didn't see anyone in the long, wide, dark room that lay before her to her right, but she heard something. Breathing. Heavy. Ragged. Her heart pounded as she took the last stair, reaching to the wall to find a plastic panel with several switches. She flicked one and a dim light went on across the room, over the TV.

"Hey!"

"Darce?"

Darcy's breath came out in a rush as the sheepish faces of Willow and Amory popped up from a makeout session on the couch. Willow adjusted her blouse and Amory swiped a hand over his lips, grinning wickedly.

"You two scared me to death!" she exclaimed.

"Scared you to— Did I miss something here? Wasn't 'watch a movie' code for each couple having a few minutes alone?" asked Amory, using air-quotes for "watch a movie."

"No!" said Darcy "It wasn't meant to be a euphemism."

"Could've fooled me, the intense way you and Jack were looking at each other. Right before you told us to go 'watch a movie' I was about to tell you to go get a room!"

Darcy shook her head, her heart still racing.

"You didn't lock the door," she said, looking pointedly at Willow, who had yet to say a word.

"Yeah, I did."

"No," said Darcy. "It wasn't locked. I just came up."

"I'm telling you. We locked it, Darce."

"Well, it wasn't locked, Willow," said Darcy impatiently, rubbing her hands together, that sense of foreboding returning in a rush.

"Is it locked now?" asked Willow, eyes widening.

"Yes," said an unobserved voice in the darkness at the top of the stairs, behind Darcy. "Yes, it is."

Lela.

Darcy gasped, turning to face Jack's sister, then backing up until she hit the couch behind her.

Her first thought was, *He wasn't lying. She's very pretty.*

Her second thought was, *She wants to kill me.*

Amory and Willow stood up and Willow vaulted over the couch to stand beside Darcy as Lela approached them slowly, a catlike, stalking motion to her movements.

Amory circled around the couch leisurely, extending his hand to Lela.

"Hey, I'm Amory. You are?"

"Not interested in you."

Out of the corner of Darcy's eye, she saw the claws dropping. She looked up and realized that Lela's fangs were dropping too. Before she could warn Amory to stay back, Lela reached out a claw and swiped it across Amory's chest, slicing an eight-inch path from his shoulder to his breastbone.

Amory gasped in shock and pain then grunted, grasping at his chest as he fell to the floor on his knees.

Willow stepped in front of Darcy.

Suddenly Lela stopped in her tracks, inhaling deeply, a variety of emotions crossing her face—surprise, shock, disbelief. Her claws retracted quickly and her nostrils flared as she stared at Willow with intense annoyance.

"What the *FUCK*?! An *Enchanteresse*? Just my fucking luck!"

Lela's eyes glowed gold as she stared at Willow, but she didn't advance any further.

Darcy's mind scrambled. *An Enchanteresse? What the heck is an Enchanteresse?*

Watching Lela from behind Willow's shoulder, Darcy flicked her glance quickly at Amory, who appeared to have passed out on the floor. A small, but growing puddle of blood soaked the carpet in front of his chest.

"Get out of my way, *Enchanteresse*."

"No," said Willow, crossing her arms over her chest.

"You think what I did to your boyfriend hurt? It'll look like a kiss when I'm done with you. I could kill you with one blow."

"Try it," snarled Willow. "See what happens."

Lela narrowed her yellow eyes at Willow, uncertainty making her features weak for a moment, her nostrils flaring in frustration. Finally she shrugged, offering Willow a thin smile.

"I don't want you, *Enchanteresse*. I don't have a fight with you. Give her to me and I will leave you..." she glanced down at Amory's body beside her, kicking his chest lightly "...and your *meat* alone."

"Over my dead fucking body I'll give her to you, you bitch."

"That can absolutely *BE ARRANGED*!" bellowed Lela, fury contorting her features, taking a wild step toward Willow.

Willow raised her hands, palms out, fingers splayed. Lela growled angrily and stopped advancing.

"Find Jack," Willow whispered to Darcy over her shoulder, her voice taut, frantic. "*NOW!*"

"It doesn't work like...I *can't* just..."

Lela cackled with laughter, hands on her slim hips, yellow eyes bright and mean. "Like a virgin with a hooker. You have the equipment but you don't know how to fuck!"

You have the equipment. Darcy flicked her eyes to Lela's face, the gut-wrenching fear making her insides swirl uncomfortably. It felt oddly like going inside.

S HE WASN'T IN THE WOODS.

She was in an inside room, hovering above the three women below.

She looked at their bodies for a moment: A light-haired woman stood behind a petite, dark-haired woman…and another—a dark, long-haired woman—stood across from them with her hands on her hips. There was a man on the floor and he was lying in a small black stain, but she could see through his chest. His heart glowed like a red lightbulb and she saw it pulse and pump. Whoever he was, he was alive.

She drifted to the window, but it was closed. She could feel the black wolf. He was far away, but coming. She felt frightened and confused so she screamed for him in a primal, reflexive way, as a baby cries for the comfort of its mother. She could barely hear the weak, muted sound, like she was screaming under water. She tried again, but it sounded hushed and strangled in her ears, like the very distant, distorted echo of a scream from long ago or far away.

She glanced back at the three women, floating toward them. The dark, long-haired woman was squatting down beside the man now, holding out a handful of knives. Suddenly the woman twisted her wrist and the knives pointed downwards toward the man's head.

The smaller woman lunged forward, drawing the attention of the long-haired woman.

OH MY GOD!

Planes of consciousness collided and Darcy realized where she was and what she was seeing.

That's Amory on the floor.

Lela is about to hurt him.

Willow can't protect all of us.

She raced back to the window, hovering behind the glass and felt the force of her desperation and fear come bubbling up out of her center like a geyser. The window shattered before her as the raw, hot power of her terrified scream broke the glass.

She found the wolf's yellow eyes on the ground below and beseeched him:

HELP ME!

"DON'T. YOU. TOUCH. HIM," WILLOW snarled as Darcy shook her head sharply to rouse herself, taking a deep breath. She'd have to process her feelings about pulling Jack inside later—with no comforting forest waiting for her when she initiated it, she didn't like it, that was for sure. She opened her eyes wide, reorienting herself.

Lela squatted beside Amory, the razor-sharp claws of her hands dangling a fraction of an inch over his unconscious head. With one plunge his brains would be impaled.

"Lela, NO!" Darcy cried, stepping forward from behind Willow. "NO! DON'T!"

Lela's hand stilled and she turned her face up toward Darcy. Jack was right. She was young. Up close, so very young. It occurred to Darcy that she might even be old enough, biologically, to be Lela's mother. Under all of that fierce anger, she was still just a girl.

"The meat speaks!" Lela declared, slowly standing.

Willow placed her hand on Darcy's arm. "Get behind me, kid."

"No, Will," said Darcy, a surprising calm blanketing her as she stood before her mate's sister. She tilted her head to the side, regarding her—her what? Her sister-in-law? She spoke softly, compassionately. "He doesn't love you like that, Lela."

Lela's brows furrowed over narrowed, golden eyes.

"He will when you're gone," she growled at Darcy.

"No," said Darcy, and a firm gentleness, such that she'd use with a truculent teenager, came easily to her lips. "No, he never will."

"I will KILL you, meat!" Lela bellowed, her eyes igniting.

"Then he will *hate* you," said Darcy with finality.

Lela threw back her head and Darcy watched as her claws lengthened another two or three inches. Her fangs also dropped and raised, from the top and bottom of her mouth, sharpening to long shards as they developed in the space of seconds. Darcy could hear the stretching as her body grew in height and girth, her muscles popping her clothes off her body. Darcy's mouth dropped open as Lela's face turned from a tan, human color to black, her nose widening like a dog's. Lastly, coarse black hair had appeared all over her body until she was covered in it—her face, down her neck, over her breasts to her stomach, her pelvis and legs. When she was fully shifted, she raised her arms over her head, her claws scraping against the ceiling of the room, and she turned to the window, howling at the moon.

Darcy's heart threatened to beat out of her chest and she panted, close to hyperventilating with the force of her terror. Lela was no longer human. She was a fully shifted Roux-ga-roux. Darcy's mouth had dropped open and her eyes burned as she unblinkingly watched with horror as her adversary transformed herself from a lovesick psychopath into a mythic creature.

Darcy felt Willow's cool hand slip into hers, and she knew what she had to do. She squeezed it, hoping that Willow would always know the depths of her love for her, no matter what happened, then released her friend's hand and, placing her hands on Willow's shoulder, pushed with all her might. As Willow fell, Darcy stepped forward until she stood toe to toe with a shifted Lela, whose sharp fangs were about a foot over Darcy's head and dripped with froth. Her gleaming eyes burned like lasers into Darcy's.

Fear threatened to buckle her knees, but she thought of Jack's face on his pillow this afternoon, staring at her with enough love to last a lifetime. And she knew: It had been worth it to love him. It had been worth it to have him again these past two weeks, even if she would never see him again. If she died now, tonight, at least she'd had a chance to tell him that she loved him.

She faced Lela's gruesome, slavering face and screamed the words that would surely be her last:

"HE BELONGS TO *ME*!"

Lela lunged and Darcy lurched back, pulled roughly out of Lela's path by Willow, who had reached up from the floor and grabbed Darcy's hand, yanking with all her strength. Darcy fell to the floor on top of Willow as Lela stumbled toward the couch. Suddenly they heard the crashing and crunching noise of the locked door downstairs being ripped from its hinges and thrown. And in one pounding step—two, three—another creature at least twice Lela's size crashed into the room, claws raised outward, howling with a deafening, blood-curdling roar.

Darcy looked up from her sprawl on the floor to see the larger creature seize, with deadly precision, Lela's neck, holding her with the V of flesh between thumb and forefinger claws, propelling her across the room until her head slammed against the far wall, cracking the glass of the big-screen TV that hung on the wall. She growled and yelped, thrashing her body violently, but was unable to break the chokehold on her throat.

Looking to the stairs, another creature appeared. He stopped, surveying the scene, and Darcy watched his eyes glow brighter as he noticed Amory's body on the floor. He approached Amory with a decisive grunt of interest but the bigger Roug pinning Lela claimed his attention with a sharp, brutal roar.

Darcy shifted to all fours and slowly pushed herself up from the floor, backing against the wall to her left. The Roug holding the thrashing Lela jerked his head toward Darcy and locked his glowing yellow eyes with hers. She gasped when she heard Jack's voice.

I'm still me.

She clamped her eyes shut, bracing herself against the wall. Her lungs constricted and she couldn't take a breath. She had known it was him, of course, but hearing Jack's voice in her head as she beheld him in fully shifted form for the first time was still shocking. She puffed in and out in shallow breaths, trying to get a deep one into her diaphragm. Close to fainting, it occurred to her that there was only one possible way to comfort and calm herself.

Slowly, she opened her eyes again and she stared into Jack's glowing, golden eyes. He was waiting for her.

It's okay, baby. You're okay. Breathe.

She wanted to close her eyes, but if she did, she'd lose the soothing, comforting sound of his voice. So she stared at the savage, inhuman golden orbs intently and was relieved to feel her heart slow down.

It's me. It's me. Breathe.

Gradually she found she could breathe again. She sucked in a deep breath, glancing down at his body for a moment. He was covered in black hair, like Lela, but the unoccupied claws of his left paw were a good deal larger, sharper, and more discolored than hers had been. Darcy raised her gaze and met his shiny golden eyes without wavering. She could finally form a coherent thought.

It's you, Jack. I know it's still you.

He nodded at her slowly, then turned his head to Julien, who was still sniffing Amory, and growled at him sharply again. As Julien slowly approached Jack and Lela, Willow scrambled across the floor to Amory's side, working quickly to tear his shirt aside and inspect his wound.

Chapter 8

WITH WILLOW FINALLY TENDING TO Amory, Darcy took a step closer to Jack, wanting to collapse against him in exhaustion as soon as he shifted back to human form. She moved softly to the front of the room, around the couch until she stood in the left corner, a good ten feet from where Roug Jack had Roug Lela pinned in front of the TV with the dim spotlight shining down on them.

Lela had stopped fighting him, her strength sapped, and her face—even shifted as she was—defeated, as she hung limply against the cracked flat screen, still pinned by the throat. Jack growled and groaned more and more gently, holding Lela's eyes, until she looked down at her feet in submission. Julien was at his shoulder now and Jack slowly loosed his grip on Lela's neck, the claws of his left hand still raised as he slowly backed away from her, toward Darcy, making room for Julien.

Roug Jack stood between Darcy and Roug Lela, but she peeked around his body to see what happened next. Jack flexed his fingers lightly at his side, his bone-like claws brushing together, a sound like wooden wind chimes catching a breeze, *clack clack clack*, a reminder that he was ready if Lela should threaten Darcy again. He kept his back to Darcy, facing his brother and sister.

Roug Julien stood naked in front of naked Roug Lela. With the fur-covered back of his hand, careful not to touch her with his claws, he gently tilted her chin up. Julien grunted softly and Lela growled softly back. Suddenly, before Darcy's eyes, just as Jack had downshifted last Thursday, she watched as their claws slowly retracted and the hair covering their bodies seemed to shrink back into their skin.

Looking immediately before her, she saw Jack's body doing the same.

The long claws weren't visible at his sides now, and his back was flesh again, dirty but smooth. She reached out a hand to tentatively touch him and he whipped around, crushing her into his arms, pulling her against his naked body and burying his face in her hair. The hard lines of his body pressed into her, as the iron grip of his arms encircled her. She leaned up to kiss him and felt him tremble.

"Darcy. You saw me..." His voice was tortured, despairing.

"I did." she whispered, holding his shaggy face in her hands, finding his eyes in the dim light.

I've seen you shifted and...

He dropped her eyes, looking down. She lifted his face, forcing him to look at her, seizing his eyes with hers again.

I've seen you shifted and you still belong to me. I still want you. I still choose you. I still love you, Jack. I love you, I love you, love you.

He shuddered from the impact of her words, his eyes closing as he pulled her back against his chest, his voice low and thick with emotion near her ear.

"My God, Darcy, if you hadn't pulled me inside—"

"You got here in time. You saved me."

"I love you," he murmured against her ear. "You're my life. If I had lost you—"

"Don't say it." She leaned back. "You didn't. I'm here. I'm yours."

He nodded and the strength of his emotions or the sheer exhaustion of his body seemed to finally hit him. He pulled her to him, sighing raggedly, as his arms wrapped around her like he would never, ever let her go.

From the safety of his embrace, Darcy turned her head slightly, looking at Julien and Lela. Julien's skin was dirty from running in the woods, but Lela's was somehow smooth and tan, supple and perfect, bathed in the moonlight filtering in from the window. Her breasts pressed against the hair on Julien's chest as she turned her neck and looked, with mournful, defeated eyes, upon Jack and Darcy's reunion.

Julien's quiet voice demanded her attention.

"*Lela Beauloup, fille de Lynette Reynard et Dubois Beauloup, je veux que tu sois ma compagne.*"

"They're speaking too fast for me. What did he say?" whispered Darcy.

Jack whispered back, his breath hot on her ear, "He wants her to be his mate."

Lela's neck had a bright red mark where Jack had held her and her shoulders were still slumped in surrender, but her eyes sparked and glowed in indignation under long, black lashes. She was fiercely beautiful, but almost feral, her black hair tumbling in wild waves around her shoulders, curling just over the tops of her breasts. She glanced at Jack again and winced before facing Julien.

"*Je ne vous aime pas, Julien,*" she said softly, like she was sorry.

"Now what?" Darcy whispered.

"She doesn't love him."

"*Voulez-vous essayer, Lela? Puis-je vous embrasser?*" asked Julien gently.

"He asked her to try. He asked permission to kiss her," breathed Jack, and Darcy's heart leapt at the touch of his lips grazing her ear as he spoke.

"*Je m'en fiche. Je veux mourir,*" Lela breathed, looking back toward Jack.

"I don't care. I want to die," echoed Jack, low and soft, translating.

"*S'il-vou-plaît, Lela. S'il-vous-plaît, faites-moi confiance.*"

"Please, Lela. Please trust me."

"*D'accord,*" said Lela softly, her voice tired and beaten. "*Je n'ai rien à perdre.*"

"She gave permission. She has nothing left to lose." Jack paused before continuing. "If the binding is true, we'll feel it. You and me. Bound couples share the energy of a true binding."

Lela finally looked away from Jack and raised her head to look at Julien. Darcy held her breath as Julien placed his hands on Lela's face, gazing at her with such poignant tenderness it made Darcy's belly leap with hope for him, and he bent to kiss her.

As his lips pressed against hers, his fingers curled, one by one, until he held her face softly with his knuckles. His lips drew back from hers, his breathing audibly ragged, before capturing her lips again with a deep groan, his hands uncurling, splaying over Lela's face with building passion, the bones in his hands stark and white as he flexed them rigidly with the force of his emotions. Lela moaned, coming to life, raising her arms, her hands running over the contours of Julien's muscular back, her back arching to push her breasts up against his chest.

Darcy gasped as her whole body started vibrating like a violin string strung too tight and plucked too hard. Dizzying waves of orgasmic-like pleasure pooled in her belly, fanning out to the entirety of her body, making her turn away from the newly bound couple to capture Jack's eyes. He was waiting for her, his body humming in tune with hers.

Can you feel it? he asked.

I feel it. I feel you.

He dipped his head and captured her lips with his, tasting her mouth, stroking her tongue, growling softly to let her know how much he loved her, how close he came to losing her. She felt it all in the heavenly vibrations that ended as abruptly as they began and she drew back, disappointed they were gone too soon, left wanting so much more than the kiss they'd shared. It was like her own binding to Jack was revalidated, strengthened, gloriously reconfirmed through watching another couple find their way.

Nice, huh? He grinned at her, his face loving and tender.

Can we attend another binding sometime soon?

His face registered a chuckle, but it was soundless.

Her body felt hot and taut and made to love. Now. She barely trusted her legs to keep her upright. All she wanted was to take his hand, pull Jack down the stairs, lock his bedroom door and impale herself on his waiting hardness.

He read this in her eyes, his eyes burning for her, but he showed extreme self-control, shaking his head at her, looking over her shoulder at the happy new couple. Darcy turned, following his gaze.

Absurdly, it occurred to Darcy, yet again, that Julien and Lela were both naked, pressed passionately up against each other—and with increasing sounds of pleasure, there was no indication they planned to stop what they were doing.

Darcy turned back to Jack, her body a mess of sensations—aroused from him shifting to save her, aroused from the binding tremors, aroused from watching Julien and Lela on the verge of consummating their binding…wet and slick and wanting and knowing of only one way to relieve the pressure of her arousal. "Jack…"

He cupped her face and kissed her lips gently. "Soon, baby."

She sighed, frustrated, turning back to Julien and Lela. "Um, are they going to…"

"It's highly likely. Maybe we should go…"

But Darcy continued to stare at them, drawn and fascinated, until he tugged her hand, leading her around the couch toward the stairs.

"Ours was nothing like that," she murmured, considering their relatively chaste kiss in the darkness of a high school stage.

"We were just kids. It was perfect."

"Humph," she grumbled, wanting nothing more than to get in Jack's bed for a long night of exactly what Julien and Lela were about to do.

They had just reached the stairs when Darcy heard a sob and looked down to see Willow leaning over Amory.

Oh, my God! Amory! With the distraction of the binding, she'd forgotten about her brother. Seeing him lying there was as good as being doused with a pail of cold water.

Willow turned over her hands, covered in blood, and looked up at Jack with watery eyes.

"I stopped the bleeding and the cut's not actually that deep, but he's burning up. I need to get him to a hospital but my cell phone doesn't have a recep—"

"LELA!" yelled Jack, looking down at Amory. "WHAT DID YOU DO?"

When he got no answer, he bellowed her name again, turning toward the passionately kissing couple. "LELA!"

Darcy looked back at the wall where Julien still had a now-willing Lela pinned with his hard body. They broke apart with a shared groan of regret and Lela peeked at Jack from over her mate's shoulder.

"DID YOU—" Jack growled.

"No!" she answered. "No! Not that! It's just a scratch."

Then she grabbed Julien's head and pulled it back down to hers.

"I'll take him downstairs," said Jack, lifting Amory's body off the floor with a low grunt. "As long as she didn't bite or lick him, I know what to do."

Willow followed behind Jack but Darcy stood dazed for a minute, unable to look away from the newly bound lovers. Lela growled, biting Julien's neck with small fangs, which made him scream and prompted him to cup her ass, lifting her off the floor with a sudden, torrid urgency. Lela locked her legs around his back, moaning in French, and Darcy's face flamed hot as Julien thrust without further ado into a screaming Lela. Darcy forced her feet to move back downstairs.

JACK LAID AMORY GENTLY ON the guest room bed that Darcy had been using as Willow quickly gathered Darcy's work into a messy pile and put it on the floor. Jack ran to his room to put on a pair of jeans, and when he returned Willow was patting the long scratch with a wet washcloth until it was a neat red line.

Jack leaned over the wound, inspecting it.

Willow's hand was on Amory's forehead.

"He's so hot, Jack."

"She didn't lick him or bite him. So she didn't directly transfer her venom. But there were probably trace amounts on her claws. It's not enough to turn him, but the next four or five hours are going to be very…*uncomfortable*…as his body purges whatever it absorbed."

"Should I go get antibiotics?" asked Willow.

"Human antibiotics won't help."

"What will?" asked Darcy from the doorway, her cheeks bright red.

Jack's erection, which had been calming down as he helped Willow situate Amory, sprang back to life at the sight of her so flushed and ready for sex. It killed him that he was about to add a delay to their lovemaking.

"*Aconitum*," he answered softly in a hard voice. He hated the thought of even bringing the stuff into his house.

"Wolfsbane!" Darcy exclaimed, her eyes clearing.

"Wolfsbane," confirmed Jack. "It's the only thing that suppresses a shift."

"It *what?*" Darcy gasped and he heard the hope in her voice.

"It suppresses a shift in a Roug and will draw out the venom from a human."

He turned to her and saw the hope in her eyes.

"But, Jack! Then you can just take Wolfsbane at the full moon and it'll keep you from—"

"It's poisonous. For me. For my body. More than a little would kill me. It killed Julien's first mate. It killed my father."

"He's right." Willow nodded. "Julien told me about it. Sorry, Darce."

"No. Don't be sorry." She smiled at Jack, looking just a little sheepish. "I love you just the way you are."

But she didn't and he knew it. She was *accepting* him just the way he was, but it was clear she wished that the shifting part of his nature could be controlled. He wished it could be too. He smiled at her sadly. *I love you too.*

"Do you know what it looks like?" he asked Darcy aloud.

She nodded.

"We only need a tiny bit. If we put a little in the wound before Willow dresses it, it will draw out any rogue bits of Lela's toxin. It'll make the fever go down faster. He'll still be uncomfortable, but it won't be as bad."

Amory murmured in his sleep and Jack turned to him, feeling sorry. Amory's cheeks were blotchy red and his hair was saturated with sweat; his eyes rolled back in his head in a state of discomfort in his unconsciousness. Still, Jack knew this was nothing compared to the process of turning a human to Roux-ga-roux. He shuddered, blocking out the upsetting images of the two times he'd witnessed a full turning.

"One of you has to go," said Jack. "I shouldn't touch it."

"I'll go," said Darcy. "I know exactly where it is. In the garden at the Second Congregational church."

Figures, thought Jack to himself, thinking of the history between his kind and that church.

He hated to see her go and let her know as much.

I'll be fine, she insisted, flicking her glance toward the ceiling where they could hear bumps and crashes and loud growls and groans. *The danger's gone now. Please stay with Willow and Amory. That's more important to me.*

She grabbed her jacket out of the closet and he watched her go, telling her where to find the keys to his car as she headed out the door.

"Maybe we should still take him to the hospital," said Willow uneasily, sitting beside Amory, pressing the rinsed and wrung washcloth to his head.

"I promise you don't need to," said Jack. "I've seen this before. He'll be fine."

"You're right. He's strong. He should be okay. I'm just worried," mumbled Willow. What she said next surprised him. "I read all about this."

"What?" Jack moved off the bed to sit on a chair in the corner of the room, facing Willow, who sat against the headboard of the bed beside Amory.

"*Le Livre de Magie*," she said. "When you came back on Saturday night, Julien and I talked for a while on the swing. He's the one who mentioned the word *Enchanteresse* and though I'd never heard it before, something about it stuck with me. I called my *Nohkom* and she admitted that yes, she's an *Enchanteresse* as well. My father wasn't, of course. He's just a run-of-the-mill horse's ass. But he must have passed the gene down to me. It was a relief to find out. I've always felt...different. I think I went into medicine to give legitimacy to the skills that came naturally.

"My *Nohkom* sent me the *Book of Magic* on Sunday special delivery and I got it this morning. I basically read through it all day. But the first chapter I flipped to was Shifters. You're not alone, you know."

Jack lifted an eyebrow.

"Roux-ga-roux. Altamaha-ha. Fouke. Letiche. Memphré. Peluda. Waheela. Wendigo." Her voice was soft, far away as she rattled off the names of the known shifter groups in eastern North America, from the swampy bayous of Louisiana and Florida to the cold wilds of Nunavet on the Quebecois border.

Her voice eventually stilled. He watched as she pressed her lips to Amory's forehead, whispering endearments as he whimpered in his sleep. Finally she looked back up at Jack.

"And you're one of them. A shifter. You've turned her life upside down, her brother's lying bleeding beside me, and I know far more about any of this than I ever wanted—or needed—to know."

A low groan turned her eyes back to Amory's face. She pushed the reddish hair off his brow and leaned down to press her lips on his feverish skin again as he quieted.

"You're okay, Brat," she whispered tenderly. "*Je suis ici. Je t'appartiens. Vous n'avez pas à attendre plus longtemps.*"

Jack looked away, trying to give them a moment of privacy. She had whispered, *I'm here. I belong to you. You don't have to wait anymore.* Jack was touched by the quiet certainty of her words, and it occurred to him that, in a manner of speaking, he was watching a sort of binding. He was watching Willow Broussard commit herself to Amory Turner. An *Enchanteresse* to a human.

While Willow wasn't a skinwalker, his kind regarded her differently from a human. She was considered mystical by his people, a superior sub-class set of humans, feared and respected at once.

As for him? Yes. He was a Shifter.

He didn't know what to say to her about the others. Did he know they existed? Of course he did. His mother had known a displaced Memphré family when he was young, but they'd lost touch once the Memphrés had resettled by a lake three hours north of Portes de l'Enfer. Since their small population shifted to the waters of northern Quebec, and the Roux-ga-roux generally steered clear of large bodies of water, they didn't have a whole lot in common geographically. Sure, he knew about other Shift-ers—in the way that the Canadian Métis might know about the Alaskan Inuit or Australian Aboriginals. They were nothing more than faraway beings with whom you had something in common, but almost no cross-over in real life.

He watched Willow in the moonlight of the small guest room, the only other light filtering in through the crack under the bathroom door. He had a vague sense of intimacy with her—nothing attractive or sexual, not at all, just the feeling that they shared something genuine and sacred in these quiet moments, waiting for one sibling to ease the suffering of another while his siblings made love for the first time above them.

Willow took a deep breath. He sensed she had more to say.

Now she raised her head to him and he caught the reflection of light in her dark eyes.

"If things had turned out differently, I wouldn't have liked you, Jack. I would have helped her abjure you." She paused, turning her attention back to Amory and running the cool cloth over his lips before kissing them gently. "But she *chooses* you. Not just because of the binding. Her *heart* chooses you.

"And I know something about waiting for the one you love. And I know how it feels when the wait is over. *Finalement.*" She took Amory's hand and pressed it to her lips before returning it to his side, threading her fingers through his.

"We have that in common," said Jack quietly.

"We do. But, we have something important *not* in common. I'm a human who loves a human, Jack. You're a Roux-ga-roux who loves a human."

He breathed in, staring at his folded hands in his lap.

"And as far as I can tell," she continued, "that's not sustainable. As far as I can tell the Roug needs to be human or the human needs to be Roug for it to work."

"I refuse to turn her," muttered Jack, trying to keep the edge out of his voice. "Don't worry."

"I *am* worried," she whispered. She kissed Amory's hand again then released it, taking the washcloth off his head and heading to the bathroom. A moment later she returned, shrugging her small, tan, bony shoulders out of her sweater and laying it gently at the foot of the bed. She crawled up next to Amory, carefully arranging the cool cloth on his forehead before lying down on her side flush beside him, propped up on one elbow so that she could still see Jack.

And suddenly he knew where she was going with all of this. Suddenly it was clear.

"*Julien te l'a dit,*" he said into the dark quiet of the room. *Julien told you.*

He barely needed confirmation, but he let his eyes burn so he could see hers clearly. They were full of accusation and sorrow. She knew about the re-binding. He closed his eyes, clenching his jaw. "I just wanted some time with her before—"

"Before what? Before they hunt her down? Kill her? Kill you? Your binding's an abomination. He said they won't allow it."

Jack swallowed hard. *Damn Julien for meddling.*

"I know what you're thinking," Willow continued. "But he didn't betray you. Not purposely. It slipped out. I asked if he felt your binding was absolute and he said he did, but he wished like hell it wasn't because of the, um, re-binding."

"I won't let anyone hurt her."

"As far as I can tell, she'll get hurt either way. If you produce her before your—your Council, you'll prove your binding but put her in danger. If you can't produce her, you can neither prove nor explain your binding which will raise eyebrows and compel a, um, what's it called? Oh. An Inquisition. From what I could gather, Inquisitions don't go too well for the accused. She loses either way, Jack."

Jack rested his elbows on his knees and bowed his head, staring down at his bare feet.

"Will you let me tell her?"

Willow took a deep breath, and when he looked up he saw the compassion in her eyes.

She nodded. "Tell her soon. She might be able to help figure it all out. She's so smart, you wouldn't believe it. And there's us too."

He looked up at her and gave her a brief, sad smile.

"Oh, you don't see, do you? She chooses you, Jack. So I choose you too. After what those two"—she flicked her eyes to the ceiling—"put you through, they'll help too." She turned her eyes to Amory, gently moving the back of her free hand across his cheek. *"Ma chérie aidera aussi."*

My sweetheart will help too.

Jack stared at her bowed head and felt his eyes prick and burn with gratitude for her words.

When she looked up, her eyes were brimming with tears. "You still don't see? *Vous n'êtes pas seul.*"

You aren't alone.

She smiled at him, grim and firm, as a tear trailed down her face. Then she dropped her elbow and nestled on the pillow beside Amory, who shivered and flinched with fever, whispering gently in his ear and carefully laying her arm over his stomach, below the red, angry slash on his upper chest.

After so many years of keeping his binding a secret, the nature of his binding, the nature of his mate…after so many years of worry and longing and solitude, her words covered Jack like a blanket. He was grateful for Willow, for the acceptance and sense of community she offered to him. He had rarely been so grateful for anyone else in his entire life. And if it meant holding on to Darcy, he'd take all the help he could get.

"*Merci, Willow*," he said quietly, his voice low and gravelly with emotion.

She didn't answer, so he got up quietly, leaving them, closing the door gently behind him.

IT HADN'T TAKEN LONG FOR Darcy to find the Wolfsbane. She'd seen it many times in the church garden, growing in the shade of a large maple tree. She snipped off several pieces with her collecting shears and put the specimens in one of several small plastic bags she always kept with her for collecting.

It was a cool and misty evening as she drove back to Jack's lodge, and her mind circled uncomfortably with the events of the evening: Lela's attack, going inside to find Jack, seeing Jack shifted, Lela and Julien's binding, Amory's injury…it was a lot to process. But headlining her thoughts—perhaps because it was the most compelling to her intellectually and the least emotionally fraught—was the Wolfsbane's suppressive properties on Roux-ga-Roux shifting physiology.

She couldn't shake the idea that it was the first building block toward figuring out a "cure" for Jack so that he could control his shifting during the full moon. What she needed was to figure out how to have the appropriate dose of Wolfsbane to suppress the shift, ingested with an antidote to the toxic properties it held. She needed something to cancel out the poison that didn't hinder the suppression.

A deer suddenly bolted out of the woods and Darcy swerved sharply to avoid it, driving several yards into the woods before pumping the brakes to stop. Her heart raced, but she hadn't hit anything. Still, she needed to get out for a second and make sure there was no damage to Jack's car. She opened her door and stepped out gingerly into the woods, slapping at her neck almost immediately as a mosquito landed for a drink. She walked to the front of the SUV and aside from a salad's worth of vegetation caught in the front grill, everything appeared to be okay. She pulled the green out, throwing it to the ground before making her way back to the car.

As she tugged at the car door, she realized she still had something stuck to her hand. She turned it over to find a stalk of *Lycopodium clavatum,* the same moss that Miss Kendrick had drawn her attention to at the greenhouse last week.

"Wolf's Paw clubmoss," she murmured, looking at it carefully. "Healing properties for arthritis. Rheumatism. Anti-spasmodic. Persistent indigestion and gastritis."

What part of the Roug body did Wolfsbane attack, she wondered, and could Wolf's Paw reverse the toxins in the Wolfsbane?

She brushed the sample off her hand and put the car in reverse, backing slowly out of the dark woods and onto the rough dirt road leading back to Jack's house, the cogs of her mind still turning.

If Wolfsbane suppressed the shift and Wolf's Paw remedied the sickness, they'd just need a stabilizer to pull the two together. She arrived at Jack's house and cut the engine. She needed to get the Wolfsbane to Amory… and talk to Will.

"WHAT DO YOU THINK?" SHE asked Willow about her Roug cure, sitting in the chair in the corner of the room as Willow extracted tiny bits of the nectaries from the Wolfsbane and placed them on Amory's wound. He flinched in his sleep and Willow grimaced.

"I think I need to pay attention to Amory now. Plus, I'm exhausted. You may be on to something, but could we talk in the morning?"

Darcy got up and moved to the edge of the bed to look at her brother's damp, pink face. "Poor Amory. You think he'll be okay?"

"Jack says he will be. And yeah, I agree. He already looks better and he's not as agitated. His kidneys are probably filtering out some of the toxin. And this should help with the rest. He'll have a nasty scratch in the morning, but I think he's already out of the woods."

"Hey, Will…the *Enchanteresse* stuff…have you always known?"

Willow shook her head. "No. I didn't know until Julien called me *Enchanteresse* on Saturday night when we were sitting on the porch. I had my *Nohkom* confirm that she's one too. She also admitted that the *legend* she told me about the Roux-ga-roux was based on the truth."

Darcy raised her eyebrows at this. "You didn't know you were an *Enchanteresse*?"

"Listen, I always had an interest in healing, of course. And I never let any of my smart professors turn me off from incorporating Métis techniques into my healing practices. I guess it was always in the blood. *Nohkom* sent me a Book of Magic. Should make for interesting reading." She shrugged lightly. "What did that little bitch upstairs say so eloquently? Ah, yes. I'm like a virgin with a hooker. I have the equipment, but I don't know how to…well, you know the rest."

Darcy shuddered, remembering Lela's fury, how close she came to ending up dead.

"You saved my life," Darcy whispered.

"You did okay all on your own, kid," Willow said softly, gently stroking Amory's sweaty hair off his forehead. "It was quite a night."

Willow finished dressing Amory's scratch and looked up at Darcy.

"You sure you want this? Jack? The life he can offer you?"

Darcy shrugged lightly, offering her friend a sad smile. "I love him."

"It's a lot to take on. Seeing him tonight like that."

"It was still him, Will. I could hear him." She felt a smile touch her face, an unexpected, almost inappropriate, but totally inevitable joy bubbling up from inside. "It's absurd, right? The stuff of fairy tales and legends. I feel like Belle from *Beauty and the Beast*…the bookish librarian who falls in love with a monstrous creature."

Willow smiled at Darcy's movie-trailer inflection. Darcy's smile faded and she faced her friend gravely.

"I'd rather die than live without him." She swallowed, her eyes filling with tears as she felt the true impact of her words.

Willow circled around the bed, reaching out for Darcy's hand, a worried expression darkening her face. She searched Darcy's eyes intently and the moment was heavy, as if Willow wanted to say something important. She finally exhaled and gave Darcy a small smile.

"I love you, kid. You're like a sister to me. If there's ever anything—*anything*—I can do for you, you just ask. I wouldn't have had much of a family if it wasn't for you. There's nothing I wouldn't do. I just want you to know that."

She reached out and clasped Darcy against her small body and Darcy's forehead wrinkled with the intensity of her friend's speech. Willow was fiercely loyal, fiercely loving, and fiercely protective, but she wasn't given to mushy speeches. *Was something going on?*

Then she recalled the events of the past three hours, and shook her head, reaching up to embrace Willow too. It had been an incredibly frightening, emotional evening and Amory still needed Willow's expertise and strength. She had a right to be a little more emotional than usual. Darcy leaned back and kissed her friend's cheek.

"You need anything else? Does Amory need anything?"

"No, kid," said Willow, sighing, then shaking her head and smiling. "Go find Jack."

Darcy took one last look at Amory then drew back, nodding at Willow, closing the door gingerly behind her.

Chapter 9

DARCY HAD BEEN THROUGH ENOUGH tonight and Jack was anxious to have her all to himself, in his room, in his bed, taking care of her for the rest of the night.

He wished she hadn't had to go out for the Wolfsbane, but she was the most logical person to go find it, and in the meantime, he wanted to think of something immediate, something special, that he could do for her.

He'd never *had* someone to take care of, so ideas didn't come quickly.

Any of the women he'd been with before Darcy had been short-lived, emotionally detached, incredibly frustrating screwing sessions that never ended in much satisfaction. He'd never had a girlfriend or a long-time, repeat lover, even. Just a handful of unfulfilling liaisons that hadn't amounted to anything memorable.

But after the night she'd had, the fear she'd experienced and her loving acceptance of him in all his forms, he wanted to do something special for her.

He also wanted to have sex with her. Badly. He swallowed hard, remembering the vibrations that had ripped through his body as Julien and Lela bound themselves. He'd heard about the sweet, hot connection that bound couples, felt at Gathering Bindings, but he'd never experienced the phenomenon for himself. And Darcy's face. Her heavy eyes and flushed cheeks so hot for him, the smell of her body dripping wet for him. He sighed. *Slow down, Jack.* He felt like after everything, he needed to earn his time with her tonight.

First he showered his dirty body, scrubbing the forest away. He cut the overgrowth of his hair and shaved his beard down to shadow and stubble, and then put on a pair of flannel pants that hung down around his hips. He had no candles—he could see in the dark, so they served no practical purpose—but his bedroom had a fireplace, so he built a fire. When he heard his car in the driveway, he started running a hot bath for her then sat down on his bed and waited. Nervously. Like a teenager who'd asked a pretty girl to the prom and was hoping to get lucky afterward. He looked around the room, his heart racing with anticipation.

A knock on the door. His heart leapt and he took a deep breath, turning the knob only to be disappointed by Julien's face peeking around the door sheepishly. He was naked and dirty and looked immensely satisfied. Jack's nose curled up from Lela's scent wafting off Julien's sated body, his expression curdling.

"*Fiche ton camp, Julien.*" *Piss off!* Jack growled at his little brother. He was in no mood to deal with Julien, or Lela, for that matter. In fact, Lela would do well to place herself as far away from Jack as possible.

"*J'ai pas de pantalon,*" Julien hissed, flicking his eyes to his groin.

"For Chrissakes," mumbled Jack, walking over to his bureau to grab some jeans and throw them at his brother.

"Tomorrow, we'll, um, straighten up the, uh—" Julien pointed his finger at the ceiling.

"Fine. Just get out of here, please."

"Um, can Lela borrow some clothes? From Darcy?"

"You have *got* to be kidding me."

Julien shrugged.

"Where is Lela, my darling, psychotic little sister?"

Julien moved to his left and a naked Lela peered at Jack from around Julien's shoulder, her face a mixture of sexual satisfaction and contrition.

"I'm good and pissed off at you right now, *petite soeur.*"

"*Je comprends,*" she murmured, casting her eyes down. "*Je suis désolée, Jacques.*"

"Your apology doesn't mean a whole lot to me right now, Lela." He trudged to the bathroom and took his bathrobe off the back of the bathroom door. He handed it to Julien humorlessly. "I'm not asking Darcy for anything. This is the best I can do for her."

Julien handed the robe to Lela and she shrugged it on over her shoulders, keeping her eyes downcast. Julien pulled her to his side protectively before looking back at Jack. "She said she was sorry."

"She tried to kill my mate. Why don't I try to kill yours and you can see how you feel?"

"Okay, Jack. You made your point." They backed away from Jack's bedroom and headed to the stairs. Jack assumed they'd be sharing the pullout loveseat in the studio above the garage where Julien had been staying. Good. He didn't even want them in the house tonight.

He plopped back down on his bed, trying to find his previous enthusiasm. The fates were kind because right then his door opened and Darcy peeked her head in, her lips tilting up into a smile as she found his face, and every thought of Julien and Lela flew out of his head. She slid around the door, closing it behind her, then ran to the bed without a word, maneuvering herself onto his lap, straddling him, her knees resting by his sides on the bed.

His hands immediately reached for her hips as she ran her hands through his hair, looking at his face with such tenderness his breath caught in his throat.

He would figure out Solstice. He couldn't lose her. He wouldn't give her up. He promised Willow that he'd tell Darcy about the re-binding, but not now. Not right this minute. Right now he just needed to be with her.

She bent her head and kissed the skin under his ear.

He counted quickly in his mind: Four weeks, five, six, seven…fifty days. *Fifty days until Solstice.*

He felt her breath, hot with hunger, and it made him shiver.

I still have time.

Her tongue darted out to flick the sensitive lobe.

Fifty days.

Fift—

Her teeth caught the lobe lightly and tugged as her hands trailed down his chest, slipping into the waistband of his soft, flannel pants, her cool fingers brushing the top of his rigid erection.

Ahhhhh.

JACK HAD INSISTED THE BATH was for her.

She had informed him that if he didn't join her, she wasn't taking a bath at all.

Hopping out of bed naked, she tugged his hand until he got up and followed her into the bathroom. She touched the pre-filled water with her fingers and must have found it cool because she turned on the hot water and perched on the edge of the tub with her legs crossed gracefully, watching the steaming water fall.

And all the while Jack watched her, leaning against the bathroom door with his arms crossed, wondering what she was feeling. Even though they'd just made love, they'd barely spoken a word other than groaning one another's names intermittently. It worried him a little. After a lifetime of waiting and longing he wanted to trust that despite what she'd seen tonight, that she really wanted him, that she really belonged to him, that she wouldn't decide to walk away—but it was hard.

She turned the faucet and the water stopped. He watched as she stepped into the tub, sinking down beneath the hot water with a light sigh, easing back until she rested against the comfortably curved contours of the large tub. She looked up at him and he watched as she spread her legs to a V.

He drew a sharp breath, looking at her face with raised eyebrows. "What next?"

"Come sit with me," she said softly, raising the hand closest to him.

"Do you want to—"

She shook her head slowly. "Nope. We're relaxing. We'll do that again… soon."

He stepped into the conventional, though oversized, tub, sitting down between her legs and leaning back against her breasts. The hot water lapped against his skin and she raised her knees to his sides. He knew she was wide open behind him and the thought made him harden reflexively.

"Darcy…" he groaned.

"Just be comfortable," she suggested, her voice low and tired, but amused. "Relax."

Relax with his naked mate behind him. Right.

He leaned back against her lightly, sinking down just a little until his head rested right above her breasts and he felt her arms encircle him, around his neck, her hands resting on his upper chest, over his heart. He took a deep breath and sighed, surprised that he was actually relaxing.

"This is nice," he breathed, closing his eyes.

"Mm-hm."

He might have almost fallen asleep if she hadn't spoken again.

"Why are you worried?" she asked.

Jack stiffened for a moment, wondering if Willow had broken her promise and said something to Darcy about the re-binding, but she continued, "I can feel it."

He took the soap in his hands then rubbed gently up and down her legs on either side of him, loving the smooth slickness of her skin under his fingers. "You saw me. Shifted."

"Mm-hm," she breathed again, leaning forward to press her lips to his wet shoulder. "I saw you shifted." She paused before speaking again. "Do you think I love you less now?"

"It must have been shocking."

"It was," she admitted, her lips still close to the skin of his shoulder, occasionally pressing against it, and he sensed it was an absentminded gesture as she gathered her thoughts. "Until I looked in your eyes. *Your* eyes. I saw you there, I heard you there…and then I couldn't see anything but you, Jack. You're still you, whether you're like this"—she rubbed her hands lightly over his chest from behind—"or like that. And I love you either way." She kissed his shoulder again.

He reached up to clasp her hands tenderly, moving the left to his mouth and then the right, pressing his lips to the freckled backs for several moments before releasing them, retuning them to his chest, and covering her hands with his own.

"You've never pulled me inside before," he said, wondering how she had figured it out.

"I didn't like it," she said after a few quiet moments. "I like it better when you do it. It felt strange. *Too* strange."

"You're just not used to it," he sighed, squeezing her fingers, knowing that *Dansmatête* didn't necessarily manifest itself identically in both mates. "It's a good tool, though, to be able to find me if you need me."

"I never intend to be further away from you than this," she said softly, kissing his neck.

He smiled, reassured and pleased by the unexpected sweetness of her words. Her lips brushed across his hot skin. He had to admit the bathtub had its benefits, but he was anxious to have her writhing under him again.

"Jack…"

"Mmm?" he murmured, eyes closed, head leaning back against her.

"What if I could synthesize different…" She paused, clearing her throat. "What if I could synthesize a cure? For the *Pleine Lune* shifting? So you wouldn't have to. So you could control it. All the time."

"I don't think it's possible, baby."

"I think it might be," said Darcy quietly. "I have an idea, but I need to talk to Willow."

He didn't say anything. He didn't want to put pressure on her by answering in a voice that would be infused with hope. His heart beat with yearning, with the fervent wish that what she was saying could possibly be true.

"Have I offended you?" she whispered and he heard her worry.

He sat up and swiveled, jostling the water around them, and turned to face her, cupping her cheeks in his hands, searching her face. He didn't trust his voice so he captured her eyes.

It would be a miracle.

She exhaled, looking relieved.

No promises, Jack.

He leaned forward to press his lips against hers, his tongue breaking through the barrier of her lips to mate with hers. He stroked it gently, lovingly, taking his time to cherish her, to let her know how much he loved her. Finally he pulled back. Her eyes were closed and he kissed each lid tenderly before turning back around and settling once more between her legs.

"Hey..." she protested, wanting more, and he chuckled.

"We're relaxing. Remember?"

She took a deep breath, which pushed her breasts into his back, and he gritted his teeth. *Tease.*

Finally she put her arms around his neck again, her fingers trailing softly along his collarbone in a hypnotic movement and he knew she was thinking.

After a few moments she spoke again. "Remember tonight when you yelled at Lela?"

"Which time?" asked Jack, running his hands up and down her smooth legs again.

"When you saw Amory. You asked 'Did you—' but you didn't finish your question."

"Uh-huh," he muttered, knowing where this was going.

"And then later you said that because she didn't lick him or bite him, she didn't directly transfer her venom."

"Right," he said, waiting for it.

"What if she had?"

"She didn't," he hedged.

"Jack..."

"It would have been too late. Amory would have already started turning."

Darcy was silent and he reached up to take her hands, lacing his fingers through hers and tightening them into double fists, resting on his chest.

"Into a Roux-ga-roux," she said.

"Yes," he answered.

"You've licked me. I mean, we've…"

"Not when I've been shifted."

"Oh."

"Things would be different if I was shifted. But, Darcy, I would never, ever—"

"Have you met any? Um, *turned* Rougs?"

He squeezed her hands. She sounded curious, not frightened. "Some."

"How are they different from you?"

"They're not in essentials. But I've been Roug since birth. I have a blooded family; I've grown up in the customs; I know the rules. Turned Rougs tend to be rogues, especially if they were turned unintentionally or out of spite and left without a mentor. No family. No understanding of our culture. Turning's strenuously discouraged. It can be a pretty messy business."

Jack suppressed his memories of the many turned Rougs he'd had to hunt down while he served as a Council Enforcer, the fear in their confused eyes. But a turned Roug without a proper, responsible mentor was a danger to the entire Roug community.

"If Amory had been turned—"

"He wasn't."

"I know. But, if he was…"

"Lela, as his maker, would have mentored him. And probably Julien, by proxy, as well."

"What about you?"

"It's possible to foster a turned Roug. But there's a bond between a turned Roug and its maker. The only thing stronger is a binding. Its maker is the organic guide."

"And right now, if Amory had been turned…"

"Darce."

"Please, I'm just trying to understand."

"Fine. You want to know what would have happened? It's not pretty. His fever wouldn't be getting better. It would be getting worse. Hotter. Until he started with seizures. They go on for a while. If he survived the fever and the seizures, his fangs and claws would start to drop. He'd be so out of it, he wouldn't know he was biting and swiping, but he wouldn't be able to help it. By about then, his eyes would start burning with fever, and his body would be expanding. In another hour or so, his beard would grow out and his hair would fill in. About eight hours from now, he'd be fully turned."

"What else?" she asked, her voice low and insistent.

"He'd need blood. He'd want it."

"So what would you have done?"

"Julien and I would have locked him in the vault and I'd have made Lela go kill a deer and haul it back here. Then I'd have thrown her and it in there with him. After he consumed it, he'd sleep, and likely shift back to human. When he woke up, he'd see Lela. He'd still have his human memories, but he'd definitely perceive the changes in his hearing and sight, his lust for blood. In his confusion, he'd still know her as his maker, so Lela's presence would be his only real comfort."

"And then?"

"And then she'd teach him our ways over the next several weeks and months. He'd live with her and learn how to hunt, how to behave, the rules, the history, the culture. And hopefully he'd be able to make a life for himself with us. But he'd be Roug, not human."

"Forever?"

"Forever. Turned, not blooded."

She took a deep, shaky breath.

"If she'd licked him…," said Darcy. "Oh, I don't want to think about it."

He heard the fear and sadness that had crept into her voice and he hated it, and he hated Lela for initiating it.

"Then don't, *mon âme*. It didn't happen. Amory's going to be fine by morning. He'll be pretty tired for a day or two and he'll have a mean scar someday. But he's fine, Darcy. I promise."

"Have you ever turned anyone, Jack?"

"Never," he replied absolutely, unlacing his hands from hers gently. He brought her fingers to his lips and kissed them. "I'd never want this for someone else."

"What does that mean?"

"It's a hard life. It's not—"

"Not that." She flattened her hands across his chest, pulling him back against her breasts, leaning forward to kiss his shoulder. "What you called me… *mon* âme."

He leaned forward and stood up then turned, offering her his hand. She took it and he pulled her up. Once she was standing naked and glistening before him, he cupped her face in his hands, gazing into her eyes with all the love in his heart and whispered,

"My soul."

MY SOUL.
            "Am I?"

The wince that swept across his face was elusive even as it imprinted on her heart in the small second that she saw it.

"You're the closest thing I have."

She reached up and took his hands in hers, stepping out of the tub. She held his eyes as he stepped out after her, and then she backed out of the bathroom, pulling him into his bedroom. In front of the golden glow of the fireplace she stopped, her heavy eyes momentarily mesmerized by the drops of water shining like diamonds on his shoulders in the firelight.

"You have a soul, Jack," she murmured.

He shook his head, but it was only the slightest gesture. She released his hands and raised her fingers to his face, tracing the contours, finally touching her fingers to his lips.

"You have a soul," she murmured again.

His lips pursed softly, kissing her fingers. One finger rubbed his lower lip, and he took it into his mouth, sucking on it gently. The wet heat of his tongue teased her fingertip as his teeth bit down, the softest pressure on her skin. His lips tightened over the digit, sucking it with increasing pressure. She felt the lovely, familiar warmth start to pool in her belly.

She withdrew her finger, and he watched as it sailed between them, into her own mouth where she sucked on it, tasting him, tasting the heat of his mouth.

Jack's eyes caught fire. He saw them, fiery copper, reflected in hers. He knew that he didn't have a soul. Not as she did—as a human being who lived in the light of life. He was a dark thing, a creature of the night, suddenly unworthy of her goodness, her trust in him.

"I don't," he breathed, looking down.

He felt her hands on his face, one damp finger near his eye, which looked at her, sorry from the depths of his soulless being that he had ever bound himself to someone so gloriously luminous when he was so dark and obscured.

"Then we'll share mine," she said and smiled at him with so much love, it hurt to look at her. It knocked the wind out of him and made his chest ache with the force of his gratitude, the force of his love.

He was a fool to ignore the Solstice.

He didn't know how to protect her. To protect them.

She offered him her body, her heart, her head…and now her soul.

He offered her nothing.

"Darcy," he whispered, his voice raw with the power of his feelings, the wholeness of his love for her, the desperation to have her, the imminent danger to both of them.

"Let your claws drop," she breathed.

It was the very last thing he expected to hear.

"What?"

"I want…" She swallowed, looking unsure for a moment before meeting his eyes again. "I want you to know that I trust you, that I love you. Every part of you. I don't want you to hide yourself from me."

Any other thought in his head was lost, gone, suddenly far away, and he felt an insane heat unfurl in his gut that hardened his cock like concrete so fast it made him feel dizzy.

I offer you nothing.

You offer me you, she answered. *And that's all I want.*

"You don't have to do this…"

"I know. I want to. I want you."

He was surprised to feel the points of his claws poking through the tips of his fingers, as of their own volition, and he raised his hands, palms up, fingers pointed at the ceiling. She lowered her hands from his face, placing them under his hands and pointing the claws at her own body. She stepped back to make space for them and cupped his palms gently, watching intently as his claws protracted forward, inch by inch until about four inches of claw had grown, lightly tapping the skin of her chest above her breasts with sharp points before stopping.

She raised her eyes to his and grinned before looking back down.

"What does it feel like?"

He looked down at her hands cradling his, semi-protracted claws grazing the soft skin of her body, and his body ran riot, his blood racing like liquid fire through his body, the pulse in his neck throbbing with the intensity of his need for her.

He lifted one shoulder in a shrug, unable to speak, unable to trust his voice to form actual words.

"Does it hurt?"

He shook his head.

"Does it feel good?"

He nodded, dazed, desperately, terribly, irrevocably in love with her. Time and space ceased to exist, and there was nothing but this moment, this pinpoint of a millisecond in the history of time, nothing but the thrilling, terrifying reality of how much he loved Darcy Turner.

"Marry me," he rasped, half prayer, half growl.

Darcy gasped in surprise and it raised her chest up, extracting two perfect drops of blood from the middle claw-tips that pierced her tender, pink skin. She winced in pain and looked down as he dropped his hands. She looked up and saw the horror in his eyes as he stared at the blood on her chest.

"Jack," she murmured quickly. "It's okay."

She reached down, grasping his wrists, and carefully raised his hands, pressing the heel of his palms against the red droplets, claws flanking her face. Leaning forward and tilting her head, she pressed her lips against his and felt the pressure of his claws retracting back into his hands.

His hands dipped lower to cover her breasts, his thumbs rubbing back and forth over her nipples as his tongue swept into her mouth. She arched her back toward him and he wrapped his arms around her, crushing her against his body, profoundly grateful for the way she was welcoming him into her life, into her heart.

But when he pulled back from her, he looked down at her chest, hating the two small smears of blood over her breasts—a reminder of the damage he could inflict on her soft, tender body unintentionally.

"I hurt you," he said, his voice breaking.

"No, Jack." She shook her head, a single tear catching on her lower lashes before slipping onto her cheek. "It's nothing."

Was he crazy? He had no right to ask her to marry him.

"I shouldn't have—I can't offer you anything, Darcy. I'm dark. Soulless. A skinwalker, a—a monster. And you...you're everything bright and hopeful. If I could go back in time—if I could release you—"

"Yes," she said, interrupting him.

"Yes..." he murmured brokenly.

"No. I don't want you to release me. You asked me a question. The answer is yes."

"Yes?" he asked, shocked, disbelieving, the growing warmth in the depths of his body making his legs weak, making his entire body tingle with anticipation.

"Yes," she giggled, and he felt the hard tips of her nipples rub lightly against his chest as her shoulders shook softly. "Y-Yes, I'll marry you."

Tears coursed down her face now, and he wove his fingers into the hair at the back of her neck, pulling her face to his, kissing every salty drop before they could reach her lips, and then finally capturing her lips with his.

He kissed a trail from her lips to her neck, whispering, "*mon âme mon âme mon âme mon âme mon âme mon âme mon âme mon âme*" in a litany, in a prayer of thanksgiving, in a pledge to protect her with his last ounce of strength and courage, in a promise to always remember that he held her heart in his hands.

He swept her into his arms and carried her to his bed, her warm, now-dry body stretching languorously across the sheets that had already been tousled and messed as they made love that afternoon. She reached her arms up to him and he lowered his body onto hers, savoring the coolness of her skin against the heat of his, the smell of her hair and skin, even the drying blood smeared on her chest that she had so quickly forgiven in a rush to reassure him.

"You belong to me," he whispered, his hands on her cheeks, his eyes burning with fire and water at once.

"I belong to you," she answered, shifting her hips and bending her knees, opening herself to him. "Forever."

He drew back then inched forward until the tip of his throbbing sex found her entry. He lowered his lips to hers at the same moment he thrust forward, fully impaling her, his eyes closing at the simultaneous relief he felt as her soft heat surrounded him, the aching that was building to a quick pitch, primed by her tenderness, by her vulnerability and reassurance and acceptance.

Darcy stole the breath from his lungs as she gasped at the sudden sensation of him fully inside of her. She was ready for him, but he stretched her with his invasion, tiny hidden nerve endings clinging and pulsing, demanding more. He answered them, withdrawing from her so slowly her fingers curled into fists in the sheets by her sides, and then pushed forward again, fully, deliberately, making her moan with the longing he created inside of her. His lips moved across hers with increasing pressure, stroking her tongue while his pelvis thrust forward again.

"Jack," she moaned into his mouth. "More."

He dipped his head to her breast, his lips finding the hard bud of her nipple and closing around it. She arched her back and his arms slipped under her, holding her up against him as he licked and suckled, thrusting faster and harder until he raised his head, her cries of pleasure mingled with his guttural groans.

The whirling in his belly was dizzying, spiraling into a tight cone that finally exploded as he climaxed, making his body shake with tremors that radiated out, his eyelids fluttering and toes curling as he screamed her name.

Growling as she ripped open the flesh of his back with her fingernails, the shock of pain only adding to his thunderous climax, his claws protracted into the mattress and he thrust into her quivering body one final time, groaning *mon âme* as every muscle tightened then released as he pumped his seed into her willing flesh.

Chapter 10

"OH, MY GOD," SHE MURMURED.
Jack could barely catch his breath. He had never climaxed in a semi-shifted state and even with only his claws out he could feel the difference in intensity.

"You have to ask me to marry you more often," Darcy breathed as he kissed her forehead, pulling out of her body and rolling onto his back beside her.

"Wow," he sighed, his chest rising and falling with the force of his breathing. *That's right! She'd said...* He turned his neck to look at her. "Did you mean it?"

"Mm-hm," she murmured, rolling toward him, onto her side to face him. "I meant it, fiancé."

He chuckled, glancing over at her red face, plastered with still-wet and sweaty wisps of light red hair, and trying out the word for himself. "Fiancée."

"But, here's something I need to know," she said, her voice taking on a serious edge.

He propped himself up on his side, worried. He searched her eyes then relaxed when he realized she was trying not to smile.

"Where's my ring?"

He had a wedding ring for her, but no engagement ring. He chuckled again, letting himself fall back. "We'll drive to North Conway tomorrow. I'll buy you whatever ring you want."

She lowered her head and pressed her lips to his shoulder.

"I have to go home tomorrow," she said softly. "Now that Lela's been taken care of."

He twisted his neck to look at her. "Move in with me."

"I will," she said. "But this is Carlisle and my mother lives in this town.

So, it'll have be a gradual sort of thing until we're married."

"Let's get married tomorrow," he suggested, frowning.

She smiled at him, shaking her head.

"Why not?" he asked. "I love you. You love me. We're already bound and we've waited long enough."

"We did the binding your way. We do a wedding my way."

"Fine," he growled. "One month. One. And I'm sleeping at your place or you're sleeping here every night until then. I'm never sleeping without you again. Ever."

She shifted herself over his chest, letting her breasts crush softly against his hard muscles and staring into his eyes.

"One month. Agreed. And if you thought you'd ever spend a night without me after *that*, you're one crazy skinwalker. You are good and stuck with me now." She lowered her lips to press them against his before sliding down and resting her head on his chest comfortably. "You're going to need a new mattress."

"We'll get whatever mattress you want," he assured her.

"Rings and mattresses," she said softly. "We're really doing this."

We're really doing this, he thought, his heart swelling with love for her. He reached one hand up to stroke her damp hair away from her face, suddenly reminded of how close he came to almost losing her.

"Darcy, I'm sorry about tonight," he murmured. "Lela…"

"She's *something*," said Darcy.

"That's kind," he sneered.

"She's young, Jack. How old is she?"

"Twenty-one."

"*So* young."

"She's wild and reckless."

"And bound to your brother. Oh. Your, uh, brother's bound to your sis—"

"Lela and Julien aren't related by blood. Lela's my father's daughter and Julien's my mother's son. But, they don't share blood."

She didn't say anything for a moment. Then, "Your mother cheated too."

Jack took a deep breath, thinking about his parents. "They were bound young. Eighteen. I think they always loved each other in their own way, and the binding made them find each other, but I don't think they were very happy."

He felt her nod. "I'm so sorry about your dad."

"I lost him a long time ago. I grieved him a long time ago. I'm glad I was able to get him back to my mother before…"

"You couldn't stay for the funeral?"

"We don't have human-style funerals. Once someone's gone, they're just…gone. There would have been a tribute and burial. But, I couldn't stay…"

"Because of me."

"Because of *Lela*." He flinched, remembering the image of Darcy in the shattered window with Lela's claw against her neck. "If she had hurt you—"

She flattened her palm against his chest and gently rubbed. "She didn't."

"I would have killed her."

She propped herself up to look at him. "Don't say that. She's your sister, and barely grown up. She didn't hurt me, Jack. You don't have to hate her." She paused before adding, "I'm sorry you missed your dad's burial."

"I got to say good-bye." He thought of his father's dead weight over his shoulder as he ran the miles and miles back to his car. He'd barely had a moment to process his passing and it felt soothing to talk about it with Darcy, but he didn't want to feel sad.

Nor did he want to talk to her about the re-binding, but he knew he should. As his bound mate and human fiancé, she had a right to know. *Fifty days. Fifty.*

He felt her breathing change to a deep and even rhythm and he knew she had fallen asleep. There was time. He would tell her tomorrow.

SHE LOOKED LIKE AN ANGEL with her hair spread out on his pillow, rumpled and shining in the morning light that filtered in through his bedroom window.

She belonged to him, and miraculously had agreed to spend her life with him. She was too good for him—too sweet and good-hearted, too hopeful and trusting. He would endeavor to earn his place in her life every minute of every day they had together from now until the end of their days as a couple. In his heart, he was already married to her, and he let himself fantasize for a moment about springs spent in the garden, winters by the fire, summers taking walks in the woods and watching the leaves change in the fall. After a lifetime of longing, she was here, she was his, and his heart swelled with recognition and gratitude. In spite of their separation and the recent revelations about his nature, she still wanted him, still chose him. It humbled him absolutely.

Getting up carefully, he took a quick shower, pulling on a pair of jeans and a plaid flannel shirt that he buttoned twice. His body was always so hot, clothes were an irritation most days, but he wore them to conform to her society. Living under the radar in human society came easily to Jack after a decade living in Boston, preparing himself to—one day, he hoped—live in Darcy's world.

He scribbled a quick message on a piece of notepaper.

Good morning to the future Mrs. Beauloup. I love you. Hot coffee. Downstairs. Come find me.

He placed the note on the pillow beside her and stared at her face for a long moment—the pink skin dotted with freckles that looked lightly sunburned, her pale lashes brushing the elegant lines of her upper cheekbones. Her lips, swollen and red from so much attention, lightly open in sleep. He'd get hard and need to mate with her if he stayed any longer, and he wanted her to sleep. He turned and left the room, closing the door softly behind him.

Julien and Lela had taken over the kitchen, undoubtedly attempting to replenish the calories they'd burned last night. By the looks of things—Lela was toasting bread and making eggs and bacon—a shitload of calories had been exhausted.

He stood in the doorway watching them unobserved, his scent masked by the frying food.

Julien sat at the table, clad only in Jack's jeans. Lela stood by the stove, a spatula in one raised hand, Jack's bathrobe closed modestly around her body. She had one hand on her hip and she was smiling and laughing that wonderfully happy, throaty laugh that Jack had heard so seldom throughout her life.

"I'll do it, Lela. I will. I'll take you right on the floor of our brother's kitchen."

"Just try it, skinwalker," she taunted, thrusting out her chest.

In a flash Julien was out of his seat, his hands inside the bathrobe, his mouth hot on his mate's.

Jack cleared his throat and they broke apart, looking over, surprised, then wary. Julien slid his hands up and out of the bathrobe and Lela used her free hand to hold it closed, keeping her eyes down.

"How long have you been standing there?" asked Julien, taking a step in front of Lela, hands on his tan, well-muscled hips.

"Long enough." Jack sauntered into the kitchen enjoying their discomfort. "Coffee hot?"

"Yes!" said Lela, opening a cabinet and handing him a cup. "I made it Tallis's favorite way, so it's good, it's…"

Her voice trailed off as Jack looked at her with cold eyes and she swallowed, looking back down.

"Jack," said Julien quietly, a mild edge to his usual cajoling tone, "she's sorry. How long are you going to be mad at her?"

Jack whipped his head to Julien, eyes burning. "She tried to kill Darcy *twelve hours* ago, Julien. I think I'm entitled to some time to process that."

"She's bound now," said Julien. "She wouldn't hurt Darcy."

Jack looked at Lela, whose shoulders were rolled forward in submission. He took a deep, loud breath through his nose.

"Maybe. But there's the troubling matter of the re-binding. Lela's rained a hailstorm of shit down on me."

"Good point." They all turned back to the doorway to find Willow leaning against it, still wearing the same simple black dress from last night, deep circles under her dark eyes. "What exactly are you going to do about that?"

Willow stepped into the kitchen, eyeing each of them one by one.

"Do you want coffee, *Enchanteresse?*" asked Lela softly, reaching for another cup.

Willow stared at her with fury and Jack braced himself for a confrontation.

"How's Amory doing?" he asked, trying to distract her.

"Better," answered Willow in a cold, tense voice, still holding Lela's eyes. "Fever's long gone. He's finally sleeping without thrashing. His chest will be scarred for the rest of his life."

"S-Sorry," offered Lela.

"I should make you more sorry," Willow burst out, taking a step forward.

Julien blocked her path and Willow looked up at him. "Oh, Julien. How quickly things change."

Lela looked around Julien at Willow, her eyes widening and glowing with realization and fury. She pivoted to face Julien. "Did you…did you…*As-tu couché avec elle, Julien?*"

Did you sleep with her?

"*Non,*" answered Willow, picking up the coffee pot and pouring herself

a cup. She added suggestively, *"On a pas beaucoup dormi."*
We didn't do much sleeping.

Willow turned her back on Lela, slowly making her way to the table, but Jack kept his eyes on Lela, whose face turned crimson. Lela leapt at her, claws protracting as she lunged. Jack caught Lela around the waist and jerked her back.

Willow didn't miss a beat as she pulled out a chair and sat down without even glancing at Lela, who writhed against Jack trying to get to Willow.

"C'est assez, Lela! Rien assez!" yelled Jack. *Enough!*

"Tell her it isn't true, Willow!" said Julien, slapping his palms on the table.

"Don't you mean…*belle Saule?"* Willow purred, taking a sip of her coffee.

Lela lunged and growled, trying to spring forward but held firmly by Jack, swiping her claws at Willow from under Jack's iron grasp.

Julien sat down at the table across from Willow, his face serious. "Please don't play with her. I'm asking you to tell the truth."

Willow took a deep breath and sighed then turned languorously to face a furious, heaving, panting Lela with a catlike smile.

"Tu es tellement bébé. Rien ne s'est passé." *You're such a baby. Nothing happened.*

Then she turned back around, sipping her coffee before saying something else under her breath in a tight, dark whisper.

"Si jamais tu touches encore Amory, je te transforme en crapaud."

That made Jack smile. Willow had essentially added that if Lela ever went near Amory again, she'd turn the young Roug into a toad. He had to hand it to Willow—she had style.

Lela fought to break free of Jack, but he hissed "Downshift" in her ear, and didn't release her until her claws had fully retracted. She fell into Julien's waiting arms.

"Promise you didn't…?"

"Lela," he said tenderly, stroking the hair out of her face. "I belong to *you.* Willow and I never—we never did anything more than chat."

Jack recalled Julien's original plan to make a move on Willow, and made a mental note to cash in on his warning to stay away from her. Julien owed him one.

Lela returned to the stove, plating the smoking eggs and bacon that had sat too long. She put the plate on the table, and Willow glanced up at her.

"Pour moi? Merci!"

Jack gave Willow a look. Things would go a lot smoother if she'd stop baiting and heckling the hotheaded young Roug. Not that he necessarily blamed Willow after Lela's behavior, but he wasn't really in the mood to keep breaking up fights all morning.

Willow rolled her eyes and shrugged, mouthing *Bien*.

Jack and Julien took the seats on either side of Willow quickly so that Lela was left with the farthest one, across from her. They scowled at one another across the table, passing the burnt breakfast.

Finally Julien spoke.

"So, what did Darcy say about the re-binding? How're you going to handle that?"

Three sets of eyes turned to Jack.

"You'll have to turn her," said Lela softly. "I'm sorry Jack."

"I *won't* turn her," he responded through clenched teeth.

"What other option do you have?" asked Willow, her face a study in concern.

He shrugged. "I don't have an answer yet. But I have fifty days to figure it out."

"The Council will hunt you down. They'll hunt *her* down," said Julien quietly but firmly, his face grim. "But, whatever you decide to do…" He reached over and covered Lela's hand with his. "Lela and I will help you."

"Me too," whispered Willow.

"I'll keep her safe," Jack repeated.

"How?" demanded Willow.

"I don't know yet," said Jack, beads of sweat running down his neck as he felt the full, terrible impact of the situation. "They can take me, if it comes down to it. But they will *never* find out about her."

"They will," insisted Lela. "You were on the Council Enforcement. You know how they are. They'd never allow this. They will find out, and when they do—"

"I will NOT turn her," Jack said, raising his voice to a growl and pounding his fists on the table.

"Turn who?"

Her voice was soft and heartbroken from the doorway of the room, and Jack bolted up out of his chair to see Darcy's face, her chin high, her eyes devastated, her cheeks more flushed than they'd been as she slept peacefully.

"Turn who?" she asked again, steel in her voice this time, eyes holding his unmercifully.

"You," he whispered. "We're talking about you."

"**W**HY?"

Willow stood up from the table, gesturing to her vacant seat. "I'll get you some coffee, kid," she murmured.

Darcy still looked at Jack. She could see it on his face. Whatever was going on, it was bad. It was really bad. And everyone in this room—including Julien and Lela—knew more about it than she did. She seized his eyes.

The garden. Now.

Ignoring the cup of coffee Willow offered, Darcy walked through the swinging door to the dining room. Opening the French doors that led onto the garden patio, she stepped outside into the bright sunshine, breathing deeply, unable to enjoy the smells of herbs and flowers. She waited for him with her arms crossed over her chest and her back to the house, bare feet warmed by the sun-soaked brick patio.

So many things were bothering her right this minute; they were talking about turning her, and Jack was insisting that he wouldn't. She had caught the end of Lela saying something about them "never allowing it"—what did it mean? And why had she seen such concern and fury in Jack's eyes? And how come Julien, Lela, and Willow seemed to know more than she did? She was so sick and tired of Jack keeping things from her.

When he placed his hands on her shoulders, she flinched, stepping away and pivoting to face him.

"What's going on?" she asked quietly, her heart heavy.

"Come sit with me," he murmured, holding out his hand.

Her days of refusing to touch him and pushing him away were over as of yesterday, but she was angry and confused. And frightened. She placed her hand in his and allowed him to pull her to the stone bench under the crab apple tree.

"I'm sorry I didn't tell you," he started, putting his arms around her shoulders and pulling her close to his side. "I wanted to figure out what to do first. I wanted you to have a day or two of just being happy, not worried."

"Do I have something to be worried about?" she asked, letting her head drop to his shoulder.

"No."

"The truth, Jack."

"Immediately, no."

She leaned back to look at him. "Tell it to me straight or I'll go back inside and ask one of them."

"Okay." Jack took a deep breath. "You and me. It's an aberration. Not like an oddity. It's totally singular. A Roux-ga-roux has never been bound to a human before. Never in the history of my kind.

"When I left you that night, after our binding, I went home to my pack to have it acknowledged. That's an important thing—it means that the pack recognizes me as an adult male who can't be re-bound. It was recorded, but never announced. I sort of flew under the radar. I worked on the Council Enforcement and spent a lot of time away from home on business. Tombeur, he's my mentor, kept an eye on me. My parents were well-respected—my mother, at least. When asked, we said that you were from one of the northern packs and refused to relocate south. That was pretty unconventional, but I was traveling so much for the Council, no one really bothered me about it.

"After the first decade had passed, I needed to figure out how to be with you. So, I found a job working for a private security company in Boston. My experience with the CE meant I knew more than most about keeping order and protection and it wasn't long until they promoted me to a high-level bodyguard position. I learned how to live amongst the humans. I made a lot of money. All I thought about for those ten years was how to make it back to you. How to have you in my life.

"I had learned how to control my Roug impulses when I was in the CE with Tombeur, and even more so in Boston. I barely returned home. Just occasionally for a Gathering. By that point, I only hunted big game. I'd go to Vermont or New Hampshire during *Pleine Lune*…hole up, stay away from humans. After ten years, I had enough money. I was even ready to try living in a small town. It had been long enough. It was time to come back to you.

"I renovated this lodge and had it decorated by a woman I knew in Boston. Amory handled the garage. He did a good job, really, but I only hired him to get to you. I found out about your cousin's wedding and asked Amory if I could join him. He fixed it with your cousin. You know the rest.

"Last weekend was the Gathering of the Northern Bloodlands. It's an annual thing when the packmasters and Council leaders and some other

Rougs show up to discuss the rules. About two hundred turn out for it, and they also read the names of the dead and the names of the bound. And anyone who wants to be bound to someone unwilling can demand a sparking."

"Lela," whispered Darcy.

Jack nodded. "Lela demanded a sparking with me. Tombeur and my mother tried to stop it. They had acknowledged my binding to you, but because I couldn't produce you, and indeed had never produced you, they were overruled. I kissed Lela, but I didn't spark to her because I'm bound to you."

"Then…it's okay," Darcy whispered, turning to look at his eyes and hating that they were so heavy and worried.

"Well, she was angry and embarrassed. So, she demanded a re-binding."

"A what?"

"A re-binding. That's when bound mates kiss in front of the assembly at the Gathering so that their binding can be felt."

"Like I felt Lela and Julien's last night."

Jack nodded. "Exactly. Our re-binding's at Solstice."

"Oh, my God…" Darcy sighed. "Oh, my God, you and I are supposed to—No! I mean, I can't go up there, Jack and be surrounded by…"

Jack put his hands on her face, making her look at him. "Listen to me, they will *never* find out about you. Never. I will die first."

"Could it come to that?"

His face was stricken and he looked down. She covered his hands with hers.

"Jack," she said, evenly, trying to keep the panic out of her voice. "Could it come to that?"

His nostrils flared as he flexed his jaw. "I don't know."

She felt her eyes widen as her breath caught in her throat. Tears sprang into her eyes. "Can we try to explain? Maybe we write a—"

"No *we*. No. They can never, *ever* know about you," he exclaimed, his hands tightening on her face. "Never, Darcy."

She saw the panic in his eyes and it made her blood run cold.

"That's what Lela was saying. They will find out, and when they do…" Tears slipped out of her eyes as she looked at him. "That's why she suggested you…that's why you were talking about turning…"

Me, she finished.

She couldn't speak anymore. It was unspeakable.

He pulled her onto his lap, wrapping his arms around her, burying his face in her hair as she cried on his shoulder.

"I won't do it. It's not an option."

"What *are* the options?" she whispered.

"We spend every minute together. Be happy. Be married. We have a little time."

"How much?"

"Fifty days," he murmured.

"Fifty! Fifty days! No, Jack, there's got to be a way…"

He leaned back to look at her face then captured her lips with his for a gentle kiss.

"There isn't. If I don't show up, they'll hunt me down. If they can't find me, they'll hurt my family. My mother, my brother, my sisters, Tombeur. If I show up without you, they'll take it out on me." He swallowed and she watched his throat bob up and down. "But eventually they might let me go…if they can't get it out of me…who you are, where you are…"

"Let's run away," she suggested desperately, swiping away the tears.

"No, *mon* âme. They wouldn't like that. My family would pay—"

"I'll go up with you," she said, gathering her courage. "We'll show them that our binding is true. We'll try—"

"They won't care. They will kill you."

She winced, feeling her face collapse, and she hid against his shoulder again, grateful for the feeling of his hands stroking her back, but desperate for a solution. Any solution. She couldn't lose him. After a lifetime of waiting for him, she couldn't say good-bye. She couldn't watch him get into his car and drive to Quebec for certain doom. For them to hurt his beautiful body and torture him. Over her. Over his love for her.

She leaned back.

"We have to at least talk about it."

His eyes clouded over. "No."

"We have to."

"I won't do it."

She wiped the last tears off her cheeks and leaned back from him, straightening her shoulders, steeling her jaw.

"Surely you're not the only one who can," she said.

"You wouldn't," he breathed, his face horrified at her veiled threat.

"I don't know what I wouldn't do for you," she said softly, but firmly. "I belong to you, and you belong to me."

"Please, baby," he besieged her.

"So you would scratch and lick me or bite me with your fangs." She swallowed, fighting to keep any tremors from her voice. "And I would have a fever. Then seizures. My claws and fangs would drop, and you'd put me in the room under the garage. I'd be out of my head. And then my body would expand, right? And I'd grow hair…everywhere. And you'd throw a fresh kill in with me. And when I emerged…" She blinked her eyes to keep the onslaught of tears at bay. "I'd…I'd be Roug."

"Darcy, please."

"Is that the lay of it?"

His face was contorted in pain, in regret and sorrow, his eyes watery and golden. He nodded, looking down, away from her.

"Anything else?" she asked.

He nodded, but didn't look up.

"What? Tell me everything now."

"The binding."

"What about it? We'd both be Roug."

He swallowed and grimaced. "Turning a human is a rebirth on almost every emotional level. I would still be bound to you. But, you—there's just no guarantee."

"There's no guarantee that I'd still be bound to you?"

"No." He pulled her face down to his and she felt the trembling of his lips as he pressed them against hers. His thumbs lightly stroked her cheeks as he deepened the kiss. Finally she drew back.

"Jack, you'd still be bound to me?"

"Yes. Until death. No matter what."

"But, I wouldn't be dead, and more importantly, neither would you. So, I would find you again," she murmured. "In the whole world there's only you for me. Nothing can change that, Jack. Nothing. We're stronger than a turning. We're stronger than anything."

"Darcy, you don't know. You'll be like an animal at first. The bloodlust at *Pleine Lune* will be stronger than anything you've ever felt before in your life. You're a different being. You're…"

"Roug," she answered. "Like you."

"I love you. I don't want this for you. I don't want to risk the binding—"

"I would rather die," she vowed, interrupting him and commanding his attention with the low fury of her voice, "than live without you. If I am your soul, then you are my heart. You are the strength of my life beating in my chest, and if you die, I die."

His eyes fluttered closed, glowing under the thin skin of his lids and she knew that he was trying not to cry. She could feel it. She could feel the depth and breadth and certainty of his love for her. She knew that he would die for her, and now he knew she would do the same for him.

She raised her hands to cradle his cheeks and her lips tilted up into a smile. A smile. Because regardless of the other complications in their life together, looking at him, she felt such joy, such completeness, she felt like life was worth living.

She pressed her lips to his, moving them softly back and forth. He raised his hands to her neck, sinking his fingers into her hair, his tongue slipping through her lips. She met his intrusion with passion, stroking his tongue as he lapped at hers, her fingers curling on his face until she held him in the grip of her fists.

She drew back.

"Open your eyes," she whispered.

HE DID. HE SAW THE courage on her face, in the set of her jaw, in the directness of her gaze. She leaned her neck to the side, moving her hair, offering him unobstructed access to her jugular artery.

Do it, Jack. Do it now.

He held her eyes with his, tilting her head back upright gently and reaching up to take her hand from his face. He lowered it, turning it over slowly, staring at the skin on the inside of her arm—her pink, soft, perfect skin into which his fangs would sink and bury. In his mind, he saw them biting down, leaving jagged bite marks as she screamed in pain. He felt his fingers clamp down on her arm, keeping it in his mouth as his saliva mixed with her blood, until he felt his heat transferred not onto her skin, but into her body. He imagined her passing out in his arms, watching her body turn scarlet as he carried her to his bed. He could almost feel the fever and seizures as his venom had its way with her.

He closed his eyes against the images, against the pain they caused him. He swallowed and looked back up at her.

You can't want this.

I want you. This is the only way.

He shook his head, gently releasing her arm.

"I won't do it," he said gently. "I won't—"

Her eyes became frantic, wild. "I'm not letting you die for me, over us.

I'm not letting you go back there where they'll hurt you and they'll—"

"Let me finish," said Jack, brushing his knuckles over her cheek. "*Yet.* I won't do it *yet.*" He paused, staring at her. "We have fifty days. Let's try to figure it out another way first."

She took a deep breath, her shoulders relaxing, and nodded.

"Okay," she agreed.

He pulled her against him and she rested her head on his shoulder as she had yesterday.

He heard the sadness in his voice. "Relieved?"

She shrugged lightly. "A little."

It made him wince to know she was still offering herself to him even though she was frightened.

"Better get to work on that cure," he said. "If you can make a cure that can control the shifting, I'll—I mean, I'd be more open to…"

She looked up at him, catching his sad eyes.

…*turning you.*

"I won't do anything else," she said, dropping her head back down to his shoulder. "I'll start thinking through the different combinations, molecular structures and fusions. And Willow. I need to talk to Willow. Perhaps there's something in the *Enchanteresse* book. I'll take a hiatus from Dartmouth. I won't do anything else but this."

He loved her for her energy, her bright mind, her willingness to work as a team to figure out how to come out on the other side of this safe and together.

"*Nothing* else?" he asked, pressing his lips against her forehead.

"Well, I have to go to bed at night," she said, and his body tensed at the low, sexy way she drew out the word bed.

He leaned back to see her lips tilt up in a smile. A smile.

"Let's go now. Just crawl back under the covers and stay there all day. Sounds like the perfect idea."

She smiled up at him, shaking her head. But her smile faded as her eyes glinted with a fierce, intelligent energy bathed in determination.

"Fifty days, Jack."

"Fifty days," he said, and pulled her back into his embrace, his heart seeking and finding the rhythm of hers—his mate, his fiancée, his soul. And he tried to keep the inevitable at bay, the dreaded words circling over them like vultures in his head:

Solstice is coming.

Part 4:
Darcy & Jack II

Chapter 1

THE DREAM WAS ALWAYS THE same.

She was running in the woods. So fast, it was like gliding. So fast, she couldn't even feel her feet as they beat a path through the darkness. Branches and undergrowth brushed at her body, but didn't hurt or slow her down. And she couldn't stop. Something deep inside of her insisted that she couldn't stop. Looking up, she saw the moon, a waxing crescent, a perfect slice of white light in the midnight sky. Her lungs burned, but she ran, like her life depended on it. She leapt over a fallen tree and slashed at a bramble. Slashed. *Slashed*. Suddenly she stopped, looking at her hands, at the long, white claws that extended outward, at the thick thatch of hair covering the backs of her hands so that they were unrecognizable. Back to the moon. The crescent. The beguiling, teasing bitch that owned what was left of her soul. As panic besieged her mind, a wretched, guttural howl gathered in the depths of her being—

Darcy's arms flailed and she bolted upright in her chair, awakened by a loud thunk. She looked down to see her once half-filled coffee cup in two pieces on the floor, lying in a small puddle of brown liquid.

Sweat covered her face and her heart raced in real life as it had in the dream. She took a deep breath, and then another, resting her hands on the desk, pushing away the book where she'd rested her tired head and fallen asleep. It happened all the time lately. She was perpetually exhausted.

As her heart slowed down, she stood up, stretching her arms over her head and looking at the warm and bright windows of Jack's house. The light cut through the darkness, making her feel less alone. She sighed, glancing at the clock on her laptop. 7:35. If she didn't go in soon, he'd come out for her. She swiveled in her chair and glanced at the loveseat against the wall, feeling her insides swirl hot as her lips tilted up in a smile.

She turned back to her desk and took off her glasses, laying them gently on one of the six or seven books spread out on the desk before her, then rubbed her tired eyes. She needed to get a towel from the bathroom and clean up her mess.

It had been three weeks since Julien and Lela's binding, three weeks since accepting Jack's marriage proposal, three weeks since finding out that her binding to Jack had been challenged by Lela.

"Solstice," she said aloud softly, the hairs on her arm standing up straight as though someone had just walked over her grave. "Four more weeks until Solstice."

Kneeling down, she moved the two pieces of ceramic cup to the side so she could wipe away the coffee with a hand towel. Then she sat on the floor against the desk leg, looking at the pieces. Almost two perfect halves and no chips. She took one in each hand and gently pressed them together, watching as something broken transformed into something whole before her eyes. It *looked* whole. It looked strong. And yet, if she withdrew the pressure of her hands, the two pieces would quickly fall apart again. She closed her eyes and took a deep breath, depositing the pieces in the garbage and holding her bent knees against her chest. With only two days before *Pleine Lune*, she and Willow were running out of time. There was no more time for research and planning. They needed to synthesize the formula tomorrow so it could be tested on Jack.

They had worked tirelessly on the antidote to Jack's monthly shift, and Darcy felt with increasing confidence that they'd nailed it. They'd taken the Wolfsbane, with its shift-suppressing qualities, added synthesized olivetol from *Parmeliaceae* lichen as a stabilizer for its calming effects and to suppress vomiting, and finally *Lycopodium clavatum* to protect Jack's stomach lining from the poisons in the Wolfsbane. Poor Jack had been stuck with more needles than a pincushion over the past three weeks, but never once had he objected or stood in the way of their progress. All day every day she poured over Métis shaman books, worked on the formula, and foraged for samples, doggedly working toward a way to suppress Jack's *Pleine Lune* shift, and maybe—someday—her own.

All day, every day, he left her alone to work.

Ah, but the nights.

Darcy's face softened and she closed her eyes, exhaling in surrender.

The nights belonged to Jack.

The nights were about hearing his heart beat under her ear and tolerating the heat of his body against her skin. The nights were about his eyes as they held hers, burning and direct, awestruck and disbelieving, sometimes, like it should be impossible that it was her body clinging to his, after a lifetime of dreaming about her. The nights were about Darcy and Jack, bound together, until it was impossible to tell where his flesh ended and hers began. The nights were about having him, belonging to him, owning his heart, giving herself over to the ecstasy—the panting, roaring rapture of his body joined with hers. Fast. Slow. Rough. Gentle. Everything.

The nights were about slipping from dreams into a relaxed conscious-ness, eyes only half opened in the darkness as she felt his hardness slip into her waiting softness. Moving slowly, filling her, rotating his hips so that the pressure of his sex pressed against the swollen, slick walls deep inside of her, he swept every nerve ending, driving her to the brink of what she could bear, keeping her in a dreamlike pre-orgasmic state of longing. She whimpered his name, arching her back against his chest as he squeezed her nipples gently, forcing her to stay with him stroke for stroke until her body finally convulsed and shattered around him. The nights were about him growling her name like thunder, arms like steel clasping her against him, and then trembling and shuddering as his seed poured hot and vital into her depths and he declared his undying love.

But always, always, hovering like a shadow in the corner, was Solstice. The longest and lightest day would invariably end in night. In darkness. At the Gathering. It was coming.

Darcy opened her eyes, trading softness for determination, and pushed up off the floor, taking the hand towel back into the bathroom and resuming her seat at her desk, rearranging her notes and opening another book. If the nights were about tricking herself into believing that what she had with Jack was strong enough to last forever, the days were about figuring out a solution to the looming matter of the re-binding. Losing Jack was unthinkable, would be unbearable, was not an option.

As far as Darcy could tell, there was only one solution.

She and Willow needed to create a potion that would control *Pleine Lune* shifting. Once Jack was convinced the full moon no longer con-trolled him, he could turn Darcy into a Roux-ga-roux, assured that her life wouldn't be at the mercy of the monthly depravity and blood lust brought on by *Pleine Lune*.

However, even with the promise of a potion that could permanently suppress shifting in any Roux-ga-roux, convincing Jack to turn her in time for the re-binding was proving to be a much bigger challenge. She stared out the window for a moment, resting her chin on her hand, remembering their conversation last night.

"I don't want to do it, baby," he'd sighed for the hundredth time, brushing her hair from her forehead in soft, monotonous strokes as she lay across his hard, naked chest.

"The re-binding's a month from today, Jack," she'd whispered, unable to keep the heaviness from her voice. "We have to talk about you turning me. At least talk about it."

"I don't want to. I just want this."

"I want this too. I want this forever. I don't want it to end at Solstice. I don't want you beaten and tortured and—" Her voice broke, as it always did when she imagined what they might do to him when he arrived at the re-binding Gathering without his bound mate by his side.

"I'm strong, Darce. I'll—"

"You'll *what?*" She leaned up and away from him, bracing her weight on her elbow, looking for his eyes in the darkness. He blinked once and when he re-opened them, they glowed a dim copper-gold.

"I'll survive. I'll come back to you."

She shook her head, tears pooling in her green eyes as she gazed at him, at his beautiful face that she loved more than any face on earth. That face that was her waking and her sleeping, her morning and her night, her light and her darkness, the beating heart of her soul.

"No. Lela and Julien said—"

"Lela and Julien have never even been to a re-binding. And neither of them ever served on the Council Enforcement. They certainly haven't attended an Inquisition. They don't know what they're talking about."

"But, you do. You have. And I can see it in your eyes. They'll hurt you. They'll punish you and I can't—"

He pulled her against him, lining her up on top of his body, her breasts against his chest, his erection pressed insistently against her soft curls. He held her face between his hands, searching her eyes with longing, with certainty.

I'll come back to you.

You don't know that.

I know that nothing could keep me away.

Except death.

He ground his jaw, dropping her eyes.

"The potion's almost ready, Jack, and it's going to work. I know it. And when it does, you can turn me. You can, and I won't ever have to shift. I'll have control over it."

He raised his eyes, staring at her with such hope, such tenderness, her breath caught in her throat. He reached up with one finger and traced the outline of her bottom lip, making her insides flood with heat. His finger trailed down over her chin and down her neck to rest on her pulse. The first place he'd ever touched her twenty years before. He breathed deeply and the flames in his eyes jumped and brightened with arousal.

"One step at a time. If I can tolerate it? Then we'll talk about…about…"

She hated that he couldn't even say it. "Turning me."

Instead of repeating her words, he skimmed his hands down the sides of her body, his palms landing on the swell of her hips to flip her onto her back. He lay on his side beside her, leaning over her, his fingers trailing softly inward, slipping over the triangular thatch of soft, pink curly hair, insistently seeking their target through her damp, quivering flesh.

Darcy's breathing changed as her eyes grew heavy and half-masted. The tips of his fingers brushed lightly over the hidden, sensitive nub, teasing her, and she moaned lightly, arching against his hand, letting her eyes fall closed. "We have to…we have to talk…Jaaaack…."

His fingers moved away as he rolled on top of her, bracing his weight, positioning himself, teasing her opening with the head of his rigid sex. She skimmed her fingers down his back until they rested on his hips. She clenched her fingers into the hard muscles under his skin, trying to push him forward, finally opening her eyes when he hovered motionless above her.

His eyes burned, snapping and sparking like flames, licking higher, devouring everything in their path. His lips tilted up.

We'll talk, baby. After this.

His lips melted into hers as he pushed his entire body forward, his swollen length driving into her body in one possessive motion, filling her to the hilt. Darcy cried out, thrusting her body upward, curving into his as her nails bit into his hips.

"Darcy," he breathed.

She opened her eyes.

Tell me.

She smiled at him, dreamily, holding his eyes. After a lifetime of waiting to hear the words, she knew they still felt raw to Jack. He told her that almost as much as wanting to join his body to hers, he'd wanted to hear those words, lying awake at night for two decades, imagining how they'd sound coming from her mouth. She knew how he'd hungered for them. For the simple, perfect reassurance they offered him.

I love you, Jack.

He trembled and she felt his sex pulse inside of her. And then he moved rhythmically, slowly, caressing her wet heat, claiming her lips, swirling his tongue around hers as the pressure built between her legs.

He leaned his head back, the message in his wild, glowing eyes clear in her head.

I will still be loving you the last second I breathe.

And it was truth. He would never, ever be free of her. His binding to her was forever, no matter what, while hers could be compromised if he turned her. She knew it was the reason he was so anxious not to discuss it.

She reached up to hold his face between her hands, seizing his eyes and forcing him to hear her.

So will I. No matter what.

His lips crashed down on hers again and she tasted his fears as he thrust into her again and again. She rose to meet him, arching her back into a vibrating bow until she finally exploded beneath him, bucking and shuddering, as he howled her name and buried his face in her neck, the aftershocks making his arms flex and relax around her until they both calmed and fell asleep, sated.

Darcy took a trembling breath, wishing she still had a bracing sip of coffee left in her broken cup. No matter how much solace and fulfillment they'd found in one another's arms, the fact remained that he hadn't agreed to do the only thing that would save him, and Darcy was running out of time.

Her phone buzzed beside her, snapping her out of her troubling thoughts.

"Hey, Will."

"Hey, kid. We on for tomorrow?"

"It's as close as I'm going to get it," Darcy said, shuffling her notes to find the formula written in a black sharpie on a piece of yellow notebook paper. "You got the phosphoryl chloride?"

"I got it."

"The a-pinene? Just in case?"

"I've got everything. Everything's just waiting for you. *I* would have synthesized it last week and tested it out on him."

"Wouldn't have mattered if it suppressed a common shift, Will. It has to work at full moon. He won't trust it any other time. He has to know it works. He has—"

"To know how it feels before he considers ever letting you try it."

"Yes," breathed Darcy quietly.

"Is that the final plan, then? He tries it this weekend during the full moon and if he stays in human form, he'll turn you?"

"He'll barely even talk about it. Whenever I bring it up, he—he distracts me...."

Willow chuckled lightly. "You two are like rabbits."

Darcy's mouth quirked up in a grin. She couldn't argue there. But she could give it right back. "And I suppose you and Amory are living in a state of chaste friendship."

"You want details? About your brother?"

Darcy made a gagging noise like she was sticking her finger down her throat. "What? I couldn't hear you. I was too busy throwing up in my mouth."

"Anyway, Amory and I aren't living together. Technically."

"Neither are Jack and I. Technically."

And yet, Darcy knew that Amory spent every night at Willow's old Victorian on Main Street, and although Darcy had good intentions about keeping up appearances, she hadn't spent a night outside of Jack's bed since Julien and Lela's binding. There were moments when she tried to reason with herself, when she tried to tell herself to hold back some small, obscure part of her heart, just in case she lost him...but such moments were overwhelmed by the force of her love for him, by her desperate desire to spend every possible moment near him until Solstice.

"Hey!" exclaimed Willow. "You evaded the question."

Darcy sighed. "That's *my* final plan, Will. If the potion can suppress Jack's *Pleine Lune* shift, I want him to turn me."

"And if he won't?"

"Then I'll have to find someone who will." The words tumbled out of Darcy's mouth before she could decide whether or not to share them with Willow. She hadn't shared this part of her plan with anyone, not even Jack. "I won't lose him. I can't."

Willow was silent on the other end of the line, and Darcy wondered what her friend was thinking. She wondered if she'd try to talk her out of it, or if she remembered Lela's attack on Amory—the fear she must have felt seeing him lying there in a pool of blood, a long, vicious slash across his chest.

"I get it, kid. Can't say I like it, though."

"Not all of us are *born* different like Jack…or you."

Over the past few weeks, since discovering her nature, Willow's skills and abilities had exploded into a full cache of spells and powers, sometimes surprising the heck out of Willow and whomever she was with.

"It's a hard life."

"Yeah," Darcy deadpanned. "You seem very oppressed by it."

"That's not a fair comparison. I'm not a shapeshifter. For me, it's like freeing something I always knew was inside of me."

"Maybe it'll be like that for me too, Will. I've been bound to Jack for longer than I ever lived my life without him. Maybe in a weird way it'll feel familiar for me too."

Darcy waited for Willow to come back with a snappy retort, but she spoke thoughtfully, softly, when she replied. "If you can even convince him. It has to be him, Darce."

No, it doesn't, Darcy disagreed in her head. *If Jack won't, I will convince Julien or Lela…*

"Right," she answered, unwilling to get into the matter further with Willow.

"Tomorrow at ten? We'll play chemistry?"

"I'll be there. You bring the magic."

"I'll do what I can. Night, kid."

"Night, Will."

Darcy pressed the red End button on her iPhone, and looked up, through the window to Jack's house. She saw him in the living room, sitting on the couch where they'd made love for the first time one month ago. He looked up at her, his eyes catching hers, his face softening with love for her.

Dinner's almost ready. Coming in soon?

She smiled at him and nodded. *Ten minutes. Coq au vin?*

Tourtiére, he told her, referring to a typical Quebecois meat pie. *But that's the second course.*

What's the first?

His eyes ignited. Copper coils of burning light held hers from across the driveway.

You'll just have to come down here to find out.

Her heart skipped a beat and her sex clenched involuntarily with need. His lips twitched and his tongue darted out to lick them. Damn him for knowing her so well.

Two minutes, she amended, forcing herself to turn in her chair, away from the window.

She straightened up her desk, placing the books into neat piles and the notes into a tidy stack with the formula on top. She looked down at the trash can and stared at the two halves of her broken coffee cup sitting forlornly. She picked them up and placed them, side by side, on top of the formula like a paperweight.

I belong to you and you belong to me, she thought. *No matter what, I will be there beside you at the re-binding. No matter what, you won't go alone.*

For what is bound cannot be broken.

Chapter 2

A FEW HOURS LATER JACK WATCHED Darcy sleeping peacefully beside him. Requiring far less sleep than her meant that he spent a good share of every night watching her. He'd waited his whole life to have her beside him and after almost losing her, he knew the bitterness of a moment spent without her. She was curled up on her side, facing him, her rosy lips parted in sleep, light lashes fanning the flushed skin of her cheeks. Thankfully, Willow had devised an oil that, combined with daily oatmeal baths, managed to control most of the burns. Jack touched her cheek lightly, watching the pink color deepen slightly, and then sighed, withdrawing his hand.

He bent his elbow, putting his hand against his cheek, using his other hand to pull the covers down just a little. He watched her beautiful breasts rise and fall evenly with her breathing and his blood headed south in a rush. He wanted her. He *always* wanted her.

Leave her alone. She needs to sleep. Between their endless nights of passion and her endless days of research, she looked exhausted all the time lately. And he knew she was worried. He tried to keep it from her, but he was too. Bodily harm or pain didn't concern him; though Jack knew that arriving at the re-binding without Darcy might subject him to torture, that didn't bother him half as much as the thought of being locked up somewhere in Portes de l'Enfer, far away from Darcy, unable to protect her, unable to be with her.

She'd tried to get him to talk about turning her again tonight but he'd managed to put her off yet again. Jack never intended to bind himself to Darcy Turner, and yet, with one moment of uncontrolled passion as a teenager, he'd bound their fates, changing her life forever in the space of a single, perfect kiss. However, being bound to him was one thing—she was still human, she hadn't lost her light, hadn't lost her soul. She was still his bright, beautiful Darcy, his creature of sunshine and goodness. But turning her? Forcing her to adopt his nature? She'd become a creature of the night, like Jack, at the mercy of an all-consuming blood lust at every full moon. No. No, he wouldn't do it. It was unthinkable. Turning her into a monster wasn't the plan.

Binding her to him was bad enough, but he'd scraped out a plan to make it work—a plan that his conscience and heart had been able to accept. He'd returned to her, a model of strength and control, prepared to love and protect her for the rest of her life. If it weren't for Lela, his plan would have worked.

But thanks to Lela and the goddamn re-binding, the thought he hated almost the most—turning his beloved Darcy into a monster like him—seemed to be the only option she would consider for their future. If her potion worked and was able to suppress his *Pleine Lune* shift in two days, her insistence was only going to get stronger.

I won't do it, he thought. *No matter what. I won't turn her.*

He took a deep breath and swung his legs over the side of the bed, walking quietly around it to stand at the French doors, which flooded the room with light from the waxing gibbous moon. Even in its not-quite *Pleine Lune* state, it affected him. He felt the pressure of his claws wanting to drop, the itch of his coarse hair wanting to grow, the gnawing in his stomach for the warm, metallic taste of blood.

He clenched his eyes shut, turning away from the window and sitting restlessly in the wooden rocking chair. He looked across the room at Darcy, at her skin, so white in the moonlight, as white as his white sheets. His breathing quickened as he stared at her, his love for her making his heart swell and eyes burn.

But I can't lose her either. I'd rather die.

He cringed at the direction of his thoughts, at the uncomfortable reality he tried to hide from himself, but which asserted its strength and made him hate himself for a selfish bastard: He allowed Darcy to believe his primary objection to turning her was changing her nature, changing her from human to monster. But in his heart, he knew there was another, more powerful, reason for his hesitancy. Turning Darcy into a Roux-ga-roux, distasteful though it was, would be a viable solution for Jack if he could be guaranteed one thing—that their binding wouldn't be compromised. But while he would remain bound to Darcy for the rest of his life, there was no guarantee their binding would transfer *with* her once turned. This was Jack's primary and most crippling fear: that she would open her eyes, blazing silver as a turned Roug, and he wouldn't be able to hear her. She wouldn't recognize him as her mate. She'd walk away from him. She wouldn't love him anymore.

The idea of losing her in such a way, being hopelessly bound to her for life in a state of unrequited longing, alone with the memories of their short, perfect time together? Knowing that she lived and breathed on the earth, but didn't love him anymore? The possibility that she could be bound to another Roug who would bring her body to the peaks of ecstasy that they had known together while he stood by, alone, deeply in love with her? The very thought was so agonizing, so unbearable to even fathom, he'd rather submit to the Council than chance it.

He winced, standing up to stretch and looking up at the shadows of branches on his ceiling, clicking and clacking like bones, like claws. He clenched his hands into fists and moved quietly back to the bed, sitting on the edge with his back to Darcy. The Council wouldn't go easy. His mother had assured him of that on the phone today.

"*Jacques, on doit parler,*" Tallis had said, without pleasantries or preamble, as soon as he picked up the phone. *Jack, we need to talk.*

He'd checked through the living room windows to be sure Darcy was engrossed in her work in the little studio over the garage. He saw her head bent over books, omnipresent pencil stuck between her teeth.

"*Oui, maman,*" he replied. "*Continue.*"

She continued in French. "There's talk of an Inquisition, *mon fils*. This is serious."

Jack swallowed then took a deep breath, muscles throughout his body flexing in response to the news. "An Inquisition? That seems extreme."

"Saint Germain is blowing everything out of proportion! He wants to make an example of you to remind the packs that binding laws are our most sacred and unique traditions. He's insisting that if you can't produce your mate, you've disrespected the binding laws and must pay for your crimes."

Jack had never liked Saint Germain, the Senior Council Elder. Saint Germain loved a show. He loved a fight to the death between two Alpha Rougs, or a disappointed sparking that led to violence. He loved playing with humans before feeding, terrifying them before shedding their blood. He was a mean, arrogant, self-centered leader who ruled with fear and cunning, and Jack had always tried to stay under his radar.

"He's quite the showman," Jack growled softly, moving out of Darcy's view, into the dining room that looked out over Darcy's well-tended garden.

"I don't know if it's all for show, Jacques. Not this time. He seems genuinely angry with you. He believes you've tricked the system. They've checked the sacred text and compared it against birth records. They cannot find a female within ten years of your birth with the initials DT, and Saint Germain is planting the seeds of doubt. I hear use of the word *fraude* more and more."

"But an Inquisition?"

"*Oui, Jacques,*" his mother whispered, and he heard the brokenness in her tone. "*Une enquête judiciaire.*"

A judicial inquiry. With Saint Germain sitting in as the judge. Jack shuddered, remembering the only Inquisition he'd ever attended. The screams, the moans, the smell of charred flesh, barely time to regenerate, under the influence of Wolfsbane so the interrogated couldn't shift to protect himself. Jack clenched his eyes shut, trying to focus and not let fear take over.

"I still have friends on the Council, don't I? In the CE?"

"You're not here, *mon fils.* You haven't lived here in years. It's well-known you don't hunt. They say you've become more human than Roug. They say you've turned your back on your pack and you think you're above Roug rules. They say you've dishonored the laws of binding."

Jack shook his head, working his jaw until it ached. "That's not true."

"But, Jacques—"

"*Non, Maman! Non!* My whole life, I have had only one goal, one ambition, one cause—to protect my binding. To honor it." He ran his free hand through his hair, unable to control his anger against such outright lies. "You cheated. Papa cheated. Tombeur cheated. *Moi? Non! Jamais! Dishonor* my binding? All I have done—my whole life—is work to *honor* it."

His mother was silent, and Jack wondered if he had offended her.

"*Je sais,*" she finally replied softly. *I know.* "What will you do?"

"There's still a month," Jack replied, taking a deep breath. "I will try to think of something."

"*Oui.* I will do the same. Tombeur too. Even Julien and that bitc—and Lela. We are all willing to help."

Jack's lips quirked in a slight smile. So, Julien's binding hadn't patched things up between the two Beauloup women. He decided not to touch it.

"Are they harassing you, *maman?*"

"*Non, Jacques.* I have lived here all my life. They would not disrespect me. They have come to see me and I have told them the birth records aren't accurate. Those packs up north are barely civilized. They are not interested in causing trouble for me unless you fail to appear. Then I know they'll…"

"I'll be there."

"If it wasn't for Delphine, I would tell you to run. We could protect ourselves, but she's so small."

Julien's daughter was only four years old. If Jack didn't appear for the re-binding, his family would face the inquisition in his place. He couldn't have their safety jeopardized by his actions.

"Don't worry. I would never run. I would never *dishonor* our family. I will be there."

"Alone?"

He didn't answer. They'd already been over this several times. He refused to turn Darcy and there was no way she could attend a Roux-ga-roux Gathering in human form. Even with him, his mother, his brother, Lela and Tombeur surrounding her like a wall, they wouldn't be able to protect her from the hundreds that would want her blood.

"Jacques." She hesitated before her words came out in a rush. "I would gladly turn her for you, if you can't do—"

"*Arrête maintenant!*" he barked. "That's not an option. You know that. I will figure something out." He paused, anxious to wrap up their conversation. "You sure they're not bothering you?"

"They only stopped by the one time." She paused. "Plus, I have Tombeur here."

"Staying with you? Have you—"

"*Non, Jacques.* We live like brother and sister, like friends. Were we to kiss…."

He heard the conflict of fear and longing in her voice as it trailed off. He finished her sentence in his head. If they were to kiss, they would initiate a binding and find out whether or not they were meant to be. Neither was prepared to accept the possibility that they weren't destined for one another. They wanted to protect their friendship, their unbound bond, their mutual affection, for as long as possible.

He wondered how Tombeur could bear it, living near the woman he loved, likely sleeping in the same bed without kissing her, without belonging to her. *Control.* That's how. He thought of Darcy's broken, exposed body on the floor of her Boston apartment so many years ago, blood seeping out of her head. The way he'd been able to pick her up, hold her, carry her to her bed, and ultimately leave her. His heart swelled. Jack knew a thing or two about control, most of it learned at Tombeur's hand.

"Your human. She is well?"

"She is."

"She doesn't breed?"

"*Maman!*"

"*Jacques*, I don't ask because I have any interest in that part of your life! I ask because to bear a Reynard, a half-bre—"

"No child of mine would be a Reynard! You forget I am bound to her." Jack's voice blazed with warning. "Darcy's and my children will be Beauloups. Just not...full-blooded."

"It doesn't work that way," she said softly. "The child would still be a half-breed skinwalker."

"Interesting that in one breath you say that the binding laws are above all, and in another you say they're not." He huffed, frustration making him tired and gruff. He softened his voice. "She's not. Pregnant. I have work to do, *maman*. I need to go now."

They had discussed pack politics for a few more minutes before Delphine had interrupted, asking for *Grand-mére*, and Tallis had hung up.

Jack turned and lay back down on the bed, glancing at Darcy, who stirred lightly in her sleep. He pulled the covers back up over her naked body, moving a little closer to share his warmth with her. With one finger, he lifted the strands of cantaloupe-colored hair that covered one eye, brushed them back behind her ear, and lay on his side, staring at her sleeping face.

He thought of what she would look like as a turned Roug. Her body would sprout reddish hair like a fox and her claws would be white and pristine for years. Even longer, if her potion worked and her hunting instincts could be suppressed. Jack stared at her closed eyelids. Were she to be turned and their binding preserved, her eyes would burn greenish-silver for him when they hunted, when she wanted him, whenever he looked at her with desire, whenever they mated. Her skin wouldn't burn from the heat of his, and their children would be full-blooded Beauloups. To Jack's shock and despair, he hardened like a rock at the mere thought of breeding with her in shifted form, in the woods, under the full moon during *Pleine Lune*, after feeding.

His blood raced hot in his veins, boiling with want. He didn't want to want it. He wanted to be satisfied with Darcy in human form, with what they had together now. He didn't want to long for more—not when it put Darcy, and more importantly, their binding, in jeopardy. But, still, he couldn't banish the image. Her claws opening his coarse skin as she raked them across his back, thrusting into her up against a tree, speaking to her with his eyes in the dark, his fangs cutting into the flesh of her neck and bathing his face in her blood. Howling his devotion, his all-consuming love for her, as he drove into her again and again, finally shooting his potent seed far, far into her depths, knowing it would find its mark. Watching for seven months as she swelled, heavy and round with his child, flaunting the result of their wild lovemaking. The image of his beautiful Darcy carrying his strong, hot-blooded Roux-ga-roux child made him groan, exhaling as his body tightened further, hungry and demanding.

He cringed, rolling away from her, onto his back, throwing an arm over his eyes. As much as he wanted to believe that their Roug-Human binding was enough, as much as he would have sworn it was, some minute part of who he was, primal and base, longed for more. Wanted everything. Wanted the full realization of every Roug-Roug binding. Wanted the violent, unparalleled ecstasy of shifted breeding. He wanted it. He wanted it with her.

He growled, throwing the covers off his body, then slipping into sweatpants and a t-shirt. He laced up his running shoes and left the room quietly, headed for the woods.

But his heart was heavy. He finally had Darcy Turner in his life. It *had* to be enough. It *needed* to be enough. He couldn't allow his darkest desires to influence his decision, to change his mind about turning her. He had to stay in control, to do what was best for her, even if his blood screamed for more.

As his footsteps moved swiftly through the woods, he tried to ignore the truth. He could exercise all the control in the world, but it wouldn't change his nature. He was soulless and monstrous somewhere deep inside. Despite his best intentions, despite his control, he'd never be able to run away from the beast within who wanted more. Not now. Not ever.

"WHAT TIME DID YOU LEAVE for a run?" Darcy asked from where she sat at the kitchen table, sipping a mug of coffee as morning sunlight warmed her shoulders. She wasn't sure how often he left their bed for midnight runs, but it seemed to be happening more often as *Pleine Lune* approached.

"Why?" Jack, who stood against the counter in ripped sweatpants and a dirty t-shirt, grinned at her. "Did you miss me?"

"Maybe." She blushed and looked away. She took a deep breath, changing the subject. "I'm headed to Willow's for the day."

Jack's grin faded and he nodded.

"Are you sure you're going to be okay trying this, Jack? Even though the compound includes Wolfsbane?"

She watched as he clenched his jaw twice before answering. "It's now or never."

"Can we go over the plan again?" she asked, trying not to get distracted by the way his pants sat low on his hips, teasing her with a peek of skin every time he moved.

"I'm so dirty," he said, his face the picture of innocence as he pointed to his shirt. "I should take a shower first."

"Jack—" she started. He put one arm over his head and tugged on the collar of his t-shirt, pulling it over his head. He tossed it on the floor then rested both elbows on the countertop behind him, thrusting his taut chest forward. Her mouth went dry. No matter how many times she looked at his chiseled perfection, she couldn't seem to control herself; she couldn't make herself look away. Her eyes trailed from his neck over his broad pecs to his six well-toned abs, to the triangle of muscle at his hips that formed a V of sinew, trailing into the waistband of his pants like an arrow.

She took a deep, shaky breath, raising her eyes to his.

He licked his lower lip then bit it lightly with his teeth, staring at her.

"I can hear what you're thinking," he teased.

"Get out of my head, skinwalker," she breathed, wishing she could look away from him. But he was so damn beautiful and he belonged to her.

He beamed at her. "Mm-hmm. And you belong to me."

"Quit it," she said, taking a deep breath and forcing herself to look away. "You can't distract me with sex every time I want to talk about something important. It's not fair."

"To whom?" he asked, his voice peppered with humor.

"I'm serious, Jack."

"Fine," he said, sauntering to the table and pulling out the chair across from her. He put his elbows on the table and waited.

She kept her eyes down. Better to avoid temptation.

"So, we'll both go into the vault tomorrow. Around four o'clock. The sun won't set until eight o'clock or later, but the urges start earlier, right?"

She looked up and he nodded at her, all traces of humor wiped free of his face. His nostrils flared and her heart surged with love for him. He must be worried. She knew he was wary of Wolfsbane, not even allowing it in his house, and yet he trusted her enough to ingest it. His love for her was staggering, profound.

"I'll give you the potion and lock you into the safe room."

"I'll lock myself in," he corrected her.

"Okay. But I'll have a password or something, right? To disable the door?"

Jack looked down, furrowing his brows.

"Jack! I'll be able to get you out, right? If you have a bad reaction, I need to be able to get you out. If anything goes wrong..."

He looked up and she could see the pain in his eyes. "It's too risky. A *Pleine Lune* shift is like—like nothing I can describe to you. I can't risk it, Darcy."

"You'd never hurt me," she insisted. "We're bound."

"It's true. It's unlikely that I'd hurt you." He swallowed, holding her eyes, and she heard it before he could look away. *On purpose.*

"On purpose? What do you mean?"

"I'd never *hunt* you. Not for your blood. But...."

"For what then?" she demanded.

"No, it's just—"

"Just what? I've seen you fully shifted. I've seen your claws several times. Your burning eyes. You've never hurt me," she insisted.

He opened his mouth to say something then closed it, staring at her with yearning in his eyes while her name buzzed in a loop in his head, blocking the rest of his thoughts. His eyes gazed back at her with untold sadness. And...embarrassment. Wait. *Embarrassment?*

"What's going on?" she asked, her voice tighter and higher with concern.

He sighed loudly, looking away from her.

"I'd want to mate with you," he said softly.

"*Mate* with me? You mean, make love?'

"No." He shook his head. "I mean mate."

Her eyes flew open. *Shifted?*

He nodded.

But, everything gets bigger. Everything about you is....

He stared at her, quirking his head to the side. He raised his eyebrows and his lips twitched.

"Oh," she breathed, her face flushing crimson. "Oh, I see."

"It's a pretty powerful instinct," he explained, reaching across the table to take her hand. "I don't know for sure that I could control it if you were...nearby."

"I didn't know," she said, flicking her eyes up to his then looking away again quickly. She didn't want him to see the doubt in her eyes. Although she loved Jack and outwardly accepted him for who and what he was, inside she still battled to embrace his strange, dangerous nature.

"How would you, baby?" he asked, massaging soothing circles on the back of her hand.

"But, what if something goes wrong? I'll be helpless. I won't be able to—"

"Nothing will go wrong. You're the smartest person I know. This is going to work." He smiled at her sadly. "I'll be in the safe room and you'll be in the control room, next door. But you can keep me company. There's a speaker built into the wall. You could talk to me and you'll be able to hear me and see me. You can watch me on the monitor. I just can't see you. The camera is mounted into the wall behind a four-inch thick piece of Plexiglas. The picture's a little grainy, but..."

"I'll be there the whole time watching."

"And I'll be like a zoo animal in a cage."

"No! Jack, no. It's not like that!"

"I'm kidding. I know it's not." But his eyes said differently. His eyes said there was so much about this that he hated. He managed to smile for her. "It's three days, Darce. You go upstairs and sleep in your office from time to time. I don't want you getting too exhausted, sick or—"

"I'm not going to leave you. Not for a minute. I'll sleep in the control room."

Jack picked up her hand and drew the back of it to his lips, pressing against it gently before tilting his head and closing his eyes, resting his cheek against her soft skin.

Her chair scraped the floor as she stood, moving around the table. When he looked up, she was standing beside him, her outstretched arm still attached to his cheek. He tugged lightly and she sat down on his lap, encircling his neck with her arms as he held her close.

"It'll work," she promised. Then, close to his ear, so close that he shivered from the touch of her breath—"Don't be scared."

"I'm not." He drew back, looking at her, surprised, before smiling tenderly. "There's only one thing in the world that scares me, baby. And that's losing you."

She smiled back at him, leaning forward to rest her cheek on his shoulder as his hands crept under her pajama top to rest on the skin of her back.

"Then you have nothing to worry about, because I'm not going anywhere." He stroked her back as she thought of the three weeks' worth of mornings she'd woken up in his bed, often in his arms.

"These have been the best days of my life, Jack," she murmured.

"And mine."

"But we have to figure this out before Solstice."

"We will."

"Tomorrow's just the first step."

She leaned back, seizing his eyes with hers.

I belong to you.

He nodded.

And you belong to me.

He nodded again.

She wiggled a little to straddle him, taking off her top and pushing her naked breasts against his hard chest, well aware that there was nothing else between them but her pajama bottoms and his sweat pants.

I want you. Make love to me, Jack.

His eyes ignited, flashing with golden heat as he leaned forward, capturing her lips with his.

Chapter 3

THEY MADE LOVE ON THE chair at the kitchen table then ran upstairs to have a long, hot shower together. She finally hopped out because she needed to meet Willow, but Jack took an extra moment alone, letting the water sluice over his skin, wishing they could be carefree, wishing that their life wasn't fraught with secrets and danger. He finally turned off the tap and wrapped a towel around himself. Stopping in the bathroom doorway, he watched her quietly, his heart brimming with love for her.

Darcy sat on the edge of the bed, pulling on her socks and shoes, and he had a sudden flashback to the first time he ever saw her.

She looked up to find Jack staring at her from the bathroom doorway. Her lips tilted up and her eyes brightened immediately until she caught his expression and her brows knitted for a moment in question.

"What?"

"*Avec elle, ma mort et ma vie. Avec elle et nul autre.*"

"With her, my…?" she asked.

He crossed the room, falling to his knees before her, laying his damp black head in her lap. He closed his eyes as her fingers fell lightly onto his hair, gently burying themselves in the thickness. His voice sounded muffled against the fabric of her jeans.

"With her, my death and my life. With her and no other."

Her hands slipped around to caress his face, her palms lovingly holding his cheeks as she righted his head, making him look at her.

"*Avec elle, ma vie,*" she replied, her green eyes serious and worried. "*La vie.*"

With her, my life, she repeated in his head. *Life. No death. We will figure this out.*

He took a deep breath then sighed, leaning forward to touch his lips to hers. She didn't open her lips and he couldn't help feeling deprived. He had half a mind to force the issue—kiss her harder until her mouth opened, until she couldn't catch her breath, until he had her stripped down and panting beneath him. "I'd keep you here all day if I could."

"You can't. Willow's waiting for me."

"Hmmph," he grumbled, pushing off her knees with his elbows to stand up.

"And don't forget we have dinner at my mom's tonight," she added, tying her other shoe then standing up with her hands on her hips. "You're a duckling now."

"A duckling." He threw an incredulous glance at her, letting his towel drop to the ground as he pulled on a pair of jeans. "I'm a Roux-ga-roux. Do you have any idea how ridiculous that sounds?"

Darcy shrugged, still grinning. "The big wolf doesn't like being called a duckling."

"He does not."

"She means well," said Darcy softly.

"I know," he answered, throwing on a t-shirt. "And you know I like your family. I just wish we could be alone tonight. Before…"

"We have all day tomorrow," Darcy reminded him, stepping into his arms to hug him good-bye.

She rested her cheek against his shoulder, and again he thought about distracting her, keeping her with him, making it impossible for her to leave him.

"And what will we do tomorrow?" he asked instead.

"Have fun together," she breathed, her words slow and deliberate, the underlying worry in contrast to the words.

"A walk in the woods?" Her favorite.

"Mm-hm."

"A picnic?" he asked.

"Yes, please," she said, her voice warming up now. How he loved that he could tell the nuances of her mood by the changes in her tone. "And you can tell me stories."

"Stories?"

She leaned back, her eyes playful and bright. "Pack stories. Or stories about you and your childhood."

"Julien's the storyteller."

"I don't want Julien," she said, pursing her lips together. Darcy and

Julien's meeting had been rocky, at best. "I'm going to lie on your chest and stare at the sky and you're going to tell me stories."

The position she was describing—her head on his chest under a ceiling of green leaves, with bits of blue sky shining through—was a common position for them when he pulled her inside, into *Dansmatête*, where he was a black wolf, and she was ethereal, like an angel. He wondered if she'd chosen the image randomly or if it had been influenced by the moments they'd spent inside together.

She smiled at him. "Subconsciously influenced."

"Get out of my head, human."

She leaned up to kiss him lightly on the lips. "See you later?"

He nodded, his chest aching, as it always did, when he watched her go.

SIX HOURS LATER WILLOW AND Darcy sat side by side on the couch in Willow's office, staring at the glass canning jar on the desk, which was halfway filled with an amber-colored liquid.

Willow nudged Darcy's side. "You did it."

"*We* did it," said Darcy, turning to grin at her friend.

"You sure about the dosage?"

Darcy shook her head. "I'm not sure about anything."

"Hey, that's not true. You're sure this'll work. I am too."

Tears sprang into Darcy's eyes and she let her weary head fall.

"Kid," said Willow, rubbing her friend's back. "What's going on? We did it. We made the shift suppressor. *Pleine Lune*'s tomorrow night and we made it in time. You can breathe a sigh of relief."

"I wish it was that simple," said Darcy, swiping at her eyes and taking a deep breath. "But Jack still refuses to talk about turning me. I mean, I don't know how it will go tomorrow. Do I think this will keep him from shifting? Yes. I do. But it's not like he's agreed to turn me. He won't even talk about it, Willow. So what's the point of making this if he won't turn me? If he goes up there…and they…they…"

"Darce. Stop."

Darcy looked up at Willow's dark eyes.

"One step at a time. Let's get through the next few days. Jack may feel differently once he's experienced a shift suppression. How can you expect him to agree to turn you when we don't even know if it'll work yet?"

Darcy took another deep breath and nodded, the logic of Willow's words a comfort to her. Willow was right. Jack might feel differently four days from now. He might. But what if he didn't?

Though Darcy had loved the last three weeks, staying at Jack's house, sleeping beside him every night and learning more about the man to whom her life was bound, it was starting to really bother her that Jack refused to discuss Solstice, the re-binding or turning her. Yes, Willow's words were soothing, but Darcy couldn't help but worry that Jack would refuse to turn her.

Darcy was unconcerned about the binding itself. She believed with her whole heart that the binding would hold. She'd never felt anything as strong as her love for Jack or witnessed anything as profound as his commitment to her. She had faith it would hold, so she barely wasted a moment worrying about their binding.

The only thing that really frightened Darcy was the possibility of losing him permanently. The thought of Jack heading up to Portes de l'Enfer alone for the re-binding and being forced to submit to an inquisition twisted her stomach and compressed her lungs until she couldn't breathe. There was only one thing Darcy held as an absolute truth: She had to show up at the re-binding. Turned or unturned, she had to be there.

One option was for him to turn her. And as much as she worried about the change in her form and nature, the last few weeks had given her ample opportunity to study Jack—his care and compassion, his kindness, deep sense of responsibility and devotion. He was her example of every-thing a Roux-ga-Roux could be, and she would be honored to be like him. He saw himself as dark and bad, but she saw his goodness, his light, and the thought of being like him didn't frighten her. Turning seemed such a small thing when held up against Jack's life. She'd still be *alive*. Yes, she'd have to learn how to be Roug, but she'd have the most loving, attentive mentor as she learned. Didn't he see? Couldn't he understand that there was only one solution and it had very little to do with the shift suppressor? The shift suppressor was just Darcy's way of sweetening the deal, of making the turning more palatable to Jack. Because while the idea of turning bothered Darcy less and less, the other option terrified her...

The only other option was for Darcy to show up at the re-binding as his bound mate in human form. A shiver went down her spine as she imagined the hundreds of fangs and claws outstretched for her blood. But if he wouldn't turn her, it was the only way to save him, and there was not one cell in her body that would allow her to stay idly behind in Carlisle while she sent him to his doom.

Turned or human, Darcy would be at the re-binding. As far as she was concerned, it was non-negotiable.

"I'm sure you're right, Will," said Darcy softly.

"No, you're not."

Darcy stood up, pursing her lips at Willow. "I won't let anyone hurt him. I can't."

"Hey." Willow stood up, cocking her head to the side. "Make me a promise?"

"What is it?"

"If…if you decide, at some point, that you're going to take things into your own hands…tell me."

"Willow, I—"

"Promise me. If he won't turn you and you decide to show up at the binding…" Willow's face contorted and she shook her head, lowering her voice to a pleading whisper. "It's a suicide mission. You know that, don't you?"

Darcy kept her face impassive. Strong. "I know it would save him."

"But you would certainly die."

"Willow," said Darcy gently. "My life wouldn't be worth living without him."

A tear snaked down Willow's face. "If you decide to go north, promise you'll tell me first."

"I'd be putting you in danger too."

"No. They wouldn't hurt me. I'm an *Enchanteresse*."

"There would be hundreds of them and only one of you."

"I don't care." Willow reached forward and grasped Darcy's hands. "Promise me. If you decide to go north, you'll tell me first."

Darcy swallowed, bracing herself to stay placid as she lied. "I promise."

Willow exhaled in a rush, her shoulders slumping in relief as she released Darcy's hands. "See you for dinner tonight?"

Taking the jar off the desk, Darcy forced a smile. "Of course."

JACK WOKE UP EARLY THE next morning, his blood surging with the promise and threat of *Pleine Lune.*

When Darcy had returned home yesterday afternoon, she'd held up the ginger jar, giving him a rueful smile. "Here it is."

"My fate," he'd said softly, staring at the liquid sloshing against the walls of the glass jar.

"*Our* fate," she'd corrected him.

He was grateful for dinner at Darcy's mother's house as a distraction, fascinated by watching the simple, traditional family life he'd read about in books but had never experienced firsthand. His own family was a fractious mess: his father dead, his mother and Tombeur living in limbo, while his mother could barely mention Lela's name amicably. His sisters were far away, living with their mates in northern packs, choosing to stay as far away from his "family" as possible. What would it have been like to experience the sort of warm, loving home that Darcy had grown up in? And how in the world could he do anything to take her away from it?

She stirred in her sleep, reaching for him, and he gathered her into his arms.

"Today," she sighed, her eyes fluttering open, "is here."

Jack nodded, tracing the lines of her beloved face with one finger as he captured her eyes. *It is.*

She reached up to cup his cheek. *It's going to be okay.*

"Hey," he said, smiling at her. "Do you think—just for today—that we could just pretend we're Jack and Darcy who are a newly hatched couple, madly in love, with no re-bindings or shifts to contend with? Just until this afternoon?"

"Are we both Rougs or humans in this ideal scenario?"

"Let's be humans," he suggested.

"Okay. We're just two ordinary humans—"

"Madly in love—"

"Madly in love," she repeated, pushing him onto his back and rolling on top of him. "And we have"—she flicked her glance to the clock—"about eight hours together. What exactly would you like to do?"

His hands trailed up the warm skin of her back—idly, gently, savoring the softness of her skin, the pliancy of her body covering his. "I liked your idea yesterday."

"The woods," they said simultaneously, grinning at each other.

"But first," he said, easily flipping her over so that she was panting beneath him. *I want you.*

I'm yours.

She arched her hips up a little and Jack thrust forward into her, holding her eyes as their bodies fused together and wishing they had a lifetime, rather than just a day, to pretend that everything was okay.

*H*IS MOOD IS OFF, THOUGHT Darcy, holding his hand as the leaves crunched beneath their boots. The changes in the north woods were subtle, but certain…fall was coming. The trees, which had maintained their green for almost all of August, were starting to color yellow, and even though the noonday sun was high in the sky, it wasn't quite as warm as it had been a week ago.

They'd made love all morning, and while Jack showered Darcy made them a picnic. While she showered, he'd packed it in a basket. It all felt so normal. It all felt so fleeting. And yet, Darcy was determined not to ruin the short time they had left with the same conversation Jack had been avoiding for weeks. They could talk about changing her four days from now when her suppressor had proven itself.

Last night at dinner, Darcy had felt a passing envy for Willow and Amory, for the way they had all the time in the world to figure out what comes next, and what they wanted from each other. They were unwrapping each other slowly like a present, and they'd have forever to savor one another. For all that she wouldn't trade the grand passion that she and Jack shared, she wondered, wistfully, what it would be like to be unrushed and unafraid.

"I never thought Amory and Willow would happen," she said softly as he pulled her gently over a fallen log.

"I think you did."

"No, really," she insisted. "For so long—forever, really—it seemed impossible. Seeing them together last night? I mean, they're really a couple. They're together."

"They've been together since the night Julien and Lela were bound," said Jack. "Whatever Willow felt for your brother couldn't be concealed anymore after that night. It was the touchstone. The turning point."

"What would have happened if you hadn't kissed me backstage that night, Jack? Would you have found someone else? A Roug girl?"

"It doesn't work like that," he said, glancing at her as they neared the clearing where they planned to picnic. "Bound couples are like puzzle pieces. You only fit together with one until that one's gone."

"So you would've been alone?"

He nodded, bringing her hand to his lips and kissing it.

"Maybe it would've been better," she lamented softly.

"Never," he said. He stopped walking to set the basket on the ground, pulling Darcy against his body. "Loving you has been the best part of my life."

"Past tense," she said breathlessly into his shoulder, tears stinging her eyes.

"Loving you *is* the best part of my life," he amended. He leaned back, smiling at her tenderly. "I thought we were going to be two normal humans today, madly in love."

Reaching down, Darcy opened the picnic basket and took out the blanket that lay on top. "That's right."

"So, normal human fiancée, should we do some..." She watched him as he tried to think of something "normal" couples did on the weekend. "...grocery shopping this afternoon?"

Darcy chuckled. "We should. And maybe stop at Home Depot. I could use some mesh wire for around the garden. The rabbits are devouring my herbs."

Jack took two corners of the blanket from her and stepped back, helping her spread it. "End of summer's almost here."

"Mm-hm."

"Perhaps we should host a BBQ? All my frat brothers and your sorority sisters?"

"They all have kids," said Darcy softly.

"Kids," he murmured, knowing their conversation had hit a painful impasse.

Her heart thudded painfully and she looked away from him, trying to be present in the make-believe of the moment. It wasn't impossible for her and Jack to have children, but having a half-Roug child wasn't something either of them was ready to discuss. "Tell me about Julien and Lela. Any news?"

Jack sat down on the blanket then leaned back, pillowing his hands beneath his head. "Come lie down with me."

She knelt first, and then joined him, resting her head inside his elbow and staring up at the sky.

"Lela's breeding."

Her head whipped to face him as she gasped in surprise. "Already?"

"Mm-hm," he murmured. "A binding *louveteau*."

"*Louveteau?*" asked Darcy, feeling happy for Lela and sad for herself all at the same time.

"It means a—a cub," Jack explained, leaning up on his side to look into her eyes. *Are you upset?*

No, I'm happy for Lela and Julien.

But she looked away quickly because she was lying. He reached for her chin and tilted her face back to meet his. *We'll have our own someday.*

"A *louveteau* or a baby?" she asked.

Sighing, he dropped his fingers from her face and rolled back beside her to stare up at the sky. They were lying so close to each other Darcy could feel the heat of his skin warming her like the sun, and yet she'd never felt quite so alone.

This is the problem, she thought sadly, feeling her deep love for him and knowing it simply wasn't enough. *We can't plan our future, and until we can, we have none.*

Chapter 4

THE REST OF THE AFTERNOON had been melancholy. For all that they wished they could just be a normal human couple for a few hours, they both knew it was impossible. *Pleine Lune* loomed over them and Solstice sat dark and mean on the horizon. Around three o'clock they started back to the lodge, but Jack had stopped about half a mile from the house.

Holding her hand, he pulled her against his chest, looking down into her eyes. "I'll meet you at home, okay?"

She searched his face. "You aren't coming back with me?"

"I have to hunt, Darcy. Just in case your potion doesn't work, I'm going to need fresh dead."

Darcy winced, her stomach turning over. "You're going to sit in a vault for three days with a dead animal?"

He shrugged. "If I shift, I have to feed."

She swallowed, dropping his eyes to hide her feelings of revulsion. "Just trust me, it's going to work."

"I do trust you. Until Amory got hurt, I wouldn't even allow Wolfsbane in my house. Tonight I'm going to *drink* it. I trust you with everything I am, baby. But not even you know what's going to happen tonight. I have to be ready…for anything."

For failure, she thought, doubts encroaching.

He dropped her hand and tilted her chin up so she was looking up at him. "I trust you, Darcy. With everything I am."

She forced a weak smile for him, swallowing the lump in her throat. "Okay. I'll head back. Meet you at the house?"

Jack glanced at the waning sun then back at Darcy, shaking his head. "Better not chance it. I'll go straight to the vault."

Tears welled in Darcy's eyes as she stared at him. She had hoped to lie in his bed for one more hour, to make love to him, to feel his arms around her before they were separated for the next three difficult days.

"So this is all we have? Right now? This is it?"

She'd gone without Jack's presence in her life for twenty years—she hated it that three days suddenly felt so terrible.

He set the empty picnic basket on the ground and reached out to cup her face in his large, warm hands. Searching her eyes, he swallowed like there was a lump in his throat too, before dropping his lips to hers.

No matter how many times he kissed her…no matter how many different ways…Darcy would never get used to his kisses. She would never get used to the feeling of his strong, hot lips moving against hers, the way his hands caressed her face like she was his living, breathing treasure. She would never grow tired of the way he poured his love for her into every stroke of his tongue, every gasp, every groan, every tightening grasp of his fingers on her flesh.

Her knees weakened and as she swayed into him, he lowered his hands to her waist, then banded them around her, clutching her to his chest fiercely. His lips strayed from her mouth, over the skin of her cheeks like a brand, sliding effortlessly to her ear, which he bit gently before whispering,

"I love you."

"I love you too," she murmured, unable to keep a tear from sliding down her cheek.

He drew back from her, reaching up to wipe the trail of moisture away. *It's going to be all right, baby.*

I know, she told him. *I hope,* her heart whispered.

Giving her a small grin, he reached down for the picnic basket and handed it to her. *See you in a little bit.*

She nodded then turned and walked away, listening to his retreating footsteps pounding faster and faster into the wilds of the woods.

AS HIS ROUG FEET THUNDERED across the forest floor, Jack turned his thoughts to the evening ahead. He hadn't given a whole lot of thought to the physical pain that awaited his immediate future for two reasons.

First of all, it did no good to dwell on an inevitability. It was a waste of time. He had promised Darcy he would try out the suppressor and once he'd made that promise, he was locked into the experience. He knew it was going to be extremely unpleasant so he hadn't wasted time thinking about it.

Second of all, the idea of completely suppressing his *Pleine Lune* shift, while something he'd always dreamed of, suddenly felt extreme. It felt like an emasculation, a castration of sorts. In a strange way, he realized that he liked exercising control over his urges without eliminating them. Even now, as he ran effortlessly through the rambles, he felt alive—vibrant, exciting, on the very cusp of whole. He loved Darcy with all his heart, but his heart—his very nature—was Roug. And now, faced with the prospect of eliminating that part of himself, for however long, he felt conflicted.

It was impossible for Darcy to live in his world as a human, so if they wanted to be together, he must live in hers. But did it necessarily follow that all traces of his nature should be subjugated?

He knew the answer.

Yes. It was necessary that his urge to kill and feed be eliminated during *Pleine Lune*. He knew it would be for the best and give them the best possible chance at a future together. Even as he acquiesced to this reality, however, it bothered him.

Catching the scent of a young buck, he turned sharply to the left. Six hundred yards. Maybe less. He slowed his pace a little so that he didn't announce himself.

If you turned her, you could hunt on the Northern Bloodlands together. She'd be like you. She'd be one of you, whispered that soft, persistent, insidious voice in his head.

His eyes ignited in protest. Jack knew that Darcy would be angry about his choice, but he had come to a final decision last night after watching her at her mother's house. He would never turn her. He would leave her the day before Solstice and appear alone at the re-binding. He would take any punishment meted out and maintain his silence. One day—with the help of Tombeur and his mother—he would be released and he would return to Darcy. They'd been separated before, he reasoned. It would be painful, but they could stand it again.

He imagined himself shackled in a cell underneath the Council hall. He knew these cells well—he'd guarded them often enough. They would torture him, but he was strong and would withstand their punitive measures. At night, he would pull Darcy into his dreams. She would comfort him, remind him of everything he was fighting for, holding on for, living for. And when the Council understood that there was no information forthcoming, they'd tire of Jack. When they thought they'd broken his spirit, they would release him.

And he and Darcy would be free.

Distracted by the steady, even heartbeat of the unaware deer, he slowed his steps even further. It was asleep. Something in him grumbled about missing out on the thrill of the chase, even though it would be an easier kill. Letting his claws drop silently, he found it resting against a log and quickly slit its neck. He closed his eyes and breathed in the comforting, metallic smell of its blood before hefting it up on his shoulders and turning back toward home.

Once Jack returned for her, they could live a "normal" life together. As long as he was a Roug and she a human, they'd never have children, of course, but they'd have each other. They'd live out their days in well-earned peace and comfort and love.

TAKING OUT HER MEDICAL JOURNAL, Darcy listed the date and time on the top line of the first page:

September 3 — 4:20 pm

Swallowing, she stared at the blank page, wondering where to begin. Like any good scientist, she needed to keep a detailed record of the potion's efficacy and Jack's reaction to it and tolerance of it. But looking at the page was like looking down a shotgun barrel, suddenly, and her nerves made her hand shake as she raised her coffee cup to her lips.

God, please don't let this hurt him.

Please let it work.

Please let him see that turning me is the only way.

She heard the upstairs door open and stood up from the desk in the small office adjacent to the vault entrance. She looked up the stairs to see him descending.

"Turn away if it's going to gross you out," he warned when he was about halfway down.

Darcy turned away from him, looking back into the office that contained two grainy TV monitors mounted over the desk, a metal file cabinet, a coffee maker, and one uncomfortable guest chair. As he passed by her, she could feel his heat and smell the musty pungency of his kill. Her stomach threatened to revolt, so she concentrated on the desk, littered with her notes, and focused on the jar of liquid standing conspicuously in the middle of them.

Glancing up at the monitor, she saw Jack relax his shoulders and the large deer slid down his back, crumpling into the corner of the room. With horror and fascination, she watched as he looked down at his blood-covered hands, suddenly lifting them to his lips and licking. The sound in the vault was turned off, but even from here, on the other side of the massive, cracked-open door, she could hear his groan of relief and pleasure.

It's almost time, she told herself.

"Do you—do you need anything else? Before we get started?" she called to him, picking up a pencil to write up his kill and arrival time, and then dropping again when she felt his hands on her shoulders.

She turned to face him, and even though sunset wasn't for another two and a half hours, she could see the bristly black hairs poking out on his face and arms. His fingers twitched with eagerness to let claws drop for the hunt, and reaching up to take his pulse, she felt the racing rhythm throbbing beneath his touch. She darted her eyes to his face, where his eyes burned like liquid gold.

I'm not turning yet, he told her. *But soon.*

Then it's time.

She started to encircle his neck with the hand on his throat to pull him in, but he reached up and clamped his fingers around her wrist, pulling it away from him and releasing it meaningfully.

Don't, his eyes begged her.

Her breath hitched and she stepped back from him, reaching for the jar on her desk with a trembling hand.

"You'll have to finish it."

He took the jar carefully, but his eyes were wide and wild as they searched hers. She saw uncertainty. She saw fear. She saw love. It all twisted her heart in the worst, most painful way and she winced, placing her palm against her chest.

"I wouldn't—" He gasped softly, as his eyes flooded then burned. "There isn't another soul on this earth who could get me to—I mean, I'd do *anything* for you."

"I know," she sobbed, a tear snaking down her face as she controlled the impulse to reach for him one last time.

"Keep me company?" he whispered fiercely.

"Every minute," she promised. "Every second."

He nodded, staring at her face for one long, hard moment.

I belong to you.

She nodded.

And I belong to you.

Then he turned away from her and she heard the keypad next to the vault beep loudly as he pressed his palm against the sensor and entered a code. A moment later, the heavy steel door slammed closed.

September 3 — 4:40 pm

Subject has ingested the suppressor.

I am watching for signs of immediate discomfort and finding none, much to my relief, which means that the *Lycopodium clavatum* is coating his stomach and the olivetol appears to be controlling the urge to vomit. Will the Wolfsbane still suppress the shift?

SURPRISED THAT HE FELT NOTHING after drinking the disgusting mixture, he sat down on the floor with his legs spread out in front of him and looked up at the camera.

"You there, baby?"

"I'm here."

It was strange, the way her voice filled the metal and concrete box where he was trapped. It was comforting and disconcerting at the same time to have her voice but nothing else. He briefly considered pulling her inside, so he could touch her as he'd desperately wanted to before, but thought better of it. There would be plenty of time for *Dansmatête* over the next three days.

"I don't feel anything," said Jack.

"That's good. That's the best possible scenario."

He chuckled dryly. "What's the worst?"

She sighed into the microphone.

"Darcy, I already drank it. Tell me the worst."

"Shakes, chills, fever…I don't know. Vomiting maybe. Anything. For as much as Willow tried to map your DNA so we could get the dosage perfect, this is still a first trial."

His stomach gurgled unpleasantly.

"I think it's coming back up," he said through clenched teeth.

September 3 — 6:50 pm

Subject has now vomited eight separate times.

This shouldn't affect its potency as enough of the potion was metabolized upon ingestion.

He is sweating and shaking as the sunset draws near, and he occasionally stalks around the cell, growling and groaning.

As of right now, his claws have dropped, but his skin is coated only with a modest smattering of growth and his face and feet remain unchanged.

"JACK?"

"*What?*" he roared, looking into the camera with wild eyes.

Darcy winced. It wasn't going well. He was about twenty minutes away from sundown now and she could see that he was struggling, his body engaged in a fierce battle between the demand to shift and the inability to make it happen.

"How can I help?"

"You could fucking accept me for who I am!" he thundered.

Darcy knew that his anger was an effect of his situation, but his words still hurt.

"I love you. You know that."

His chest heaved up and down and he vomited up some bile that clung, in ugly yellow strings of drool, to his beard.

"S—S—Sorry, Darcy."

"No," she said gently. "Don't be sorry. I'm so sorry you have to go through this."

Suddenly he clutched his chest, throwing back his head and scratching at his shirt with his claws until the shirt was shredded and he was bleeding.

"Jack, stop!"

His claws stilled and he dropped them to his sides, leaning forward to brace his palms on his knees as pieces of his tattered shirt floated to the floor.

September 3 — 7:04 pm — sunset

Subject is angry and agitated.

With ten separate instances of vomiting, we can be assured that the *Lycopodium clavatum* and olivetol weren't effective for protecting his stomach, though we can't guess how much more damage would have been sustained without them.

Sunset has arrived.

The moon is full.

With the exception of golden eyes and dropped claws, the subject's form is almost entirely human.

THE BURNING WAS EXTREME.

The hairs beneath his skin jabbed at the underside of his flesh but didn't burst forth, and Jack realized what a holy, orgasmic relief it would be if they would. Right now, as they poked and jabbed, just short of developing, they itched and burned like a colony of fire ants fighting beneath the surface of his skin. Additionally, the bones and muscles in his body, which longed for growth, were kept just at the cusp of developing. They strained and ached, pregnant with expansion, yet restrained from growth. His stomach, which had to be empty, still rolled and rebelled, and Jack gasped for breath as another wave of bile filled his mouth. He spat it onto the floor with disgust.

His jaw unleashed a sudden, powerful, gnawing pain that made his head feel like it was trapped in a vise, and he reached into his mouth to find that the fangs he expected to feel hadn't dropped. They were neatly concealed in his gums, but the waves and spirals of pain to his head originated where they should now be exposed. He whimpered, the sound more canine than human in his ears, as his trembling fingers massaged the soft, wet gums that throbbed.

His chest, which had already healed neatly, held within it a deep, sorrowful howl of longing and pain as he felt the sun slip below the horizon.

Like a sharp blow to the body, like being hit by a truck, the pain was suddenly so intense, so unbelievable, the cell around him spun wildly, and the last thing Jack remembered was his head hitting the cold cement of the floor.

September 4 — 3:00 am

Subject has been asleep (passed out?) now for about four hours, but he writhes and cries out in his sleep. He is sweating and shaking, but has not shifted beyond the initial stages.

His fangs never dropped.

His body never expanded.

He is not covered in fur.

His claws are receding about an inch every hour.

There is still a burning golden light behind his eyes, but it's not as bright as the hours move slowly forward.

I can now safely say that the *Pleine Lune* shift was suppressed.

But the emotional and physical distress to the Subject was extreme.

Additional tinkering with the formula is required to make it more comfortable for the Subject.

DARCY WOKE UP WITH A jolt, gasping as she flipped over her wrist and realized it was seven o'clock in the morning.

Straightening in the desk chair, she looked up at the screens, standing to get a better view. What she saw astounded her.

Jack was still asleep, curled into a comfortable ball, and he appeared to be breathing and sleeping peacefully. He wasn't shaking anymore and he looked almost entirely human.

"Jack?" she whispered into the microphone.

He stirred lightly, but didn't wake up.

It occurred to Darcy there was only one sure way to connect with him. She pulled him inside.

FLOATING GENTLY OVERHEAD, SHE STARED down at the black wolf, curled up on a grey carpet beneath her.

"Jack?" she whispered, the sound so soft in her head, it was a wonder she could hear it at all.

The black wolf whimpered and she let herself drop to the floor beside him, the flexible, floating nature of her being surrounding him like a cover of mist.

"Jack?"

The wolf whimpered, licking its white teeth and opening its black eyes. *Paaaaaaain.*

Still? she asked.

No, he answered, his eyes mournful and exhausted.

It worked, she told him.

Yes, he answered, his voice soft and defeated. *It worked.*

Wrapping her essence around his brokenness, she rested the beating sound of her heart against the beating sound of his, and stayed beside him as he fell back to sleep.

Chapter 5

WHEN THE VAULT OPENED ON Friday morning, Darcy threw her arms around Jack, covering his haggard face with kisses.

He tightened his weak arms around her, burying his face in her sweet-smelling hair.

"It worked, Jack," she said near his ear in a half-whisper, half-sob. "It worked."

Yes, he thought, still holding on to her, but not yet ready to speak. *In theory, it worked.*

But the pain had been extreme and his whole body was exhausted from the suppression. For the entirety of his adult life, he'd always felt rejuvenated after a *Pleine Lune* shift. Today he felt like he'd been hit by a car. It had been like dying, only not as merciful, every square inch of his body screaming in the most excruciating pain he'd ever experienced.

If Darcy's goal in testing the shift suppressor on Jack had been to prove to him that she could be turned and live a normal life suppressing her shift every month, this trial had closed the door on that possibility. Not only was it inconceivable to imagine letting Darcy experience the sort of pain he'd just endured, Jack wasn't sure if he himself would ever submit to it again. He didn't know how he'd survive it again, and he certainly wouldn't risk Darcy's safety by ever letting her try it.

"I have so many questions!" she said, her voice low but excited. "How did it feel? What needs to be changed or modified? Do you think it would be possible to have an EKG machine hooked up to your body next time, or—"

There won't be a next time, he thought.

He leaned back, reaching up to cup her face in his hands, and lowered his lips to hers for a gentle kiss. When he drew back, his smiled had faded and her eyes searched his.

What, Jack? What is it?

He looked away from her sharply. He wasn't ready to share his feelings with her yet, because he knew how hard she'd worked and how much she'd wanted her potion to succeed.

Releasing her face, he took her hand, pulling her toward the stairs.

"Jack?"

"I haven't showered, slept in my own bed or eaten in almost two days, Darcy. Can we talk in a little bit?"

"Of course," she said, following him up the stairs, but he noticed the dip in her voice. "You shower and rest. I'll make you some lunch, okay?"

Jack's usual self would have teased her about showering with him, but he was too exhausted to contemplate sex with her right now, and the realization frightened him. It was one of the most basic Roug urges: to hunt and to mate. With the suppression of one, need he fear the elimination of the other? He squeezed Darcy's hand tighter as he pushed his code into the keypad at the top of the stairs and pulled her through the door into the garage.

"Jack...?" she asked softly, her voice tentative. "You're so quiet. Are you okay?"

He glanced back at her as they neared the garage door, which he opened by pressing a button beside the stairs that led up to her study. Careful not to maintain eye contact for more than a moment, he nodded, watching the garage door rise slowly, allowing sunlight to flood the dim room.

"I'm just tired," he said, the need for a hot shower and sleep even bypassing his need for food. "We'll talk in a little while, okay?"

And then, because his disappointment and exhaustion and fear were so extreme, he dropped her hand and walked back to the house on his own without looking back.

DARCY STAYED ROOTED TO A spot under the risen garage door and watched Jack's body as he walked to the house and let himself inside. His gait was unfamiliar to her—lacking the confident stride he generally employed, he moved carefully, almost cautiously, like everything hurt. His hands hung limply by his side and his neck bent forward, as though weighted down.

Her heart twisted as she realized that his power of rejuvenation didn't seem to be kicking in. If anything, it almost seemed as though he'd been stripped of it.

Oh, God, what have I done? she thought, absentmindedly pressing the garage button and following him slowly to the house.

She took a quick inventory of his behavior.

The potion had suppressed the *Pleine Lune* shift, but it had obviously been incredibly painful for him to endure. He'd passed out, but still writhed in pain. And for the ensuing day and a half, he'd slept. But instead of appearing rejuvenated now, he seemed to be more exhausted than ever. Aside from the gentle, somewhat chaste kiss he'd given her, all he'd done was hold her hand. After three days apart, she'd have expected him to rip off her clothes and take her on the floor of the vault, or at least drag her up to his bedroom. But he'd released her hand and almost staggered to the house alone. And even more troubling, he wouldn't talk to her, either verbally or with his eyes—almost like he was avoiding her.

Her first words when he exited the vault had been "It worked!" but now she questioned that statement. *Had* it worked? At what price to Jack?

She looked down at her arm where goose bumps rose, despite the warm sun on her skin. What if—in her quest to suppress his change and convince him to turn her—she had somehow modified his body in some terrible, irreversible way? What if the potion had taken something away from him that she hadn't foreseen?

Closing the front door behind her, Darcy shucked off her shoes and stepped barefoot into the living room just as the shower turned on upstairs, the water running through pipes over her head. Her heart raced and her hands started to sweat as she recognized something that she'd been unable to fully comprehend through her tunnel vision of research and formulas: What if she'd hurt Jack in her blind ambition to convince him to turn her?

She swallowed uncomfortably, her hands shaking.

She was a scientist, and yet she'd made a very dangerous decision to administer the potion to him without figuring out another way to test it first. Her feelings for him, her desperation over their situation, was making her reckless, making her risk what she loved most of all in the world: Jack.

In a flash of consciousness, Darcy suddenly realized that for most of her adult life she'd held her own counsel and made her own decisions. As a result, she'd had few regrets and even less contention. But now, in the course of a few months, her inner GPS, her always reliable self-guidance, had been skewed.

Bracing her hands on the kitchen counter, she knew what she had to do. She flicked her eyes to a notepad on the counter under the phone and slid it in front of her, pulling a pen out from a drawer beneath the counter. She looked up at the ceiling, as if confirming that Jack would remain in the shower for some time, and because he was so incredibly exhausted, she was fairly certain he'd pass out in bed for a while before coming back downstairs.

She needed to take her fate into her own hands.

The note didn't take long to write, and she grabbed her purse and keys off the counter, slipping into her shoes and heading back out the front door before Jack could realize that she'd gone.

As she started her car, her heart flip-flopped desperately. They'd already been separated for three days, and she was about to add many more days to the tally. She brushed away tears as she stepped on the gas and rounded Jack's driveway, heading over the bridge and into the woods.

Somehow she knew in her soul that Jack would be even less apt to discuss turning her now that he'd endured the pain and privation of the potion, and if Darcy showed up in human form on Solstice, she'd be torn apart.

She was left with no other choice.

It was time to go north.

AN HOUR LATER, DARCY GLANCED over at Willow. They were a good forty miles away from Carlisle now, speeding farther and farther into Canada, and Willow had finally decided they were far enough away to call Amory.

"Hey, Brat," she said, smiling as Amory answered.

Darcy couldn't hear her brother's muffled answer, but Willow chuckled softly. "You too." She paused for a second, smiling at whatever Amory was saying.

"Hey," she said. "I can't make dinner tonight. No. Your sister wanted to head to Boston for a night. Mm-hm." She paused, shooting a grim glance at Darcy, but keeping her voice light. "Nope. Just a bunch of boring wedding stuff."

As Willow continued her conversation with Amory, Darcy realized how grateful she was to have Willow by her side. As though she'd known Darcy was coming, Willow had been standing in the open front doorway as Darcy pulled into the driveway, dark eyes serious and worried with her hands on her hips.

As Darcy strode toward the house, Willow had nodded. "It's time?"

Darcy lingered on the bottom porch step looking up at her best friend. "You're not going to stand in my way?"

Willow shook her head. "Would it do any good?"

"I'm going either way," Darcy had stated, ascending the porch steps and pushing past Willow to jog upstairs. She was packing a bag when she heard Willow's footfall in the hallway.

"I'm coming with you," she said softly from behind Darcy.

"I know. But I wish you wouldn't. Neither of us knows if you'll make it out alive."

"I will," Willow insisted, stepping forward to place a comforting palm on Darcy's back. "But you—"

Darcy swallowed the lump in her throat and turned from the duffel bag on her bed to face her friend. "The potion didn't work right."

Willow searched her face. "It didn't suppress the shift?"

"It did," said Darcy, sitting on the bed. "But it was...horrible. He was in terrible pain. Writhing, screaming in anguish for over twelve hours. Vomiting until all that remained was bile. And when he left the vault this morning, he was so haggard, Will...so defeated and exhausted. I just—I can't—"

Willow sat down beside Darcy, reaching up to push her friend's head onto her shoulder. "We could work on it."

"Not in time," sobbed Darcy. "Solstice is in three weeks. And anyway, I couldn't make him—I wouldn't ever ask him to go through that again. Not when...."

"Not when what?" asked Willow.

Darcy lifted her head, her eyes seizing Willow's. "Not when there are other alternatives."

Willow sighed, standing up and shaking her head. "They'll kill you, Darcy. If you show up as his bound mate and try to reason with them, they'll kill you."

"That's not the alternative I'm talking about," said Darcy, shoving her toiletry bag into the duffel and zipping it closed.

"What if you can't find someone to turn you?" Willow whispered.

Darcy hefted the bag on her shoulder. "His mother will do it. His mother will want to save his life, and if turning me will save it, she'll do it."

Willow's eyes, usually so steady, swam with sudden tears. "There's nothing I can say? To talk you out of it? Jack's strong. Even if there is an Inquisition, he would survive it—"

"You don't know that."

"What if you don't survive the turning?" demanded Willow in a desperate shriek.

It surprised Darcy that the small smile she had offered Willow came so easily. "Then I'll know I died trying to save him."

Willow took a deep, ragged breath, and then reached up to swipe at her eyes. "Give me ten minutes to pack and change."

"I don't have ten minutes," Darcy had said, heading to the stairs. "I'll give you five."

"Well," said Willow, ending her call with Amory and turning to Darcy. "Amory bought it. He said to have fun and be safe and he'd see us on Sunday."

Darcy nodded then turned back to the road, switching highways to follow the signs for Quebec.

JACK HAD BARELY MADE IT to his bed after his hot, soothing shower, and when he woke up, the first thing he noticed was that the house was quiet. Completely quiet.

No hum of activity downstairs or the faint sound of the TV. He took a deep breath and sat up in bed, his lips tilting up when he realized that he'd been lying on top of his comforter completely naked for the past six hours. His body still ached, but not as fiercely as before. Flexing his fingers in front of him, he let his claws extend, relieved that they didn't strain with leftover pain. Spearing the leg of his jeans on the floor, he retracted the claws and stood up, pulling on the pants and stretching.

"I need another ten hours of sleep," he muttered, but he had to acknowledge that the sleep he'd never needed before was proving to be the antidote to the exhaustion of the suppressor. His stomach growled and he crossed his room to take a t-shirt out of his dresser, breathing deeply through his nose. Darcy wasn't in the house. She was probably in her study over the garage.

Pushing aside the curtains as he shrugged into his shirt, he looked across the driveway, surprised to see the garage completely dark. Accustomed to seeing her red head bent over books, he furrowed his brows to find her office unoccupied. Only then did he realize her car was missing too.

He couldn't explain why this made the hairs on the back of his neck stand up, but they did, and he surged through the door of his room and down the stairs, his heart beating faster as he realized the house was dim and cool, as though it had lain empty for hours. Flicking on the light in the kitchen, he remembered what she'd said about fixing him something to eat, and a quick sniff told him she hadn't.

Out of the corner of his eye, he noticed a note on the counter, and grabbed at it as his heart raced and his breathing hitched.

> *Dear Jack,*
>
> *I was wrong. It didn't work. Seeing you in that kind of pain was unbearable.*
>
> *I knew weeks ago that you weren't going to turn me. I could see it in your eyes, feel it in your heart, in the way you touched me, in the way you love me.*
>
> *But, we've run out of options now.*
>
> *Please don't follow me.*
>
> *I love you more than life.*
>
> *Darcy*

He tried to take a deep breath but he couldn't, and his claws emerged, tearing the slip of paper to shreds as his eyes burned gold.

"Oh, my God," he murmured, swallowing slowly, his eyes darting up to the clock to reconfirm what he already knew. She had a six-hour head start on him. There was no way to get to her in time.

"IT'S TIME TO CALL HER," said Darcy, pulling into a gas station and looking at Willow. "I don't even know where to go from here."

"But you know we're close?" confirmed Willow.

Darcy nodded. From everything she'd learned from Jack, she knew that she was within thirty minutes of his pack's Bloodlands. She just wasn't sure how to get there from here.

"You have his mother's phone number?"

Darcy picked up her phone from the console, swiped at the screen and the name "Tallis" came up. "I took it off his phone last week. I don't know why. I have Julien and Lela's numbers too."

"Maybe you should call Julien," suggested Willow, staring out the rain-spattered windshield at the dying light of late afternoon. "At least you know him."

Darcy shook her head. "Julien might try to talk me out of it. Tallis won't. I know it. She'll come and get me, and she'll turn me. And that's what I want, so…" Darcy hit Send and listened as the phone rang once, twice—"*Oui?*"

"Madame? Ms. Beauloup?"

"Yes." Her voice was low and smooth, her accent thick.

"This is—"

"I know who you are. My son is half mad with worry."

Darcy's heart clenched, but she forced herself to ignore it. "I need to speak with you. Urgently."

"Where are you?"

"A gas station. At Stoneham-et-Tewkesbury."

"You're close." She sounded a little surprised.

"Can you give me directions and I'll come straight to you?"

She heard Jack's mother mutter something in French that sounded very much like "imbecile."

"It's not a good idea for you to come here."

"But I need—"

"I will come to you. Go north on 73 until the highway ends. It will turn into Route 175. Go another thirty minutes and you'll see a weigh station at Sainte-Brigitte-de-Laval. I'll meet you there." The line went dead.

Darcy sucked in her first breath since dialing the phone and turned to Willow. "She's meeting us. Thirty minutes up the road."

"And Jack?" asked Willow.

Darcy swallowed. "Beside himself."

JACK SLAMMED HIS FOOT ON the gas, but he still had hours to go. As a precautionary measure, he called his mother as he was leaving Carlisle, but Tallis had no information about Darcy. She hadn't been in contact, nor had she—as far as Tallis knew—made it to Portes de l'Enfer yet. He tried calling Julien and Lela too, but neither picked up the call.

The biggest problem was that Jack wasn't actually sure of what Darcy was going to do…was she going to walk into the Bloodlands and introduce herself as Jack's bound mate? Try to convince the Council to leave them alone? The very thought made rivulets of sweat slide down his face. The next time he saw her, she'd be dead.

His mother had promised to try to protect her if she showed up, but Jack knew that was a dim hope, at best. Tallis was respected as a Council member, but even with Tombeur as backup, Darcy wouldn't have a chance.

"Shit, shit, *shit!*" He banged on the wheel, clenching his jaw as he came up on the international checkpoint. He rifled through the glove box for his Canadian passport, showing it to the Canadian police, who looked at it lazily before waving him through.

You should have turned her, said a voice in his head. *You know that's what she wanted. You should have just done it and taken your chances with the binding.*

Shaking his head as he zoomed north, Jack searched his heart but still couldn't find a quorum that would have supported turning Darcy. He had unwittingly drawn her into this life. He had stolen any chance of the happiness she could have found with one of her own kind. He had placed her in danger the moment he reemerged in her life.

But through it all, he'd loved her, planned for her, living his life in one trajectory, with one goal: to have a life with her eventually. And now, when it had seemed so close, he felt it slipping through his fingers.

DARCY PULLED INTO THE SMALL vacant weigh station at Sainte-Brigitte-de-Laval, noting only one other car in the parking lot parked two spaces away from hers. She reached for her door handle, but Willow grabbed her hand quickly, and Darcy turned to face her.

"Listen," said Willow. "Stay behind me a little. They won't hurt me."

"This is Jack's mother," explained Darcy gently. "She won't hurt me either."

"No matter what happens, kid," said Willow, her eyes clear but infinitely grieved. "I will be with you."

Darcy nodded, feeling her courage slipping a little.

"It's going to be okay, right?" she asked Willow.

Willow swallowed, but nodded. "I hope so."

Darcy squeezed Willow's hand before getting out of the car. The driver and passenger doors of the other car opened as well, and two figures emerged.

"Ms. Beauloup?" asked Darcy, standing against the door of her car.

"Tallis," said a woman's voice, her stride sure as she stepped around her car toward Darcy.

Darcy couldn't help offering a smile to the striking woman who she'd know for Jack's mother immediately. With her tall, strong, trim figure, spare movements and black hair cascading in waves around her shoulders, Tallis Beauloup was every bit the fierce "warrior" that Jack had described to Darcy, and so beautiful it was evident that Jack got all of his looks from her.

"I—I'd know you anywhere," said Darcy softly.

Tallis took a deep breath through her nose, her eyes registering a bit of surprise before her lips tilted up in a very slight smirk. "I smell my son on you."

Darcy's cheeks flushed with fear and she turned her eyes to a man, standing slightly behind Tallis, to her left. "You must be Tombeur."

"I am," he said, a soft twang in his lightly accented English. He leaned forward and held out his hand. "And you're Darcy…from the Southern Bloodlands."

She nodded, taking his hand. She registered the heat he threw off his body, but she'd long past accustomed herself to Jack's heat, so she didn't flinch. His hand was warm and solid, and for a moment her longing for Jack tripled in intensity. She hushed it. It would do her no favors to be weak now.

"You've brought the *Enchanteresse*," remarked Tallis, looking at Willow, who stood next to Darcy against the car.

"*Enchante*," offered Willow, extending her hand.

Tallis grimaced, her nostrils flaring slightly, before taking Willow's hand. "*Saule*."

"That's what Julien calls me," said Willow.

"*Je sais*," answered Tallis, her eyes smoldering slightly as she stared at

Willow.

"Actually, he calls you *Belle Saule*," corrected Tombeur, taking Willow's hand from Tallis gently but firmly, and offering her a small grin. "It gets Lela all riled."

Willow smiled at Tombeur, and Darcy realized how charming he was, how grateful she was not to be meeting the intimidating Tallis alone. She gave him a genuine smile before turning back to Tallis, whose eyes narrowed.

"Save your smiles," she said, her voice almost edging into a scowl. "What do you want?"

Darcy took a deep breath and sighed, holding Tallis's eyes with a certain and steady gaze. "I've come to ask you to turn me."

Chapter 6

"WHAT?" DEMANDED TALLIS, HER FACE a mix of confusion and shock as she stared back at Darcy. She shot a brief, stunned look to Tombeur then Willow, before looking back at her son's mate.

Darcy tried to keep her voice level. "Solstice. Th—the re-binding is in twenty days. If I show up in human form—"

"*Impossible!*" exclaimed Tallis.

"Impossible, I know. But if Jack shows up alone—"

"*Une enquête judiciaire.*"

"Yes," murmured Darcy. "An Inquisition."

"But, if you're turned—your binding—"

"I know," said Darcy, her heart beating faster as she heard the hope in Tallis's voice. For the first time, she realized that though she'd told Willow she was convinced of Tallis's complicity, she wasn't certain until this very moment. Part of her must have wondered if Tallis would send her away, tell her to go home...but she heard the change in Jack's mother's voice. The slight warmth, the tentative hope. "I know I risk the binding. But Jack will live. Either way."

Tallis reached out her hand without a word and pressed it against Darcy's chest, holding it still over Darcy's heart.

"Your heartbeat is strong."

Willow spoke up for the first time. "You think she'll survive it?"

Tombeur stepped forward, pushing Tallis's hand to the side, and pressing his own against Darcy's chest, staring down at the ground in thought before lifting his eyes and nodding. "She has a better chance than most."

"*Pourquoi?*" asked Willow.

"Because," said Tallis, removing Tombeur's hand and lacing it within her own. "Because her body can withstand the heat better than most humans. You can Eyespeak, yes?"

Darcy nodded.

"You know *Dansmatête?*"

Darcy nodded again.

Tallis turned to Willow. "Because she knows some of our ways. The turn will be a shock to her body, but not her mind. She won't be as frightened. The chance of a heart attack is less likely."

Darcy swallowed, her heart racing as she understood their full meaning. "You're saying most humans have a heart attack before they've completely turned."

Tallis nodded slowly. "*Oui.*"

Tombeur gave Darcy a half-smile, half-grimace. "You asked Jack to turn you, didn't you?"

"Yes," said Darcy.

"He knew," said Tombeur. "He knew the chances of you making it were good, but not guaranteed. But mostly, I imagine he feared—"

"Breaking the binding," whispered Darcy.

"We can't tell what will happen," said Tombeur sadly. "Good chance you'll lose it."

"But, there won't be an Inquisition, and I won't be killed. I can be the turned Roug he was bound to when she was a human. Right?"

Tombeur took a deep breath and nodded. "They still won't like it, but yes, theoretically if we explain everything, both you and Jack should remain unharmed."

"He worked all his life to honor your binding," said Tallis, her eyes welling with tears. "All he ever wanted... was you."

Tears slipped over the well of Darcy's eyes and she let them roll down her cheeks without swiping them away. "Then don't you see why I must do this? *This* will honor our binding. I want his love. But I *need* his life."

Tallis reached for Darcy's arm, turning it over, eyeing the blue veins that coursed up her arm. "There can be no turning back."

Willow grabbed Darcy's arm back and took her shoulders, turning her so that they faced each other. "You're sure? God, Darcy, you're sure?"

She pulled Willow against her body and clasped her tightly. "I'm sure."

Darcy released Willow and turned back to Tallis, gesturing to the parking lot. "Are you just going to do it here?"

"Yes. And then we'll put you in the back of the car and take you to..." She glanced up at Tombeur. "Tombeur's cabin. It's in the woods, while mine is in a settlement. You'll need space to turn."

Suddenly Tombeur grabbed Tallis's arm and pulled her away from Darcy and Willow. For several long seconds, they appeared to be having a fairly bitter quarrel. When they stepped back toward Darcy, Tombeur stared at her, but it was Tallis who appeared to have won the argument.

"Are you ready?" she asked.

Willow blurted out, "I'm coming with her!"

Tombeur flicked his glance to her. "No need."

"Don't tell me what to do."

"Tallis and I will take care of her."

"I'm coming. You can't stop me."

"Well, I could, but I imagine you might get feisty about it." Tombeur shook his head, looking at her with respect. "It's going to be ugly."

"Which is why I want to be there. Maybe I can help."

Tallis's phone buzzed persistently in her pocket, but she never looked away from Darcy's eyes. She asked again, "Are you ready?"

"Yes."

"Then say so."

"I, Darcy Turner, bound mate to Jacques Beauloup, human from the Southern Bloodlands, asked to be turned."

"So be it," said Tallis, reaching for her arm.

Darcy closed her eyes, concentrating on an image of Jack's face, feeling his phantom arms encircle her as she tried to steady the fierce beating of her heart, assuring herself that there was no other way. But suddenly Tallis's fingers were wrenched from her arm, and stronger, larger fingers clamped around her skin. Her eyes flew open as she felt the unworldly, agonizing pain of Tombeur's fangs sinking into her arm.

"*Tombeur!*" shrieked Tallis from where she was sprawled out on the concrete. "NON!"

Like the rest of the world moved in slow motion, Darcy stared down at the dark, wavy head of hair bent over her arm, the way her blood dripped in two strong streams from his lips to the ground. The initial sharpness at the site of the bite subsided and she started to feel dizzy, light-headed, even, as the pain changed course. It sluiced through her veins like white-hot lightning, electrifying her, burning her from the inside out.

She felt the shock of darkness coming and turned her desperate eyes to Willow, who stood, fixed and loyal, beside her.

It's okay, she mouthed, tears sliding down in her face.

Darcy's eyes rolled back in her head and images of Jack suddenly filled her dying consciousness: a dark-haired boy sitting alone at a table in the library, a teenager kissing her on a high school stage, a grown man eclipsing the sun at her cousin's wedding, in the woods, in bed by the fire in her heart, in her soul—

A gnawing ache, so hungry and brutal, it bypassed everything Darcy felt happening in her bones and her blood, started in the innermost reaches of her heart and swirled outward like a tornado destroying everything in its path. Her throat couldn't swallow. Her lungs couldn't breathe. Her knees gave out and strong arms—*the wrong arms. The right arms?*—caught her as the ache grew stronger and more unbearable until it broke in a massive explosion, covering her body in waves of unimaginable pain.

Darkness.

JACK HAD BEEN IN CANADA for one hour when he felt the first tremor zap through his body, preceding his own personal earthquake. His hands went lax on the steering wheel and his car swerved off the road into a ditch flooded with rainwater. His muscles convulsed in pain and fury, and Jack desperately tried to catch his breath, but it felt like someone had reached into his chest and pulled out his heart.

His eyes rolled back in his head.

Darkness.

SNIPPETS OF CONVERSATION, GARBLED AND dissonant, as though under water, surrounded her.

…should have let me!…knew why I had to…Leave her with the Enchanteresse…Darcy? Darcy?…elderflower and thyme…will never forgive you…

Her body felt heavy and hot then freezing cold and shivering. Her skin itched and burned and her jaw and fingertips ached like they'd been cut open and left bleeding and seeping. Her heart beat so fast, it was like a drum in her ears, and visions of her mother and Amory, her father and Willow scuttled through her head. And someone else. Someone else, but who? She couldn't see him. His was a murky, undefined face from long ago, fading like chalk drawings in the rain.

She was forgetting something, losing something—something important that she couldn't—

A blast of intense heat and pain ripped through her and her body started convulsing as she lost consciousness again.

WHEN JACK'S EYES OPENED TO the dim dawn light, he jolted upright in his seat with a start, which he instantly regretted. His head throbbed almost worse than his chest, pounding with a steady and debilitating rhythm that made his breath catch. He'd never experienced anything like it before in his life, and his body had experienced the gamut of pain and deprivation during his years preparing for service on the Council Enforcement.

Pushing open his car door, he gulped in deep breaths of the cold, fresh air, trying to orientate himself. His car was on an angle, the right front wheel still on the pavement of the breakdown lane while the two back tires were mired in mud. Twisting his body, he stepped from the car, his boots sinking into the wet sludge. He looked back and forth along the quiet highway, feeling disoriented, trying to remember what had happened before he drove off the road.

Driving north. Sudden pain. Darkness.

In his heart, Jack knew—in a moment—what it meant. He could feel it in the way his blood burned his veins, in the way his heart throbbed and head ached in protest, but after twenty years of feeling her every minute of every day, he refused to admit that she was gone. Bracing his hands on the top of his car, he leaned his forehead onto the metal roof and closed his eyes.

Hundreds of times he'd pulled Darcy inside. All he had to do was zero in on the feeling of her in his gut, in his blood, in his bones, and he'd feel the swirling start. He still felt her, and it was a comfort of sorts for that split second, that Darcy remained a part of Jack. He clenched his eyes tighter, desperately hoping for the lightning-fast shift that would instantly transform him into a black wolf. He listened, despairing and wretched with every second that passed, for her heartbeat, loud and strong, like a beacon.

The swirling didn't start.

There was no transformation. No heartbeat. No beacon.

Tears of anguish coursed down his face as, with a keening cry, he faced the truth.

He still felt her inside, but she wasn't there anymore.

They were unbound. Which meant that Darcy had been turned.

Sobbing with agony and a deep, hollow misery, Jack swung his body back into the car, turned the key in the ignition, and slammed his foot to the gas. Feelings of worry, pain, desolation, and fury fought for dominion, but one thought silenced them, pushing Jack onward with a searing single-mindedness: she *belonged* to him.

He wouldn't let her go.

WHATEVER IT WAS, IT TASTED good and right and *Oh, God*, it soothed the cramping and twisting in her belly. Warm, metallic juice sloshed out the sides of her mouth, dripping onto her feverish skin as she leaned forward to drink more.

"Go slow," she heard a masculine voice warn, its deep rumble tightening every muscle in her body, forcing her to slow her pace, to obey.

"Mmm," she moaned, barely able to open her eyes, her fingers curling into the sheets beneath her hands. She tried to reach up but realized her wrists were bound to the bed, prohibiting movement.

She moaned, but it sounded like a growl in her ears, animalistic and yearning, and the bowl pressed to her lips was tilted back farther, allowing more thick, warm liquid to fill her mouth and run down her throat.

"She's taking it better than most," commented the deep voice. "She's lucky to have you."

A familiar voice answered near her head, "We worked weeks on that potion. I never thought I'd be using it to help ease her…transition."

Willow. Willow was here. But where was…*here*? And what was happening to her? She ached everywhere, her body itched and burned like fire, and her fingers and jaw were in agony. Nothing helped except the juice. She needed more juice.

"M-M-More," gasped Darcy as she felt the bowl being pulled away.

The deep voice chuckled and Darcy's insides clenched with longing, darts of erotic yearning zinging through her body, making her skin tingle, making her nipples pucker and tighten, as though reaching toward his voice.

"Gimme a minute, *petite*."

"Is this…normal?" asked Willow.

"No. Normal is hunting. Normal is eating a…well, a—"

Darcy couldn't hear the last word that he said. The bowl of warm liquid had been pressed back against her lips again. Her eyes rolled back in her head in bliss and the world scuttled away as the most visceral, most sensual, most important voice in the world commanded her to "Drink."

IT WAS ALMOST NOON BY the time Jack arrived in Portes de l'Enfer, but upon entering the small village, he drove straight to his mother's cabin, barely cutting the engine in his car before jumping out and striding to the front door. Over the past four hours, his shredded heart had wheezed and ached in protest of Darcy's loss; it seemed to know that while it still beat for her, hers had ceased beating for him several hours before. And yet, Jack wouldn't let himself believe that the binding—a twenty-year binding—could be broken so easily. It couldn't be true that he could have her love one day, only to lose it so completely the next.

And the horror of what she was experiencing made Jack clench his fists with frustration and sorrow. His only mission in life, for all of his life, had been to protect her. How had he not seen her single-mindedness about being turned? How had he failed to see that she would take matters into her own hands if he stood in her way?

He fisted his hand and banged on the door with all his might. His mother had done something utterly unforgivable. Without his permission, she had turned his mate, and he was here to settle accounts with her.

Raising his hand to knock again, the door whipped open and instead of connecting with the wood of the door, his fist connected with Lela's nose instead. She reeled back, stumbling into the rustic kitchen table behind her as her nose exploded in a shower of red and she gasped in outrage and pain.

"*Merde*, Jacques! What is the matter with you?" she demanded, covering her bleeding nose.

"Lela! Where's Darcy? Where's my mother?" When she didn't answer immediately, his gaze flicked to the hand covering her belly protectively. "Oh, God. I'm sorry."

"You punched your pregnant sister. Nice job, shithead." She turned her back to him and headed for the bathroom, returning a moment later with a washcloth pressed against her nose.

He stood in the doorway with his hands on his hips, smelling deeply. Neither his mother, nor Darcy, were at the cabin. Nor were they in the village.

"Where's Darcy?" he demanded, entering the cottage and closing the door behind him.

"How the fuck should I know?" asked Lela, sitting down in Tallis's rocker in front of the dark fireplace. "In Carlisle? At Dartmouth?"

Jack shook his head. "She's not. She came up here."

Lela leaned forward, eyebrows furrowing. "To Portes de l'Enfer?"

"Yeah. She…I think she…" The exhaustion and pain of the past three days suddenly came to a head and Jack stumbled as the room swam before him. He reached out to steady himself on the edge of the table.

Lela was up in a flash, her arms around his waist as she guided him to the other rocker by the fire. It smelled of Tombeur, and Jack let his eyes flutter closed.

"Jack, that's impossible," said Lela, squatting in front of him with her hands on his knees. "If Darcy came here as a human, without your protection…I mean…"

Jack bowed his head, his chin touching his chest, embarrassing tears flooding his eyes. He managed to speak, though his voice broke on the words. "She's not human anymore."

Lela gasped and a moment later she was on her knees looking up at him, her hands cupping his wet cheeks as she searched his eyes. "What happened?"

"Where's my mother?" he asked her.

"I—I don't know. She got a call and left right before dinner last night. I got up at three in the morning to go to the bathroom and she wasn't here. I assumed she was staying up at Tombeur's."

"She stays there a lot?"

Lela nodded. "It's…better that way."

Jack swiped at his eyes. It made sense for his mother to turn Darcy at Tombeur's cabin. It was remote, hidden in the woods. Tombeur's pack was wilder, more spread out, covering more territory than in Portes de L'Enfer, which functioned more as a centralized village. Turning a human to a Roux-ga-Roux was something best done in a controlled, remote environment, as far as possible from other humans.

He started to stand up, but Lela's hand on his thigh stopped him.

"Let me make you something to eat first. You look—Jack, you look terrible." She shook her head, her face etched with worry. "Why do you look like this?"

As he sat at his mother's table while Lela reheated last night's leftovers, he told Lela about how he'd refused to talk to Darcy about turning her, how she'd created a potion in an attempt to prove to him that she could be turned and live a "normal" life, how the shift suppressor had worked, but not in a way that made it a viable option for Darcy, how she'd left him when he was exhausted and weak, and how he'd lost consciousness and driven off the road en route to find her.

Lela's face fell when he told her that he couldn't reach Darcy through *Dansmatête* anymore.

"Tallis turned her," said Lela, lowering her hands to her stomach in understanding. "She'd do anything to protect you."

Jack nodded as the food in his stomach threatened to revolt. He took a long sip of water, grateful when it settled.

"When you find her...she won't know you," Lela murmured, shock and sorrow making her voice tremble.

Jack's lungs froze as she said the words, his breath catching until his chest ached and he finally expelled breath in a long, jagged stream. "No."

"But you still love her."

"Like I always have."

"Oh, Jack," she whispered, reaching for his hand across the table as she understood the hell on earth that her brother was experiencing. "I'm so sorry."

Jack looked up at his sister's eyes, but he felt none of the fury toward her that he was entitled to. Had she done this to him and Darcy? Yes. But, he couldn't hate her for it. Lela hadn't taken Darcy away from him. His mother had done that. He was saving his anger for her.

Pulling his hand away, he stood up. Even though he knew that Darcy was unbound to him, somewhere in his heart, he believed—as she had once—that their binding was stronger than her turning. He hoped, stupidly yet desperately, that she'd look into his eyes and their strong, strange, beloved bond would be restored.

"I have to get to Tombeur's."

Lela stood up and placed his bowl in the sink then crossed the small room, reaching for her jacket. "Assuming we're driving?"

"You're not coming," said Jack flatly.

"Fuck you, Jack. You're about to kick Tallis's ass, right? I've been waiting for this day my entire life."

Chapter 7

THE FIRST THING SHE HEARD was a hum.

It was loud and distracting, soon eclipsed by the sound of footfalls moving in a jittery, clicking motion very close by. Her eyes opened wide, taking in the bright afternoon sunlight streaming through the window, and she shifted her head toward the sound. On the wood-hewn wall next to her head she saw a fly making its way toward the ceiling, and each time it moved, Darcy heard another distinct footfall, *click click click*, and the hum of its buzzing wings. It finally launched itself off the wall, flew around the room in a fast circle, and through the open door.

Sitting up straight, she swung her legs over the bed and stretched her arms over her head, taking a deep breath. Instantly she wrinkled her nose, assaulted by smells that she catalogued quickly in her head: dust, wood, bacon grease. Sweat, human. Sweat, me.

Wait. Sweat, me.

Darcy slowly lowered her hands in front of her face, staring at the backs of her hands, at the fingers pointed up to the ceiling. Me.

The simple word circled in her head.

Me me me me me me.

She felt the burning in her eyes as her heart started beating faster, and she watched—partly in fascination and partly in horror—as sharp points broke through the skin of her fingertips and slowly rose, higher and higher, until ten bright white, foot-long claws pointed straight up at the ceiling.

She screamed, her hands shaking but her body motionless as she stared at the claws that had just protracted from her hands.

"Darcy?"

Willow's voice. Close. And then suddenly, there she was—Willow—standing in the doorway of the room.

"I have claws," Darcy murmured, flicking her glance to her friend then back to her hands.

"Calm down," said Willow gently. She looked as if she wanted to enter the room, and then checked out the claws again and stayed put. "You're still you, kid."

"I am definitely not still me." Darcy couldn't catch her breath as she still stared at the sharp, white, pristine claws. Experimentally she waggled her fingers, and they click-clacked against each other. It sounded vaguely familiar. Somewhere, in the very depths of her mind, she knew she'd heard the sound before, but she had no idea where or when.

"If I come in and sit next to you, will you keep those to yourself?"

Darcy nodded, slowly lowering her hands to her lap, the sharp points extending well beyond her knees.

"Oh, Willow, you stink," she blurted out as her friend sat down on the bed beside her. "What have you been doing?"

Willow wrinkled her nose, leaning down to sniff one arm, then the other. "I don't stink. I smell normal."

"Believe me, you do *not* smell normal. You smell like...what is that? Ammonia?"

"Ammonia? I don't smell like ammonia. But you?" Willow leaned a little closer to Darcy. "You don't even want to know what you smell like."

Darcy mimicked Willow's sniffing from a moment ago on herself. "I smell fine."

"You smell like wet dog and vomit."

"Do not," argued Darcy. "And even if I did, it would be an improvement on formaldehyde."

"So you're basically saying I smell like death," said Willow.

"Yeah," said Darcy with a little bit of wonder. "You do."

Willow nodded, chuckling lightly. "No wonder."

"No wonder what?"

"No wonder they don't eat *Enchanteresses*." Willow tilted her head to the side. "Want me to go sit on the other side of the room?"

Darcy shook her head. "I'll get used to it."

They sat in silence for several long minutes until Willow spoke again. "What do you remember?"

Darcy took a deep breath and sighed. "We left Carlisle and drove up here. We met a man and a woman at night. The man...oh—" She suddenly remembered in a flash—the man's fangs sinking into the flesh of her arm, the burning pain, the fever and chills. Turning over her arm, she looked at the underside, but there were no bite marks.

"They're gone," said Willow. "You rejuvenated."

"I'm a...a...Roux-ga-roux," said Darcy. "The—the creature...that your *Nohkom* told us about. Is that what I am?"

Willow nodded. "Are you scared?"

Am I scared? Darcy searched for fear in her body, but she didn't find any. She didn't feel frightened of anything. She couldn't actually imagine something that would scare her. Suddenly she pointed her claws at the ceiling and concentrated hard, and they slipped quickly and quietly back under her fingertips.

"No," she said, reveling in the words. "I'm not scared of anything."

"Okay," said Willow carefully. "That's good, I guess. Um, do you know where we are?"

"Yes," said Darcy. "Canada."

"And why did we come here?"

"We were looking for someone."

"Yes. Do you know who? Do you know why?"

Darcy searched her mind for the answers to these two questions, but it was as though the answers were shrouded in mist. She shook her head. "No. But I think it was important."

Willow nodded. "It was. It was very important to you."

"Did we find the person we were looking for?"

"We did."

"And I asked for this," she said, holding up her hands again and watching as the tips broke the skin, the claws shooting out of her fingertips like white lightning.

Willow shifted away slightly. "You did."

"Where is he?" asked Darcy, looking back and forth at the ten shiny claws, marveling at their newness and symmetry.

Willow's hand on Darcy's face was sudden and unexpected, and Darcy felt her eyes ignite like cold fire, like dry ice, like melted silver.

"Sorry!" said Willow, drawing back quickly.

"You just surprised me," said Darcy.

"I was excited...you remember him? You remember Jack?"

"Is that his name?"

Willow's brilliant, happy smile faded as she stared back at Darcy, searching her eyes, desperate for Darcy to answer her own question. "Darcy. Tell me you know who Jack is."

Jack. Darcy watched Willow's face, the stricken expression, the disbelief and desperation, and wondered who Jack was.

"Jack," she said, trying out the name, finding it wasn't unfamiliar to her lips, even though it carried no personal meaning.

"Should I know him?"

"Oh, kid," gasped Willow, standing up and crossing the room. She stood in the doorway with her back to Darcy.

"Jack?" She bit her lip, thinking hard, but her mind was a blank.

Willow's shoulders were shaking and Darcy concentrated again, watching her claws snap back with a satisfying swoosh, before standing up to place a soothing hand on her friend's shoulder. Willow turned around, distress covering her face as tears poured from both eyes.

"You know him, Darce. Concentrate really hard. Please. Concentrate on the past."

The past? Okay. Jack. Jack in the past. Something dinged in her head and she looked up at Willow.

"Wait! Yeah. I...I remember this kid, Jack, from high school. I had a crush on him, remember? He was a, um, a senior, I think? Right? Do you remember him? Is that who...?"

Willow's face was almost frozen, staring back at Darcy in utter and complete shock.

"Breathe, Will," said Darcy, and Willow gasped sharply, turning away from Darcy and walking into a small common room.

"Sit down," said Willow, gesturing to the loveseat in front of the fireplace.

Darcy looked around quickly—it looked like they were in a log cabin, small but comfortable, located in the woods. Through the windows she could only see trees, and the plethora of sounds she heard were all typical of a woodland.

"Where are we?"

"The Northern Bloodlands," said Willow. "In a cabin, owned by another Roug named Tombeur."

"Tombeur," said Darcy, trying out the name and loving the way it slipped across her tongue. "Where is he?"

"Hunting. He'll be back soon."

Darcy nodded, her stomach growling at the thought of fresh meat. She looked up at Willow for a moment, but her nose wrinkled and her hunger receded.

"Darcy," said Willow, her face still fraught and serious. "Jack from high school. Do you have any *recent* memories of him?"

Darcy thought about this for a moment. Something nagged at her—she sensed that something small and uncertain buried very deep in her head wanted a louder voice, but she simply couldn't hear it. She shook her head. "No."

"Oh, my God," gasped Willow, turning her head to the front door of the cabin as it suddenly burst open.

JACK STOOD FROZEN IN THE doorway of Tombeur's cabin, his eyes drawn effortlessly to Darcy, who sat on a loveseat, facing Willow, in front of the fireplace.

She was beautiful.

Strong and vital, he could hear her heartbeat, different from before, her blood coursing faster and hotter through her expanded veins.

Her smell was different too. It was still a derivative of her human smell, but deeper, muskier, infinitely sexier and more powerful. The bolt of white-hot desire he felt for her threatened to buckle his knees right there. He fought to catch his breath as she stared at him, her eyes, surprised by his sudden intrusion, burning greenish-silver, as he'd known they would, as he dreamed they would.

Darcy? Do you know me? he asked her, his own eyes scorching an unseen path across the room.

She stared back at him, her face blank. The silver burn of her eyes receded and she sat back in her seat.

"You're not Tombeur," she said, turning away from him.

Willow leapt up from her seat and crossed the room, placing a hand on Jack's forearm. "Kid, this is Jack."

Darcy turned her head and her eyes flicked to Willow's, then to Jack's, as her face registered a mild curiosity.

"You're Jack from high school?" She looked at him more closely then, her eyes caressing his forehead, his cheeks, his lips and eyes. He watched, holding his breath, as her face softened. "Oh, wow. It's you."

It's you.

Sagging with relief, Jack lurched from the doorway, stumbling across the room and falling to his knees before her. "Oh, baby, I'm so relieved.

I'm—"

He reached up to cup her cheeks with his hands, but she whipped back quickly, holding her hands up in the universal sign for "stop" and Jack watched, mesmerized, as her claws snapped out, pointing straight up at the ceiling in warning.

"Hey," she said, standing up and taking a sidestep away from him, her eyes confused and wary. "Nice to see you again and all, but…"

Still on his knees, Jack swallowed painfully.

It was true.

She didn't know him.

"Jacques, *mon fils!*"

Jack turned and looked back at the door, jumping up from the floor as his claws and fangs dropped.

"*WHAT DID YOU DO?*" he screamed at his mother, charging her.

He knocked into her as the hair burst out across his body, his clothes tearing and dropping to the ground like confetti as he shifted. She was thrown from the cabin by the strength of his blow. Groaning and growling at her, he swiped at her face, but she rolled to the side in time to avoid his blow.

"Jacques!" she screamed, trying to stand. "*Non!*"

Reaching down, he lifted her off the ground. He pulled back to throw her against a tree when she was grabbed from his arms and thick, sharp claws slashed into his back.

He snapped and howled in pain as he turned to find a fully shifted Tombeur standing before him, fangs frothy, claws extended in an invitation to fight.

Fight me instead, his eyes burned, holding onto Jack's.

My fight isn't with you, Jack grunted, looking behind Tombeur's back for his traitorous, despicable mother, and advancing on her, standing—still unshifted—behind Tombeur.

Tombeur slashed his claws down Jack's chest to get his attention. Jack roared as blood spurted, hot and sticky, into his fur. He looked back at Tombeur in confusion and growing fury.

Yes, he growled at Jack. *It is. Your fight is with me.*

Jack took a step closer to Tombeur, seizing his eyes. *You did this? You turned her?*

It was me, confirmed Tombeur. *Not your mother.*

Jack roared with anger and pain and agony for his lost binding, his rage white and fierce as he drew back his arms and swiped at Tombeur's chest with all his might, sending the older Roug flat on his back.

"NO!" screamed Darcy, breaking through the haze of Jack's rage. "NO!"

His body went limp at the sound of her scream and he watched, dumbfounded, as she quickly shifted, racing from the cabin. Punching and pushing at Jack's chest with the surprising strength of a newly turned Roug, she growled like a wild thing, forcing him away until she was shielding Tombeur with her body, standing in front of him, facing Jack.

Don't. Hurt. Him, she said, her trembling claws extended out toward Jack, her eyes a burning silver, staring at him as she would a monster.

Jack watched as Tombeur downshifted quickly into human form, standing up directly behind Darcy. As though he had no control over his own downshift, he felt the fur recede while his claws sank back into his fingers. He stared at her, disbelievingly, as she stood her ground, only shifting back to human once his own shift was complete. Though the world had suddenly been turned upside down, Jack was forced to acknowledge the truth: His recently unbound mate was protecting her maker from Jack, at the possible expense of her own life.

"Darcy," he said softly, his voice hitching with the pain of her unknowing betrayal. "Baby, please...."

"I'm not your baby," she said, lifting her chin. "I haven't seen you in twenty years."

From behind her, Tombeur stalked back into the cabin, and Tallis and Willow followed, leaving Jack and Darcy alone. Her eyes flicked to his hips and her cheeks colored.

Jack allowed himself a leisurely gaze up and down her naked form before capturing her eyes. "I know you think you don't know me, but—"

"That's right," she said. "I *don't* know you."

Jack scrambled to figure out something that would jog her memory, that would somehow tap into the tiny part of her heart that must—*must*—still belong to him. He reached for her, but she stepped back quickly. "We're—we were...bound to each other. You belonged to me and I—"

"No." She shook her head, looking away from him, back at the cabin where Tombeur waited for her.

"Please try to remember," he begged her, his eyes burning with despair, with human tears, with a deep, terrible dread such that Jack Beauloup had never known. "It's you."

She looked up at him again and her eyes burned bright, like molten silver, like burning magnesium, white and hot, stark and empty.

"I'm so sorry," she said softly, like she really meant it.

Then she turned and walked back into the cabin, closing the door behind her.

Chapter 8

Three weeks later

"TOM?" SHE ASKED, LOOKING UP at him with a grin. "Did I do that right?"

"Like a pro, Darcy," he answered, nodding proudly and smiling at her in a way that made muscles deep inside her body tighten with hope. "Best stalking I ever saw from a newbie."

He had no idea the impact his words had on her heart. It leaped joyfully at his praise.

For three weeks, Darcy Turner had been learning how to be a Roug. She'd also been falling in love with Tombeur Lesauvage.

He was her maker, her touchstone—a mentor, a best friend, a father figure, even, and yet, his body, so hard and toned and bronze, kept her awake at night, her eyes burning with jealousy as she heard the grunts and moans of his lovemaking with Tallis emanating from his adjacent bedroom. She wanted him fiercely, but uncertainly, like she didn't really have a right to him, but she couldn't help the deep longing that made her heart ache and eyes burn with every moment she spent with him.

"Always room for improvement, *petite*," added Tallis Beauloup dryly. She reached forward, taking the antlers in her hands and twisting effortlessly. The sound of a cracking neck rent the air and the buck's pathetic cries tapered off.

Darcy looked down at her claws, still deeply embedded in the jugular of the beast, and withdrew them, running her tongue up the side of one while she held Tallis's eyes provocatively. Tallis chuckled lightly and turned away from Darcy, rubbing against Tombeur as she passed him.

Darcy's eyes narrowed. The ever-present fly in Darcy's ointment, Tallis never gave her a moment alone with her maker. For three weeks Tallis had been there every time Darcy turned around. She said she was helping Tom to "mentor" Darcy, but Darcy felt certain that Tallis was keeping an eye on Darcy's increasing infatuation with Tombeur.

Either that, or she was keeping an eye on Darcy for her son, Jack.

Tombeur had followed Tallis in the direction of the cabin, leaving Darcy alone in the woods with her kill. She dropped her fangs, leaning down to let them sink into the hot, wet fur of the creature's neck and then sucking strongly. The blood ran in a gushing stream from the jugular artery into Darcy's mouth, and her eyes rolled back in her head with bliss. Of all the things she liked about being Roug—her increased sense of hearing and smell, the freedom of Roug running in the dark woods, night sight, rejuvenation, strength, and vigor—what she liked best was how she felt when a torrent of fresh blood flooded her mouth and poured down her throat in greedy gulps. It was like she could feel her body revitalizing with every swallow, invigorated with every lick. She imagined it was what an orgasm would feel like. Someday. With her bound mate. With Tombeur, if she had any say in the matter.

Sated, she stood up, sheathing her fangs and closing her eyes. She focused on Tallis and Tombeur, specks in the distance now, moving steadily away from Darcy with every step. Concentrating hard, she listened for their voices.

"She's in love with you," said Tallis.

"I have a responsibility to her and you know it."

"Yes. But, be careful you don't encourage her. Remember Jacques and Lela. These young Rougs are hotheaded."

"She knows you're my woman, Tallis."

"I still don't like it," came the sharp crack of Tallis's voice. "Her eyes burn for you."

"Well, *mine* burn for *you*." Tombeur paused. "Anyway, she's not mine."

"Nor am I," said Tallis.

"But you will be," said Tombeur, and Darcy heard the steel in his voice, the strength, any option for refusal eliminated by the searing certainty of his intent.

"Make certain she doesn't kiss you, *mon coeur*," warned Tallis. Darcy's eyes widened.

Why would it matter if I kissed Tombeur? she wondered, stepping around the carcass to follow behind them. Thus far, aside from assuring Darcy that she was once bound to Tallis's son and would be bound to him again one day, Tom hadn't really talked to her about bindings, except to tell her they were an almost-divine, unbreakable force.

Except in my case, she thought with annoyance, pushing Jack Beauloup's broken, desperate eyes from her mind. She knew very little about her forgotten binding to Jack—no one would tell her much about it, and when she asked, Tombeur and Tallis reprimanded her that she should concentrate her efforts and attentions on hunting and shifting. But Darcy saw the heavy, loaded looks they gave each other every time she asked about Jack. There was a story there, and they were keeping it from her.

Darcy leaned against a tree, deciding to give Tombeur and Tallis a few minutes before she returned. She stopped concentrating on their footfalls and voices; she didn't want another front-row seat to their passion.

Huffing softly, she furrowed her brows as she tuned into the sounds of the forest, thinking about Proctor Woods at home, about how much she'd like to return home someday to see her woods through her Roug eyes.

Darcy had explained to her mother and Amory that she was on a research expedition in Canada for the next couple of months as she lived with Tombeur, learning the ways of the Roux-ga-Roux. As a turned Roug who still had strong ties to and feelings for the human world, Darcy had opted not to "break the seal" between the blood of animals and the blood of humans, and decided that she would fuel her body with animal blood only. Tombeur had approved of this decision, and helped her learn how to hunt, warning her that her bloodlust for a human kill would need to be carefully managed during *Pleine Lune*. Ironically, he had also helped Jack Beauloup learn the same kind of control many years ago, so he was well positioned to help her. With *Pleine Lune* still a week away, Darcy was confident in her animal hunting skills now.

Tomorrow, Tombeur had informed her, something called a "Gathering" was taking place in the settlement where Tallis lived, and Darcy would be introduced to the packs of the Northern Bloodlands for the first time.

Make certain she doesn't kiss you.

As she picked her way through the woods slowly, Darcy wondered if there was any correlation between this Gathering and the kiss that Tallis so feared.

For no good reason, this made her mind turn to Tallis's son, Jack. She hadn't seen him since the day of her turning, but his handsome, worried face lingered in her mind, haunting her at odd moments. Stronger than his desperate words, his burning eyes had raked up and down Darcy's body like she belonged to him. The strength in his naked body had touched something inside of her, even though she tried to deny it.

Sometimes, when she overheard Tombeur and Tallis making love, Jack's face would unexpectedly dominate her mind as her fingers slid down her body, rubbing her secret valleys, trying to find relief, coming frustratingly close, but never quite able to pitch herself over the edge into bliss. Angry and confused by the way her brain would turn to Jack at such moments, she'd force his face from her mind and concentrate on Tombeur instead— his strength and speed and wisdom, the way he taught her and cared for her, and a different ache would begin, one that still couldn't be assuaged as she petted herself into an almost frantic frustration.

Approaching the cabin, Darcy tuned into the voices again, relieved to position them inside by the fireplace and not in the bedroom. She leaned quietly against the side of the cabin, listening to them talk.

"...another text from Willow," said Tallis. "She'll be here tomorrow morning. I told her she must leave well before sundown. Even an *Enchanteresse* won't be safe during a Gathering."

Willow is coming up tomorrow? Darcy self-consciously ran the back of her hand across her lips that still dripped with warm blood. She hadn't seen Willow since the day she turned, and desperately missed her friend. This was good news.

"Before Darcy comes back, I have to ask. How is he?"

Darcy held her breath as she listened for the answer.

"How do you think?" asked Tallis, her voice dark and soft.

"Bad."

"Very bad," confirmed Tallis.

"He understands, though? Why we did it? That she wanted it?"

"He understands, but he doesn't agree. He worshipped her. He would have gladly died for her. So it's a terrible blasphemy that we—"

"Is he angry with *you, chérie?*"

"No," said Tallis. "But he rages about you. Your...betrayal."

"I knew he'd want to kill whoever did it. Better me than you."

"You didn't think I could hold my own?"

"Tallis, you're strong, but he's full grown and male." Tom paused before asking, "Is he drinking?"

Darcy imagined Tallis nodding her head as she answered, "*Oui.* Too much."

"Shifting?"

"Often."

"Feeding?"

Tallis sighed. "*Des animaux.*"

"Good. Then he's still under control. He wouldn't forgive himself if he…"

"He wouldn't do that. He sees humans differently. And he still—he still believes that she belongs to him."

"Can you clean him up by tomorrow?"

"It won't be a problem. He wants to go to the Gathering. He hopes for it and fears it at once. He knows, in his heart, that it's the last chance."

"Will he force her?"

"*Non,*" said Tallis, her strong voice breaking. "He will not. He wants her to be willing. He wants her to…remember."

"And Willow is bringing the—"

"*Oui.* But there are no guarantees. It's an untested potion meant for humans, not us."

"She's a smart little *Enchanteresse.* My money's on her," said Tom.

"Oh, God, Tombeur, what if he loses her—what if—"

"Shhh. *Calme-toi, chérie.* It will happen. When they kiss, it will happen," Tom insisted. "Just like it will for us."

Darcy closed her eyes as she leaned back against the side of the cabin silently, a sudden image of Jack Beauloup's lips filling her mind. They descended with certainty toward hers in the darkness, an old smell of velvet suddenly filling her nostrils like a dead memory. Her fingers fluttered to her mouth and she kissed the tips, whimpering softly as bumps rose on her skin, making her eyes burn. A strange swirling started, like a vortex, in her belly, making her feel nauseous and wobbly, like she was physically being pulled somewhere, not just in her head, but her whole self.

What was this strangeness? she wondered, panic making her feel cold and confused.

Her eyes flew open and she pressed her palms against the rough logs of the cabin, pushing away with all her might, and dropping her fingers from her lips.

It's you, a phantom voice whispered, as she lurched forward.

Shaking her head to clear it, she focused on the tree line in front of the cabin, pulling away from whatever force had been drawing her…where? She took a deep breath as the swirling ebbed away and she looked down at the fingers that had just caressed her lips. This had happened one other time when she overheard Tallis and Tom talking about Jack, and Darcy didn't like it. It made her feel out of control, weak and unstable. She didn't understand it, and it frightened her.

Distracted by the sound of Tallis and Tombeur's farewells, she leaned back against the side of the cabin to listen.

"I'm leaving, *mon coeur*," said Tallis, and the soft sound of bodies clasped together followed. "I will see you tomorrow night."

"Tomorrow you'll be mine, Tallis. Forever."

"À demain, Tombeur. Je serez à toi, toujours."

"*Je t'aime, femme*," he whispered, his voice husky and emotional as he told his woman that he loved her.

"*Je t'aime aussi*," she replied softly, assuring him of the same.

Darcy's stomach flipped over and her fear ratcheted up a little higher. Her only focal point, her only source of comfort in this new world was Tombeur, and Darcy couldn't bear the thought of Tallis taking him away from her.

The door opened suddenly and Tallis exited the cabin, looking immediately to her right and spying Darcy.

"*Ecoute, petit*," she said, reaching forward with uncharacteristic tenderness to cup Darcy's cheek. "I won't see you again until...after."

"After what?"

"The Gathering," said Tallis.

Darcy shrugged, wishing Tallis would drop her hand and leave so that Darcy could finally have some time alone with Tom.

"I am grateful to you. I know you don't understand everything that's happened to you, but when you came to me, I was—it doesn't matter. Whatever happens...thank you, Darcy Lesauvage, turned not blooded." Tallis leaned forward and pressed her lips to Darcy's forehead, and then dropped her hand and walked the short distance to her car, looking back once to lock eyes with Tombeur, who stood in the doorway to the cabin.

Darcy watched her drive away, puzzling over her words and actions.

"I thought she didn't like me," said Darcy, turning to Tom, feeling her face and body soften as she took in the hard, masculine lines of his body behind a t-shirt and jeans.

"She doesn't," he said softly. "But she's still grateful."

"For what?"

"You don't remember," he said, turning back into the cabin. "But I guess it's time for me to tell you."

"About Jack Beauloup."

Tom nodded, sitting down in front of the cold fireplace and gesturing for her to sit across from him. His fiery brown eyes were tinged with moss but didn't burn as he gazed at her, and Darcy's fingers curled into themselves with frustration. She didn't want to hear about Jack. She wanted Tom.

"I don't want to hear about—"

His voice was hard. "I don't care. It's time."

Instantly chastised by the sharpness of her mentor's voice, she sat back in her chair and looked up at him through lashes lowered in submission. "Of course."

"Jack was your bound mate."

"So, I've heard, but—"

"Shut up and listen." He paused, clenching the muscle in his jaw as he stared at her. "I know you remember him from high school. You were in a play together. What you don't remember is that one night, he kissed you, and for the first time in the history of our race, a Roux-ga-Roux was bound to a human. This was no half-binding or imagining. This was a full, legitimate binding of one heart to another. Yours to his. His to yours. Forever."

Darcy looked down at her lap. It wasn't that she had any memory of her binding to Jack, but her body reacted to his words, leaning into them, her heart and belly fluttering as though on the precipice of something huge she didn't quite understand.

"Being with you, loving you…his longing for you put Jack in jeopardy. So he left you for twenty years, and he learned control. He loved you every moment you were apart. His only goal, the only purpose of his life, was to return to you." Tombeur breathed heavily, wincing before continuing. "He built a lodge on the Southern Bloodlands and found you three months ago. When you found out what he was, you were horrified. He left you again because you were frightened of him, but his half-sister Lela made matters worse. Convinced she was in love with Jack, she demanded a forced binding and when it didn't work, she demanded a *re*-binding."

"Between me and Jack."

Tombeur nodded. "But there was no way."

"No way?"

"No way a human could attend a Gathering, a re-binding. You'd be torn apart. But if you didn't attend—"

"Jack would be punished."

"*Oui.*"

It wasn't exactly a memory, but suddenly Darcy had a sharp sensation of *déjà vu* or intuition. She didn't remember driving to Portes d L'Enfer and asking to be turned from human to Roug, but she somehow knew it had happened. She had asked for this.

"I asked you to turn me...to save him."

Tombeur nodded once, holding her eyes. "Do you remember?"

"Not really," she said. "But I still know."

Tombeur tilted his head to the side. "Does anything I've been saying sound...familiar?"

Darcy shrugged. It was like hearing a fairy tale she hadn't heard since her childhood. It wasn't exactly familiar to the being she was now... it was like something from another time, another plane, through a fog; another person's memories, even, like a totally separate consciousness.

"I don't know," she said helplessly.

"At the Gathering...you will kiss him."

Her heart seized with panic and she exclaimed, "NO!"

"Yes," he said, narrowing his eyes at her. "I beg you."

She could imagine refusing him nothing but this. The thought of being separated from her maker, her mentor, the only comfort in an unfamiliar world—it was too unbearable. She appreciated that Jack had been part of her past, but she wanted Tombeur to headline her future.

"Tom," murmured Darcy, falling forward to her knees on the floor and crawling to the older man. She placed her hands on his knees, locking her eyes with his for a moment before flicking her glance to his lips. "Why can't I kiss *you*?"

Tombeur stared at her with sympathy, his eyes flat. "Because I love Tallis. Because I have always loved Tallis."

"If we were bound, you'd love me, wouldn't you?"

"Yes," he said simply. "But I believe that I am meant for her."

Darcy slid her palms up his thighs, slowly, gently, higher and higher. "You could be wrong."

"I'm not," he said, but she saw it in his eyes, the faint hint of heat, the tiny crackle of flame, that urged her to pursue him.

"If you're so sure," she said, leaning forward to brush her breasts against his knees, "what do you have to lose from kissing me? It won't work, right?"

He swallowed, staring at her, his eyes growing brighter as his glance darted to her lips. Her fingertips touched the hardness at the apex of his thighs with satisfaction—he was growing inside the tight denim of his jeans. She was affecting him.

"Tom," she gasped softly, leaning forward, her lips a breath away from his as she closed her eyes. "I don't want Jack. I want you."

"No!" he growled, placing his hands firmly on her shoulders and pushing her away, her arms swinging back just in time to brace her body from falling.

"Tom, please…" she whimpered, frustrated by his refusal, frightened by his anger, hurt by his rejection.

"Didn't you hear me? I *love* Tallis. Jack *loves* you. You—"

"Love no one!" she bellowed, jumping up from the floor to stand before him with her fists clenched by her sides. "And I won't be forced into a binding!"

"Darcy, you don't know our rules. Gatherings are the only times when a binding kiss *may* be forced. You're one of us now, which means if Jack compels you, you'll be required to comply…or fight."

"Then I'll fight," she vowed through clenched teeth. "You and Tallis—and even Willow—think he should mean something to me, but he doesn't. I *don't* know him. I *don't* love him."

Tombeur stood up, his gaze flat but searing as he looked deeply into her eyes. "You're lying."

"I'm not. I love *you*! I do!"

"Why are you fighting this so hard?" He tilted his head to the side, still searching her face. "You're frightened of the feelings that draw you to Jack. You don't understand them. Maybe you don't even want them. But I can see it in your eyes, Darcy. He *does* mean something to you."

"He won't force me," she sobbed in a broken voice, uncertain of where the words came from, or why they felt true.

Darcy's muscles went slack and she fell back into the chair behind her in defeat, tears flooding her eyes as her head and heart tangled in confusion. He was right. She couldn't deny this strange pull to Jack. But Jack was really and truly a stranger to her. She didn't want to be drawn to a stranger, and she certainly didn't want to be intimate with him. So much of her existence was strange now. She wanted familiarity. She wanted comfort. She wanted Tombeur.

His hand was heavy and warm on her shoulder, and made her heart twist with raw yearning for him.

"Maybe he won't," said Tombeur gently. "But consider what I've said… how much he loves you. He'd be a good mate to you, Darcy, I promise. Submit to him."

"I don't want—"

Tombeur continued undeterred. "Willow will be here tomorrow. She's bringing a serum."

Darcy's breath hitched, but she didn't move.

"Its purpose is to help you remember."

"I don't want to remember," she sobbed.

"Jack would do anything for you," he said quietly, withdrawing his hand. "Whether you know him or not…whether you want him or not… whether you love him or not…that's got to be worth something."

"How can it be worth anything when I *know* and *want* and *love*…you?"

He shook his head at her sadly and sighed, and then he turned away, heading for the door. Tears streamed down Darcy's face as he left her alone in the cabin, letting the wooden door slam softly shut behind him.

Chapter 9

JACK HAD CONSIDERED KILLING HIMSELF more than once over the last three weeks.

His life was an obscene, unique, custom-made torture, a stark and desperate hell with no light, no love, no hope, nothing to live for, except for the small possibility that Darcy might submit to a binding kiss that wouldn't even guarantee their re-binding.

His mother kept him well apprised of her progress—how she hunted with ease and skill, how she had embraced her Roug self and how closely she and Tombeur had bonded. Though Jack was still angry about Tombeur's decision to turn Darcy, he was grateful that Tombeur was proving to be a devoted mentor. If Jack separated Tombeur's betrayal from the equation, he knew that Darcy's training was in the best possible hands and she was learning from a master, just as Jack had so long ago.

But the bottom line was this: He missed her desperately.

For twenty years, her light had been his constant companion, infusing his body in every possible way. She was so much a part of him that even now, he couldn't help trying to pull her inside, every day, several times a day.

It had become an obsession, a compulsion—he would find the piece of her that still lived inside of him and focus on it with every drop of strength he possessed. He would torment himself with memories, feeling her hair run through his fingers, gazing at the green of her eyes, touching the cool softness of her skin beneath his palms. Closing his eyes, alone in the joyless sanctuary of the deep woods, he would try to pull her inside.

It was like trying to turn over a dead engine. He could lay his foot on the gas and turn the key in the ignition over and over again, but the engine wouldn't catch, wouldn't start, wouldn't engage. No matter what he did, he couldn't reach her. He poured all of his energy out, but it wasn't enough to pull her in, to touch the part of her that used to belong to him.

Every time he tried—hundreds of times over the past three long weeks—he would fail.

Until today.

This morning, with the Gathering bearing down on him tomorrow, his hopes and fears caught in a desperate struggle for dominion, he had leaned against a tree in the deep forest, closed his eyes and concentrated on their binding kiss. He remembered the eager welcome of her eyes, the touch of her lips beneath his, the way his heart had stopped beating and then started again. His emotions had hit a fever pitch as he reached for her with his mind, his claws dropping, his eyes burning, the hair under his skin prickling, his body expanding. The strangled, desperate growling sound of the words, *It's you,* clawed its way up from the depths of his being, filling his head so loudly that it ached and throbbed, reverberating with the first words he'd ever said to his mate. For just a millisecond—for the amount of time that the very tip of the sun breaches the horizon, he felt her. Not the memory of her inside of him, but *her.*

For that moment, it was like they were bound once again.

But as quickly as it had started, it stopped.

The swirling, the growling sound, the intense, visceral connection. Gone.

Jack had trembled against the tree, tears coursing down his rough face as his claws slowly retracted and his body shifted back to human form. When he opened his eyes, the forest was quiet and still, oblivious to what had just happened inside of him, in his consciousness, in his heart.

Of one thing he was certain: He had reached her. Only for a second, but he had connected with her. With the Gathering tomorrow looming like a curse, teasing him with hope, his heart had managed to connect with hers for a second, and it was enough to renew his strength.

Reaching for the omnipresent flask in his torn jeans, he had snapped open the top and poured the fiery liquid out onto the ground. He couldn't deny what he'd felt, and he knew that wherever she was, she had felt it too. But what did it mean?

Was it some remnant channel leftover from their binding? Was it a fluke? Or—his desperate heart wheezed with hope—was it possible that some small part of the binding was still intact?

Clutching his tattered clothes, he headed back to his mother's cabin, surprised to see Tallis pulling into the driveway. She'd been living with Tombeur since Darcy had been turned, only coming home for short periods of time to pick up clothes or check on Delphine. Family harmony was better maintained when Tallis and Lela had a good deal of space between them and Tallis had seemed anxious to assist Tombeur with Darcy's training.

"*Maman*," he greeted her. "*Très bien?*"

"*Oui*," she answered. "But with tomorrow's Gathering, I must be here for Council business."

"And Tombeur?" he asked, his voice tight.

"Excepted from reporting since he is mentoring a turned Roug."

"So they'll be alone. All night," he answered grimly.

Jack strode into the cabin, heading for the room he used to share with Julien and pulled on some fresh jeans. He grabbed his keys from on top of a dresser as he pulled a t-shirt off the floor.

"Jacques," said Tallis. "Where are you going?"

"I'm not leaving her completely alone with him." Tallis shook her head, her eyes pained. "She…"

"What?" he demanded, looking up at his mother.

"She still doesn't know you."

Jack swallowed painfully, his brief connection with Darcy from earlier suddenly feeling more tenuous. "She *does*…it's just buried deep inside of her."

Tallis shook her head. "I don't think so."

"I connected with her today. It was only for a moment, but I—"

"What do you mean?"

"*Dansmatête*. I reached her."

The flood of compassion in his mother's eyes made him feel small and young. "Oh, Jacques. I don't think so. I think it's like the body twitching after it dies. An electrical impulse, but nothing substantial. Nothing meaningful."

"It was *Dansmatête*." Jack drew a deep breath, desperately holding on to hope. "I *felt* her."

Tallis's eyes lingered in sympathy for just a moment before they hardened. "You're going to need to force her."

"I won't," he answered softly. "I can't."

"You must, Jacques. She thinks—" Tallis winced before steeling her jaw. "She thinks she's in love with Tombeur."

"No," he gasped, the pain to his heart almost leveling him to the ground. "Have they—?"

"*Non, mon fils. Non.* But I can see it in her eyes. She wants him." Tallis sighed. "It's not uncommon between a turned Roug and her mentor. It's happened before."

"I'm going to her. I need to talk to her. She has to know—"

"I wouldn't," Tallis said softly. "She doesn't know you. Tombeur said he would tell her your story today and Willow arrives tomorrow with a memory potion. But, son, you will have to force her tomorrow night. She will not come to you willingly. Not as she is now."

Jack, who was halfway across the room, standing by the door, turned on his mother. "*Force* her? Force her when I have made her life a nightmare? She was an innocent young girl when I kissed her. I stole twenty years of possible happiness with that kiss. She could never find fulfillment with another man. For her, *Dansmatête* was a mystery that made her wonder if she was insane for two decades. I reenter her life and she discovers she's bound to a monster. And now? Her destruction is complete. She *is* a monster...who craves blood, who hunts in the woods like an animal, who will have to battle the horror of her deepest, darkest desire at *Pleine Lune* every month for the rest of her life. I stole her light. I orphaned her. I destroyed her. Me. I did this to her. And now you would demand that I force her to submit to me when I have taken everything from her—her family, her home, her memories, her very being...her soul!"

"Jacques—"

"*Force her*? You must be mad," he spat, his eyes burning with fierce defiance of her words. "No! She will come to me willingly, or I will let her go."

"And live the rest of your life in this agony? This anguish?"

His eyes fixed on hers.

"Yes," he gasped, leaving his mother to the furious silence of the empty cabin.

DARCY DIDN'T KNOW HOW LONG Tombeur had been gone, but it was dark when she finally stood up from her chair, made herself a plate of dinner, and built a fire. No matter what time he came home, she needed to talk to him again. She needed to get through to him. He had to understand that while Jack may have been an important part of her past, she wasn't interested in a future with him.

Falling asleep by the fire an hour later, Darcy had vivid and troubling dreams. Fragments from her life with Jack entwined with the last three weeks she'd spent with Tombeur played in her mind, Jack's dark eyes effortlessly shifting to Tombeur's mossy-flecked brown, Jack's lips touching down on hers, Tombeur's palm heavy and comforting on her shoulder.

When the door opened and shut behind her softly, she woke up with a jerk, immediately aware that it wasn't Tombeur's scent in the room with her, but Jack Beauloup's.

She turned to find him standing against the door, his face dimly lit by firelight, staring at her.

"Darcy," he whispered, making no move toward her. His voice was reverent and gentle, and pinged in her head—familiar, and yet not.

"Where's Tom?" she asked.

Jack took a deep breath through his nose then looked back at her. "Not close."

"You shouldn't be here," she said softly, turning away from him, dismissing him.

He took a tentative step into the room and when she didn't stop him, he took another, and then another, until he was standing behind Tombeur's chair by the fire, across from her. He placed his hands on the back of the wooden rocker and tilted his head to the side.

"Can I ask you something?"

She shrugged. Tombeur had been gone for hours now. Was he coming back? Had she alienated herself from him by sharing her feelings, by throwing herself at him?

"Darcy. Today…earlier today," continued Jack, forcing her to concentrate on his words. "Did you experience something strange?"

Darcy raised her eyes to his, glancing at his mouth, the very lips that haunted her dreams, waking and sleeping. "Strange?"

"Like, being pulled into a dream?"

She had, of course, experienced something like that—against the side of Tombeur's cabin—and her fingers moved, of their own accord, to touch her lips.

"It's you," she murmured.

"Yes," said Jack. "It was me."

"How?"

Jack shook his head. "I don't know exactly."

"I know that..." She stopped, unable to hold his gaze, which was so searing, so desperate. She picked up an iron poker and knelt in front of the fire, rearranging the crackling logs. "I know that we were bound."

"Yes. We were."

Jack cleared his throat and stepped around the chair to sit down but made no move to reach for her or touch her, which was relieving.

"Tombeur said you loved me," she said.

"I love you right this minute, right now, more than ever," he whispered in a rush, and her traitorous heart leapt.

"But, truly..." she said, finally meeting his eyes. "I don't remember you."

"Nothing?"

Darcy thought about her dreams and shook her head, feeling frustrated and wishing she could cut bait with the past and sever whatever threads still bound her to the strange man sitting in front of her so she was free to follow her heart. But something about the way he looked at her made it impossible for her to lie to him out loud.

"Your face. I see it in my dreams. And your—" She placed the poker against the flagstone fireplace and pressed her fingers to her own lips, speaking in a whisper. "—lips. I feel them. I smell old velvet. I hear your voice. I don't know you, but...something inside of me does."

He exhaled strongly, licking his lips before pursing them together. "Will you let me kiss you tomorrow? At the Gathering?"

Panic sluiced through her veins like ice water and she shook her head quickly, sitting back in her chair and leaning away from him. "No."

"You dream of me. Some part of you is holding on to me. Why won't you give me a chance? Give *us* a chance, Darcy? Please, baby...."

His voice had grown stronger and more desperate, making her heart throb with fear and confusion.

"Because I don't *want* you," she snapped at him.

"Some part of you does."

"But more of me wants Tom."

"He's binding himself to my mother," Jack growled between clenched teeth.

"Not if I kiss him first," gasped Darcy.

Jack roared his disapproval and suddenly he knelt on the floor before her as she had knelt in front of Tombeur hours before. He reached for her face, palming her cheeks firmly but gently, and taking advantage of her shock to force her to look at him.

"Look at me!"

Her surprise wore off quickly and she struggled to release her face from his grip, but he was much stronger than she. To release herself she'd have to shift, but Tombeur had been teaching her to control her emotional shifts, and she evened out her breathing, sheathing her claws and staring into Jack Beauloup's furious eyes.

"I will not force you," he vowed. "But I love you more than my own life. I will belong to you until the day I die. And I am *begging* you to give us another chance."

Moved by his words, her jaw went slack, her lips parting as she flicked her eyes to his mouth then back to his eyes. Something in them was familiar, heartbreaking even, and her own heart throbbed and ached, as though in grief or with longing, even as her brain couldn't conjure a single strong memory of her time with him. Hot tears escaped from her eyes and rolled down her cheeks as she stared back at him, feeling helpless, confused, and frightened.

"*Please* go," she sobbed.

His breath caught as his thumbs gently stroked her cheeks, wiping away her tears. The deep sadness in his eyes was so profound, she thought she'd drown in it before he bent his neck and dropped his hands. A moment later the sound of the front door slamming reverberated through the small room.

"DARCY? HEY, KID, WAKE UP."
Willow's voice invaded the tumult of her dreams, a welcome reprieve from reliving Jack Beauloup's intense, immense sorrow.

"Willow?" she said, focusing on her friend's dark eyes in front of her. Just as Jack had knelt before her last night, Willow took his place now, her hands on Darcy's knees and her expression worried.

"Did you sleep in this chair all night?"

Darcy looked around the small room. The fire had burned out hours ago and thready morning light streamed through the windows. "I was waiting for Tom to come home. And then Jack..."

"Jack?"

"It felt like a dream, but I know he was here."

"Did you talk to him?"

"He mostly talked," said Darcy miserably. "He speaks to me like he knows me, like he loves me..." She sighed heavily. "And sometimes I feel like I know him. Like from another life. Like a *déjà vu*. But nothing solid, nothing real. He wants to kiss me, and I can't imagine just kissing a stranger, let alone kissing him and suddenly being bound to him for life. I can't. It's too..."

"Scary," said Willow, slipping onto Tombeur's chair, where she perched on the edge.

Darcy winced at her friend. "It took you a lifetime to let Amory into your life, into your heart. I'm supposed to let a total stranger kiss me? Sleep with me? Have sex with me? I'm supposed to have his children? Spend my life with him when I don't know him at all? How am I supposed to do that?"

Willow tilted her head to the side, biting her lower lip. "Do you remember anything about Lela and Julien's binding?"

Darcy searched her mind, forcing it to delve deeply, making it ache as a hazy memory surfaced. No solid images, per se, but she suddenly had a cold and overwhelmed feeling that slipped away quickly.

She shook her head. "Not really. When you said their names just now, I felt...something cold and elusive. But I can't hold onto it. I don't—"

"It's okay," said Willow. "You know who they are?"

Darcy nodded.

"Lela thought she was destined for Jack. She was sure of it. So sure, in fact, when you weren't present at the last Gathering beside Jack, she demanded a re-binding."

"Tom told me a little about this. And I know the Gathering is tonight and Jack wants—"

Willow held her hand up and continued. "Don't worry about that right now. Just listen. Lela, she was so sure that she was destined for Jack, even when Julien had her pinned against a wall in Jack's house—"

"Pinned against a wall?"

Willow nodded. "Yes. Even then, she stared at Jack desperately. She could see that he was bound to you, and yet she wanted him so badly, her desire almost made her miss what was right in front of her."

Darcy raised her eyebrows.

"Julien," said Willow. "Julien loved her. He asked if he could kiss her, and she was so sad, so alone, she submitted."

"Then what happened?" murmured Darcy, drawn into Willow's story.

"It was crazy intense. One second they were two separate beings, then next, they *belonged* to each other. If I didn't hate her so much, it would have been fucking beautiful."

A chill went down Darcy's spine as she looked at Willow. "Why did she submit?"

"Because she couldn't have who she thought she wanted. She had nothing to lose."

Tombeur's strong body and kind eyes flashed through her head. "Well, I'm not out of options. I want to be with—"

"Tombeur doesn't love you like that. Never has. Never will." Willow shook her head with finality, her eyes sorry. "Jack, on the other hand, has loved you like that since the first moment he ever saw you."

"In the library," whispered Darcy.

"Yes," Willow nodded. "In the library."

Darcy took a deep breath, remembering her fifteen-year-old self leaving social studies with two friends and heading to the library for study hall. The only reason she had a clear memory of that day was because she'd walked into the large room talking and laughing, only to be blinded by the sun from a skylight shining directly in her eyes. As a cloud passed over the sun, she'd looked straight ahead, into the dark eyes of a new student who sat, intense and alone, across the room.

In all her life, she'd never seen anything as beautiful as Jack staring back at her. He'd gazed at her fiercely, his beautiful face chiseled and stunned as he stopped her heart with his eyes. She'd been pulled over to a table by her girlfriend and lost contact with him, but she felt the heat of his eyes on her back long after she'd sat down. She knew he was watching her, and it had been the single most exciting day of her life as her blood raced hot and electric through her veins. She'd captured the notice of the most beautiful boy she'd ever seen, and after that, she'd been obsessed with Jack Beauloup.

Except that it hadn't led to anything.

They'd been in a play together. He'd mostly ignored her and then he'd moved away, never to be seen or heard from again. So, how was it, over twenty years later, that Darcy Turner was expected to feel something real for him?

And yet.

She knew that their story hadn't ended that day in the library. She knew that there was more to it, because what her brain couldn't remember, her heart wouldn't forget. Did she love him? Of course not. Was there more to the story? Yes. In her heart, she knew that what Jack, Tombeur, Tallis, and Willow insisted was true—she and Jack had history. The question was, did Darcy want to resume that history or start over again? Surely there was bad with the good—if she could remember it, would she choose it? Would she choose Jack or would she choose a fresh slate?

"How do I know I want that life?" Darcy asked her friend as tears flooded her eyes. "I don't remember it. I don't know if—if it's—"

Willow leaned forward, reaching her hand out to Darcy, and Darcy grasped at her friend's fingers, securing them, entwining them, through hers.

"Will you let me help you?"

Darcy searched her dark eyes helplessly.

Willow swallowed, reaching down to her bag with her free hand. When she raised her hand, she held a ginger jar half-full of green liquid, which jostled as she hefted it onto her lap.

"What is that?" asked Darcy.

"A memory potion."

"Do you mean—?"

"Yes. It should work like a movie in a dream. When you drink it, sit back, close your eyes, and open your mind."

"And I'll remember."

"I don't know exactly what you'll see, kid, but you should see your life with Jack. You should see your memories."

"And I'll be able to hold onto them?"

"I don't know," admitted Willow. "My *Nohkom* said this is strong magic. And it's meant for humans, not shifters. It could be unpredictable." She released Darcy's hands and took the ginger jar carefully, holding it out to Darcy like an offering.

Darcy held her friend's eyes for a long moment before accepting the strange liquid. She held it up to the light, watching the swirls of green that seemed alive to her, that seemed to move purposefully in a circle, as though gathering, holding, and waiting.

"Will you stay with me?" asked Darcy softly, pushing a tear from her cheek into her hair.

"Of course."

THIS WAS HER FAVORITE PART of the entire play.

She knew if she stayed concealed behind the thick velvet, that she'd be left in peace to watch from the wings.

His fingertips pressed against the pulse in her throat. His lips dropped to hers. Her heart stopped. Her heart started again.

It's you.

Long years apart, haunted by fiery copper eyes and then...

...his face eclipsed the sun.

Quid pro quo.

A bear and a wolf and an inhuman strength.

Control.

His hands everywhere. Touching, loving, learning, memorizing, seeking, taking...and she was giving, rising, offering, finding, desperately holding on to him, to them, to this feeling.

You belong to me, and I belong to you.

A monster.

The claws retract in the sunlight and fear and anger break her heart.

He is gone.

He is drowning. He is dying. And I watch him die. He shuts me out. He doesn't love me. And I can't bear it...because I love...I love...

In love. In danger.

Atrocious pain. For me.

I leave him or he will die because of me.

Now I am drowning. Now I am dying.

And I love him. I belong to him. I am bound to him.

What is bound cannot be broken.

"JACK!" SHE SCREAMED, BLINDED, GASPING, reaching.

"Darcy! Darcy, breathe! Darcy! Oh God, kid, please breathe!"

Darkness.

Chapter 10

THE DYING LIGHT ON THE horizon told him that the Gathering was beginning soon, but the constant influx of cars, trucks, and motorcycles all afternoon would have been just as reliable a cue. Rougs were coming from near and far to witness Jack's re-binding.

A re-binding that probably wasn't going to happen. Jack knew that appearing without Darcy by his side meant a possible Inquisition into the terms of his original binding. It meant pain and imprisonment. It meant the possibility of torture or death, and yet after Darcy's loss, it seemed trivial somehow. If he left the Gathering Hall tonight without her in his arms, he didn't care if he was in chains—his heart would be dead. What they did to his body simply wouldn't matter.

He took a deep breath, heading back into the settlement from the woods where he'd spent the night after leaving Darcy.

Her feelings for Tombeur had cut him deeply, and he had shifted outside the door of Tombeur's cabin, running through the woods with helpless, hopeless abandon. Happening upon the campsite of a human family, his mouth had watered. Watching them through the branches, he had considered—just for a moment—slaughtering them like meat, the part of himself so closely bound to humanity wanting payback, wanting to hurt humans for the way he was hurting. And the blood of their children, so sweet and hot, called to him, beguiling him, teasing him. She didn't love him. She didn't want him. It would be so easy to revert to wild Roug ways, kill them, drain them, feel their souls, the essence of their beings coursing through his veins like fire. He'd be stronger than ever. He'd stride into the Gathering Hall, compel her, force her to kiss him, and then—

The human child lifted her chubby arms to her mother, and a red-headed, green-eyed woman gathered the baby against her breast.

Jack stared at them, mesmerized, and hadn't realized that he was downshifting until he was in human form once again.

He watched the family settle into their RV for the night, guarding them until the lights were dark and the campfire was cold.

It was their very humanity that had shattered the madness of his thoughts.

They were so vulnerable. So trusting of the world around them. So ignorant of the dangers that lurked nearby, the horror that they'd so narrowly avoided.

For Jack's entire adult life, he had protected humans. And in a blinding flash of understanding, he realized that it was his searing love for Darcy Turner that made it impossible for him to hunt them now. In his heart, Jack knew that even *Pleine Lune* was no longer a risk to his control. He had fully evolved into a new creature. A creature that might even have…a soul.

Pressing his hand to his chest, he felt the heaviness, the too-lateness of such a revelation. He would always need blood to fuel his Roug side, but it needn't be human, and for the rest of his life, he wouldn't be a danger to those Darcy so loved.

His mastery of control complete, the danger to them now, he grimaced, was her.

Except that Jack, among all Rougs, was in the unique position of understanding what it was to love so hard, so deep, so irrevocably, that he could change his very matter, his nature, his desires. And though he couldn't explain it, it gave him the strength to put one foot in front of the other in the direction of the Gathering.

An hour later, he walked into the Gathering Hall, flanked by Julien, Lela, and Delphine on one side, Tombeur on the other. With Tallis handling council business, it was Tombeur who had been waiting for Jack when he arrived home from his walk in the woods.

"Why are you here?" Jack demanded. "Why aren't you with Darcy?"

"I left her yesterday. She was talking crazy. She knows how to get here. Hell, just follow her nose. Too many of us to miss."

Jack nodded. He was grateful to Tombeur for staying away from her, for not risking a single moment when she could have pressed her lips to his. Jack brushed past Tombeur and headed into the cabin, changing into fresh jeans and a clean shirt for the Gathering.

"Jack," said Tombeur, his neck bent and eyes sorry as he leaned against the doorway of Jack's bedroom. "She gave us no choice. She *wanted* to be turned."

"There is always a choice," said Jack.

Tombeur nodded halfheartedly. "If anyone was going to mentor her, well…I'm glad it was me."

"You don't get it. She didn't ask for this life."

"Son, nobody asks for the life they get. It's good luck or shit luck. It's accidents and mistakes, trying your best and hedging your bets. *She* didn't want this life? Did *you?*"

Jack fastened two buttons on a plaid flannel shirt and left the rest open.

"I was born into it."

"Argument could be made she was too." Tombeur sighed, shrugging as he shook his head. "You didn't choose her. The world tilted on its axis for a moment and revealed her to you. You had no say in the matter."

"I could've left her alone," Jack lamented.

"No more'n I could've left your mama alone once my own mate died. Didn't even matter that Dubois was alive. All I could see was Tallis."

"The difference being," said Jack, with steel in his voice, "your woman will belong to you by tonight."

"So will yours," said Tombeur.

"No guarantee for me."

"Jack," said Tombeur, wincing as he shook his head. "You gotta have more faith than that. The day I told you that you couldn't lay eyes on her for ten years, you looked up me, all furious and young, and told me I wasn't going to be able to brainwash her out of your head. And I didn't. I couldn't. Ain't never in my life seen anything as strong as your binding to that girl."

Jack clenched his jaw, unable to speak.

"Tallis told me you felt her. Yesterday."

Jack nodded, looking down.

"But you won't force it?"

Jack shook his head, staring at Tombeur with flat, resigned eyes.

Tombeur sighed. "Never been a Roug like you. A Roug-human binding? That was a first. But *Dansmatête?* With someone you're not bound to? Never heard of that either."

"Mama said it was just electrical impulses."

"Aw, son, you know as well as I do…whether she shows up tonight or not, what you got with Darcy ain't even close to over."

Then Tombeur had slapped him on the back and walked out the door. Jack followed, finding his brother, Lela, and Delphine waiting just outside, and they headed in a solemn mass to the Gathering Hall together.

As they entered, Tombeur locked eyes with Tallis, who had saved him an empty seat beside her at the Council table. He turned to Jack. "Darcy's not here yet. I'll buy you some time, though. We'll see if she shows."

Jack nodded gravely and Tombeur pulled him into a quick, hard embrace.

"I love you like you're mine," he whispered in a gravelly voice. "Whatever happens, Jack, you stay alive. We'll do whatever we can for you."

Tombeur pulled away then, looking at Jack with his eyes on fire, and nodded before turning away.

Jack followed his brother to the set of bleachers designated for the Portes de l'Enfer pack, taking a seat in the front row, which had been roped off and marked "Beauloup."

Casting his glance around the room, he realized that it was a standing-room-only Gathering, the bleachers full to bursting and Rougs of all packs still flooding the massive room. All eyes were drawn to Jack, but he kept his head mostly down, breathing deeply, seeking Darcy's scent and unable to find it in the sea of strong smells that surrounded him.

"Uncle Jack," asked Delphine from beside him. "Is Darcy from the Southern Bloodlands coming?"

He gave her a small smile. "I hope so, *louveteau*. I sure hope so."

Looking over Delphine's head, Jack's eyes smashed into Lela's and she winced, her usually tough eyes flooding with tears. "*Je suis desole*," she mouthed softly, looking miserable.

Jack grimaced, shaking his head gently and looking to the center of the Council ring where Tallis and Tombeur were in deep conversation. Jack knew that they hoped to dissuade the council from an Inquisition, should Darcy fail to attend. He didn't think they'd be successful—Jack's binding, if left a mystery, would be a troubling chapter in the history of the packs. Saint Germain had been vocal in his "quest for truth" campaign, and should Jack's binding still be unexplainable after tonight, an Inquisition would surely follow. He took a deep breath, shoving the image of the Inquisition cellar out of his head. He'd know it intimately soon enough.

In his heart he felt certain: She wasn't coming. He knew that Willow had visited her and had planned to bring a memory potion, but it must not have worked, after all. If Darcy had remembered who they were to one another, surely she would have run to Jack straight away and re-bound herself to him with haste. In the best case scenario, they'd be sitting side by side tonight, holding hands, ready to share their bound status with the Bloodlands. But Jack was alone.

The roar of the crowd took a sharp dive as Marcus Saint Germain, the First Wolf, followed by his cadre of Council Enforcers, swept into the Hall, wearing a full-length coat decorated garishly with the scalps of his many victims: blond hair, bright red, dull browns, some white and grey mixed together for a tapestry of horror. Jack felt his stomach turn over, further evidence that he'd lost his lust for human blood.

The chatter in the Hall dwindled to the barest hush, every Roug waiting on the edge of his and her seat to see what would happen next, and then Saint Germain exploded with a greeting.

"*BIENVENUE!*"

The packs went wild, stomping, howling, growling with glee.

After a moment for revelry, Saint Germain swung his coat off his shoulders and placed it gently on the largest chair at the Council Table, left empty for him.

"We have serious business this evening," he said, his showmanship on extra wattage tonight as he swept around the ring, claws extended, grinning at the packs.

Stopping in front of the Portes de l'Enfer bleachers, he looked up at Jack, sitting alone with his family, and raised an eyebrow.

"Lela Beauloup, you've been bound?" he asked, flicking his glance to Lela's growing belly. Lela stood up with Julien beside her, and Saint Germain clapped his hands together with glee, his claws clacking together. "To the other brother!"

The crowd howled its approval as Saint Germain toyed with them, pointing back and forth at them and then at Lela's belly. "And it seems Julien Beauloup wasted no time with his new mate!"

Lela's face flushed and she cast her eyes down, but Julien's lips tilted up just slightly. "Were she yours, *Premiere Loup*, would you have wasted any?"

"Ah ha ha!" chortled Saint Germain and the crowd went wild, demanding that the newly bound couple kiss by pounding their feet on the floor faster and faster, louder and louder.

Lela looked up at Julien, and Jack's own heart clenched to see the love in her eyes. As their lips touched, Jack, like every other bound Roug in the room, felt the tremor of intimacy pass through him. Short gasps and small sighs could be heard around the room, as other bound couples reaffirmed their bond with a touch or kiss.

Saint Germain narrowed his eyes at Jack. He'd noticed the shudder of Jack's shoulders, a telltale sign of a bound man. He whispered, just loud enough for Jack to hear. "And your mate, Jack Beauloup? Where is she?"

"Not here yet," he answered quietly, standing up.

"So you will *push* this to an Inquisition."

"No, sir. I could try to explain."

"Explain *what*? You had one simple instruction: to bring your mate here to be re-bound. And here you are. Alone," he spat. "You disrespect our—"

"No, sir. I have nothing but respect for our ways."

Saint Germain looked annoyed for a moment, and then grinned with delight, raising his voice. "*Felicitations, Julien et Lela!* But you will all notice…Jack Beauloup sits alone. I do believe it's time—"

"Saint Germain!"

All eyes turned from Saint Germain to look at Tombeur Lesauvage, who stood beside Tallis Beauloup at the Council table. Hand in hand, they stared at Saint Germain, and he had no choice but to turn away from Jack and direct his attention to his mother instead.

"Tombeur and Tallis. Do you have something to say?"

"Yes. We wish to be bound," said Tombeur.

A gasp could be heard around the entire hall, and Jack clenched his eyes shut in relief, sitting back down, grateful for the extra minutes. A new binding, especially between two such well-known and respected Rougs, was certainly cause for celebration. Jack's re-binding would wait.

"A new binding!" exclaimed Saint Germain, moving away from Jack to face Tombeur and Tallis. He turned to the crowd, waggling his bushy gray eyebrows. "What do you say?"

The roar of approval was deafening as Saint Germain urged Tombeur and Tallis away from their seats and into the center of the Council Ring. Saint Germain placed a hand on each of their shoulders, standing before them, and the crowd quieted down immediately.

He waited until the room was silent before reciting the ancient words: "IF SHE BE FOR ME, LET MY HEART STOP BEATING. IF I BE FOR HER, LET IT BE BORN AGAIN."

For years, Jack had witnessed the bond of love between his mother and Tombeur, so he knew what they risked tonight. If their kiss didn't bind them, it meant that they weren't supposed to be together—it meant that they'd never achieve Eyespeak, *Dansmatête*, or ultimate physical pleasure. They'd be destined to friendship, and all romantic flirtation between them would die swiftly.

Tombeur reached for his mother's face, cupping her cheeks gently, and Tallis covered his hands with hers, looking deep into his eyes. Tombeur's eyes burned golden and green and Tallis's answered with a fierce, burning copper.

From where Jack sat, he could see Tombeur hesitate for a moment, perhaps realizing that this was the ultimate moment of fate—would his soul be bound to Tallis for life, or would he lose the woman he'd loved for so many years?

Tombeur's voice shook as he whispered, "*Je t'aime, femme.*" *I love you, woman.* But Tallis's voice was strong and certain as she whispered, "*Je t'aime, aussi,*" back.

Almost unable to bear the tension, Jack watched as Tombeur's head lowered, coming closer and closer to his mother's lips until they touched for the first time, and then parted. And Jack felt it. It ripped through his heart, through his newly formed soul, like a bullet, like a drug, like a song. As Tombeur lowered his lips again, binding himself to Tallis and she to him, every bound Roug in the Hall felt the earthquake of emotion, and amidst sighs and gasps of pleasure, Jack's mother was bound for the second time in her life, to the man she'd loved for what seemed like forever.

"WHAT IS BOUND CANNOT BE BROKEN!" declared Saint Germain as the crowd exploded in approval. Tombeur and Tallis, who'd waited half their lives to feel their lips pressed against each other, kissed long and hard, arms holding, fingers grasping, entwined around each other, barely under control.

They may have kissed forever but for the loud, single, earth-shattering howl that rent the dark of night outside of the Gathering Hall. Chatter abated in waves, and a strange silence descended on the hall as every Roug in attendance recognized the call of an unbound female, newly turned, coming closer with every passing second.

Jack's eyes widened and he bolted out of his chair, flicking a quick glance to Tombeur, who ripped himself away from Tallis in recognition of his progeny's call. Taking a deep breath, he tilted his face to the open sky and released his own howl, guiding her, telling her where to find him. The Gathering Hall, waiting with bated breath to see the curiosity of a newly turned Roug, shifted their eyes to the far side of the Gathering Hall, where the large entrance lay still.

Darcy howled again, this time much closer, and Tombeur's answering cry was more mellow, more assuring, less directive.

And suddenly, she appeared.

Wearing jeans and a T-shirt, red hair tumbling over her shoulders in defiant waves and eyes burning silver-green, she strode into the Gathering Hall, beelining for Tombeur. The crowd watched in fascination as she approached, only to stop short in her tracks and inhale sharply, jerking her neck to look at Tallis.

DARCY HAD RIDDEN WITH WILLOW as far as the weigh station on the boundary of Portes de l'Enfer before tucking her clothes under her arm, shifting and running the fifty miles back north to try to make the Gathering in time. She howled to Tombeur to let him know that she was coming, praying, with every footfall on the hard earth, that she wouldn't be too late.

The change in Tallis's scent was unmistakable. Darcy shifted her eyes to her maker. "You're bound."

Tombeur nodded. "I told you."

Darcy leaned forward and kissed his cheek and then drew back, offering him a small, contrite smile. "I'm sorry I didn't believe you."

"Such excitement!" declared Saint Germain, who still stood in front of Tombeur and Tallis. Extending one yellowed claw toward Darcy, he asked, "Who. Are. You?"

Tombeur stepped forward, shoulder to shoulder with Darcy, and raised his voice to introduce his progeny to the waiting packs.

"She is Darcy Turner Lesauvage, lately of the Southern Bloodlands, turned not blooded."

"Of the...*Southern* Bloodlands," mused Saint Germain, grinning at her. "A turned human? From Carlisle or Colebrook?"

"Carlisle," she said, her voice even and strong.

She looked up at Tombeur, a clear question in her eyes, and he flicked his chin to the right, where she found Jack Beauloup standing in the first row of bleachers, watching her with rapt attention. His face—familiar, yet strange, beloved, yet unknown—was unreadable, and yet she may have seen hope beneath the burning of his eyes.

"How fascinating," murmured Saint Germain. "Why do I feel like there's more to your story, Darcy Lesauvage?"

"Because there is," she said softly, her eyes welling as she stared back at Jack, unable to look away.

It wasn't that the memories she'd seen were suddenly a firm part of her history. It wasn't that simple. Although she'd been touched on a visceral level as she'd watched hers and Jack's love story unfold in her mind, she'd still felt a certain detachment from it, almost as though she was watching someone else's story and deeply affected. So affected, in fact, she hadn't noticed when her heart, overloaded with sensations, had sped up so fast that it finally stopped. For all intents and purposes, Willow told her, she'd died in that rocking chair by the fire.

And when she did, the only face Darcy saw, the only touch she felt, the only voice that she heard…was Jack's. And as her heart started beating anew, her lungs sucked in a huge breath, and the only person she wanted to see was Jack Beauloup. Memories or not, he was her past and her future, and she wasn't frightened anymore. She knew it was true.

Her feet moved noiselessly but surely toward him and he ducked under the railing, stretching his body, then straightening to stand before her. Tall and impossibly handsome, his eyes seemed to reach out to her, trying to speak to her, and she suddenly knew that's exactly what he was doing, and it made her lips tilt up just slightly as she closed the distance between them.

When she was about foot away from him, she stopped, her heart thundering in her chest.

"Jack."

"Darcy. Do you remember me?"

She licked her lips and shook her head. "No. Not exactly."

His eyes, which had seemed so hopeful a moment ago, flattened into dark copper circles. She couldn't bear it. She reached out, touching his forearm with her hand, aware of his breath hitching softly as he took a small step toward her.

"Then nothing's changed."

"*I've* changed," she whispered, her voice a mix between a sigh and a sob.

"How?"

"I don't remember us, but I saw us. I saw us together. That first night on the stage when you kissed me. At my cousin's wedding. In your house. The pain of separation. The joy of reunion." Her eyes fluttered closed as her fingers tightened around his skin. He stepped closer to her, placing a hand on her waist, and she opened her eyes again, taking another step closer to him. "The love, Jack. The—the binding. I felt it."

"You did?"

A tear slipped down her cheek as she nodded. "I did. I'm here because

I know I loved you once. I'm here because I want that love again."

"I'm bound to you," he said, holding her eyes. "I belong to you. Right now. Right here. Forever."

"I know," she sobbed. "I'm so sorry I made you wait for me."

"Darcy Turner Lesauvage, turned, not blooded," he said gently, his other hand falling to her waist and pulling her against his strong, broad chest. His eyes swam with tears, with exhaustion and hope. "Will you re-bind yourself to me?"

"Willingly," she murmured.

Looking away from her, Jack turned to Saint Germain, who was watching them with fascination.

"But she's newly turned," Saint Germain observed, narrowing his eyes. "How can you be *re*-bound? It would mean that you'd been bound to a—"

"Does it matter?" Jack interrupted quickly.

"I don't know," answered Saint Germain, looking back and forth between Jack's copper-colored fiery eyes and Darcy's own silvery-green. "You're both Rougs now."

"You called everyone here to confirm my binding," Jack hissed through clenched teeth, impatient to kiss his mate again. "Let me confirm it for you."

"And answer my questions…?"

"Another time," confirmed Jack.

"Very well," said Saint Germain. He turned to the crowd, raising his arms over his head theatrically. "Did you come here for a binding?"

The roomful of Rougs, which had been patient as Jack and Darcy reconnected, thundered its approval, banging the floorboards of the ancient bleachers with their feet and howling.

Saint Germain looked back at Jack and Darcy and intoned, "IF SHE BE FOR ME, LET MY HEART STOP BEATING. IF I BE FOR HER, LET IT BE BORN AGAIN."

Jack turned away from Saint Germain, facing her. He lifted one hand from her waist and pressed it to her throat as he had so many years ago.

As he inclined his head, she heard his voice, raspy with emotion, whisper, "Darcy Turner, it's you." And as the heat of his lips touched down on hers, Darcy died for the second time in one day.

FOR THE SECOND TIME IN his life, Jack felt his heart grind to a stop, and under his fingertips, he felt Darcy's pulse still as he leaned back from her. He searched her eyes, which blazed like an inferno as her hand reached up to clasp the back of his neck and demand his lips again. As they touched down on hers, pressed flush against their beloved sweetness, a thunderous thumping started under his fingertips as her heart awoke re-bound to his, and in his own, pounding in recognition of the mate he'd missed so desperately these long, lonely weeks apart.

Dropping his hand from her throat, he wrapped his arms around her, pulling her tightly, fiercely against his body as he parted the seam of her lips with his tongue. As though they'd been apart for far longer than three weeks, he savaged her mouth, claiming it, unable and unwilling to allow the hot satin of her tongue to leave his, and reveling in her own domination of him—the way she flexed her fingers in his hair, razing his skull with her nails, tasting him, demanding him, pressing herself against him to let him know how much she wanted him and that she was completely his for the taking.

And how his heart thrummed and rejoiced in belonging to her again, just as she had always belonged to him. His red-headed girl from the Southern Bloodlands, turned, not blooded, who belonged to him forever, from whom he would never be parted, for the rest of his life.

The energy in the room buzzed with excitement as Saint Germain exclaimed, "WHAT IS BOUND CANNOT BE BROKEN!"

The howling and foot pounding celebration faded to white noise as Jack drew back from Darcy and she slowly opened her burning eyes. His heart clutched with relief when he heard her voice in his head, saying,

Jack. I remember everything. I love you. I belong to you.

His heart erupted with love for her, and he felt the smile split his face as he wiped away her tears and tenderly cupped the cheeks of his woman, his bound mate, his heart, his soul, his love, his bride. Recovered to him. Somehow delivered unto him. This time, forever.

I love you, Darcy. I belong to you. Forever.

Her answering smile told him everything he needed to know, but he read her eyes anyway. *Forever, Jack. Forever.*

And then, holding her face as he would every day for the rest of his life, he touched his lips to hers again.

Epilogue

THEIR WEDDING IN CARLISLE WAS a mere formality after the Gathering binding at Solstice, but it made Darcy's mother happy to see her only daughter finally walk down the aisle of the Second Congregational Church of Carlisle. And Jack, who was determined to start a new Carlisle pack and reclaim their lands in the Southern Bloodlands, understood the need to blend into the human world in order to coexist peacefully together.

For three cycles of *Pleine Lune* shifts, Jack had helped Darcy control her cravings, staying with her in the vault as she sated her hunger on the blood of animals only. There would never be human blood shed in Carlisle as long as Jack Beauloup was the *Premiere Loup*, and any Rougs who wished to live a more modern lifestyle were welcome in Carlisle. Others would be dealt with harshly.

Although the Council had considered an Inquisition to examine the rumors of a Roug-human binding between Jack and Darcy, Saint Germain himself had been the one to tamp down the gossip, declaring it outlandish and impossible. Jack sensed that the older Roug was curious, but that opening such a conversation could be dangerous. And besides, what Jack had said at the Gathering was true: With Darcy a turned Roug now, how they found their way to one another was all but irrelevant to everyone but them.

Still, Tombeur and Tallis encouraged Jack and Darcy to stay away from the Northern Bloodlands for a few years at least, until the strange binding of Darcy and Jack Beauloup had been forgotten.

Occasionally, in the dark of night, in the north woods above the small town of Carlisle, New Hampshire, the howl of a wolf is heard, followed by the answering call of its mate. At first, the townsfolk were worried, but over the years a tacit agreement has been formed: The elusive wolves don't bother the town, so the town leaves the wolves alone.

Though anyone walking on Main Street, happening by the porch of Willow Broussard and Amory Turner, might catch the good doctor's change of expression when the wolves howl—how the corners of her mouth turn up as her dark eyes look with affection toward the woods.

Only Willow knows…it's just her best friend, Darcy, and Darcy's true love, Jack, living happily ever after.

The End

Also Available

from Katy Regnery
via Boroughs Publishing Group

THE HEART OF MONTANA SERIES
Sweet, small-town, contemporary romance

By Proxy
The Christmas Wish
Midsummer Sweetheart
See Jane Fall
Meeting Miss Mystic
What Were You Expecting?

About the Author

NEW YORK TIMES AND USA Today bestselling author Katy Regnery started her writing career by enrolling in a short story class in January 2012. One year later, she signed her first contract, and her first novel, *By Proxy*, was published by Boroughs Publishing Group in September 2013.

Twenty-five books later, Katy claims authorship of the multititled *New York Times* and *USA Today* Blueberry Lane Series, which follows the English, Winslow, Rousseau, Story, and Ambler families of Philadelphia; the six-book, bestselling ~a modern fairytale~ series; and several other standalone novels and novellas.

Katy's first modern fairytale romance, *The Vixen and the Vet*, was nominated for a RITA® in 2015 and won the 2015 Kindle Book Award for romance. Katy's boxed set, *The English Brothers Boxed Set*, Books #1–4, hit the *USA Today* bestseller list in 2015, and her Christmas story, *Marrying Mr. English*, appeared on the list a week later. In May 2016, Katy's Blueberry Lane collection, *The Winslow Brothers Boxed Set*, Books #1–4, became a *New York Times* E-book bestseller.

In 2016, Katy signed an agreement with Spencer Hill Press. As a result, her Blueberry Lane paperback books will now be distributed to brick-and-mortar bookstores all over the United States.

Katy lives in the relative wilds of northern Fairfield County, Connecticut, where her writing room looks out at the woods, and her husband, two young children, two dogs, and one Blue Tonkinese kitten create just enough cheerful chaos to remind her that the very best love stories begin at home.

Sign up for Katy's newsletter today: **www.katyregnery.com**

Connect with Katy

KATY LOVES CONNECTING WITH HER readers and answers every e-mail, message, tweet, and post personally! Connect with Katy!

Katy's Website
www.katyregnery.com

Katy's E-mail
katy@katyregnery.com

Katy's Facebook Page
www.facebook.com/KatyRegnery

Katy's Pinterest Page
www.pinterest.com/katharineregner/

Katy's Goodreads Profile
www.goodreads.com/author/show/7211470.Katy_Regnery

Boroughs
Publishing Group

DID YOU ENJOY THIS BOOK? Drop us a line and say so! We love to hear from readers, and so do our authors. To connect, visit www.boroughspublishinggroup.com online, send comments directly to info@boroughspublishinggroup.com, or friend us on Facebook and Twitter. And be sure to check back regularly for contests and new releases in your favorite subgenres of romance!

Are you an aspiring writer? Check out
www.boroughspublishinggroup.com/submit
and see if we can help you make your dreams come true.

CPSIA information can be obtained
at www.ICGtesting.com
Printed in the USA
LVOW13s1547080217

523626LV00010B/976/P

9 781541 362833